REVENANT

# MERE JOYCE

## ORACLE OF SENDERS

FOR THOSE WHO CAUGHT THE SPARK.

Despite the warm sun above us and the turquoise water glistening beneath the speeding boat, my head is brimming with thoughts of death. Which would be weird, if my friend Dylan wasn't leaning over the railing, squeezing his eyes shut and trying not to retch over the side of the water taxi.

"I thought you weren't affected by spirits," I say, leaning in so the driver won't hear us.

"I'm not," Dylan mutters, pressing a hand to his forehead. "At least, I never used to be. I guess it's gotten worse."

I fold my arms across the railing. The breeze is warm, and my stomach is unfazed by the nearby canine ghost I am thankful not to see.

"I told you we should have waited for the next boat." I smirk.

After two days on route to Camp Wanagi, Dylan was so excited to reach the islands of Vava'u, he didn't mind boarding the water taxi. Not even once he discovered the spirit of a terrier curled into a ball near the bow. He claimed we couldn't wait for another boat, not when the driver had been holding a cardboard sign with *Dylan Benowitz* and *Callum Silver* scratched in black pen. The names looked like they were written in two seconds, probably when the guy realized he'd have trouble pronouncing our names. But Dylan said he'd always wanted to have a sign waiting for him upon arrival to some exotic locale, and he insisted the dog wouldn't be a big deal.

Now, his usual sickly complexion is grey-hued, and his arms are dotted with goose bumps despite the blazing sun. "Not the time for a lecture," he mumbles, opening his eyes and wincing at the harsh light.

When he's adjusted to the brightness, Dylan glances down to where I imagine the spirit sits next to his leg. As soon as it noticed Dylan, it bounded over to him. As far as I can tell, it hasn't left his side the entire trip.

"Sorry," I say, suppressing a smile.

Dylan wasn't prepared to see a ghost today. He's been talking about the tropical paradise awaiting us since L.A., where we met for a connecting flight the Oracle of Senders was nice enough to put us on together. The scenery here is beautiful, and *tropical paradise* is a fully adequate description for what we've seen of the Kingdom of Tonga. But for someone convinced his second summer at Camp Wanagi would be as free of spirits as his first, this early ghost sighting is an unfair—though perhaps necessary—reminder to Dylan that he is not here for a vacation.

Still, as amused as I am each time the taxi driver jokes about him being sea sick, I can't fault Dylan for his surprise. Even I've found it hard to remember that we've come to Tonga to learn about ghosts, not to swim with whales and lounge on the beach for ten weeks.

Everything is a complete flip from last summer, when I arrived exhausted and nervous about attending Wanagi for the first time. I'm no longer a fourteen-year-old, scared he won't fit in when he meets the other campers. Now, our impending arrival sends excitement fluttering through me, like an orchestra playing Rimsky-Korsakov's "Flight of the Bumblebee" under my skin.

The easiness is a tease. It feels like a trap to be somewhere so picturesque, given the nature of this camp. Which is why I'm tethering my hopes to the railing of the boat as I watch Dylan's hand flick in an automatic petting motion through, what to me, is only empty air. I'm trying to keep from floating too high with excitement by repeating a single question in my head.

*How many people have died on this island?*

The population is small, but I'm guessing Vava'u has at least a few lingering spirits. Maybe more than a few. A place like this might be hard to give up, even in the afterlife.

"Look," I say, pointing over the boat's edge to give Dylan some relief. "The shore. We're almost there."

Dylan glances up from the ghost dog, squinting against the sun's reflection on the water as he sighs. "This is what I'm talking about," he says, his words thin but enthusiastic. "Can you believe we get views like this all summer?"

I smile, studying the domed roofs of the small

houses—fales—resting mere feet away from the white sand of the beach.

"A little different from France, eh?" I laugh.

Dylan shakes his head. "Forget France, Cal. *This* is what summer camp should be like."

I wonder if Dylan's ever been to a normal summer camp. I have, and I've certainly never attended one in a location this nice. We haven't seen our lodgings yet but, if the dots of people milling around the fales are any indication, this set-up is going to be incomparable to last summer's dreary château.

"Everything seems alive here, doesn't it?" I ask. The swell in my stomach matches the soft crash of the waves against the not-so-distant shoreline. "The dog aside, of course," I add with a sympathetic shrug.

Dylan nods, his hand reaching towards the canine. Watching him pet it, even while he works to keep from being sick, is strange. In a year of knowing him, this is the first time I've seen Dylan interact with a spirit.

"Think the girls are here yet?" he asks with a breath of relief as the taxi driver reduces the throttle and the boat starts to glide alongside the dock.

"I feel like we've been travelling for a week," I groan. "It wouldn't surprise me if we were the only ones who haven't arrived."

The trip was long, with two stopovers and endless hours on cramped planes. But I haven't seen any spirits since I left Toronto, and I've had company for a good portion of the trek. All things considered, it's one of the better trips I've taken.

"I'd do it again in a second, if it got me back here." Dylan grins, petting the air a final time before lurching from his seat to stand on wobbling legs. His hair is slicked back with gel, the hold strong enough to withstand the whipping breeze coming off the boat. I haven't been so lucky. As soon as we're on the beach, I'll try to minimize the damage to my shorter, lighter brown strands.

"The summer hasn't even begun yet," I say, grabbing my bags as the boat comes to a bobbing stop. "If the first minutes have been any indication for you, the next ten weeks could be horrendous."

"No way."

Dylan hauls his suitcase onto the dock before climbing awkwardly out of the unsteady boat. One polka-dotted high top catches on the railing, and he stumbles into his bag.

"You sure?" I laugh, lowering my duffel bag, backpack, and violin case to the dock before disembarking more carefully.

"This doesn't count," Dylan says, untangling his shoelace from under the suitcase's wheel. "I was still under the influence of the dead—all that howling wind threw my balance off. Now that my head is quiet and I'm not about to heave my guts out, I'll be fine. Besides, didn't you say the camp is cleared of ghosts before we arrive?"

I sigh, picking up my things and waving as the taxi driver pulls away.

"I'm not sure that applies to dogs," I admit. "And camp wasn't totally cleared last summer, anyway. Just… Don't get your hopes up too much."

"Yeah, yeah, I know," Dylan mumbles, not bothering to tie his shoe before starting towards the beach. If he trips again and ends up in the water, I'm not going to feel the slightest bit of sympathy.

Dylan's unwavering cheerfulness pays off when we're three quarters of the way down the dock. Two members of the Shade Sector must have spotted us pulling in. That, or one of them sensed we were close. Kornelía Tumisdottir and Mim Castillo step onto the dock together. Then Mim breaks into a run, her stride so quick, I'm nearly the one in the water when I sidestep as she flings herself at Dylan.

I've emailed Dylan since last August but, around December, he stopped mentioning Mim in his messages. I figured they'd lost interest in one another. Evidently, I was wrong. Now, Mim wraps her legs around Dylan's waist, and he fumbles to drop his suitcase in favor of holding her up. Her lips soon crash into his, and I avert my gaze, skirting them to say hello to Kornelía instead.

She gives me a knowing smile and envelops me in a much gentler embrace. "Hey, Cal," she says, her voice high, but not quite as mousy as it used to be.

I didn't talk much to Mim while we were all at home, nothing more than liking posts and exchanging well wishes around the holidays. But Kornelía and I kept up regular correspondence, trading not only emails but pictures, too. Which is why I don't feel shy pointing out the pearly green, thick-rimmed glasses covering her tawny eyes.

"The glasses look great," I say, which is only a partial lie. They'd be nice if they were half the size, or if Kornelía's features weren't so large. I'm not sure whether there was a lack of options, or she made a significant error in judgment when trying them on. Either way, she's been moaning about the spectacles since she got them three months ago. I've done my best to assure her they're not as hideous as she insists, but my efforts have been in vain.

"Thanks," she says, although I'm sure she doesn't believe me. Talking to someone who has a knack for knowing when you are lying isn't always easy. She's even eerily good at pulling the truth from a coyly worded email.

"Woah, what's with the glasses, Korni?" Dylan exclaims as he and Mim join us.

Kornelía ducks her head, trying to hide her face with the curtain of her long hair.

"She wanted to take them off before you got here," Mim says with a grin.

"I didn't even know you had them. When did this happen?" Dylan asks.

"March," Kornelía sighs. She lifts her face and gives Dylan a meek smile. "But I should have started wearing them sooner. My sight got blurry around November."

Hurt flickers in Dylan's dark eyes. "Oh," he says, the word clipped and unsure, like he can't decide if he should be disappointed or annoyed. When Mim tugs on his arm, however, he blinks away his troubled expression. "Well, I like them." He smiles.

Under the giant, round rims, Kornelía's eyes brighten. But then Dylan tilts his head to one side, nodding as he adds, "They're very... *you*."

I shoot him a look he doesn't notice. Then I try to think up a quick subject change to wipe away the deflated resignation sweeping over Kornelía's face.

"How long have you two been here?" I ask, turning to Mim to give Kornelía a moment to regain her composure.

"Three days," Mim says. "A bit of a change, huh? Last year, we all came together. Now, they let us show up whenever we can. The new recruits are arriving this evening, though, and I think they're all coming together. Which means initiation will be tonight."

Each of us has travelled from a different part of the world to be here this summer. But seeing the girls and hearing about the newest campers warps our foreign surroundings into something familiar. Being together solidifies the fact that Camp Wanagi is about to begin.

"Are you kidding me?" Dylan looks astounded. "You've been relaxing for the last three days and, now that I'm finally here, we have to go straight into camp mode?"

"Tough break," Mim says with an exaggerated pout. She pinches his chin, her dark hair catching the sun as she moves. This summer she's streaked pink throughout the black strands. The style is a little longer than it used to be as well, though her bangs are still cropped short above her eyebrows.

"I'm sure you'll have plenty of time to see the beach," Kornelía offers, her smile back to normal. "We're here until the middle of August."

"If ghosts don't hinder my ability to bask in the tropical sun," Dylan adds.

"You don't see them, anyway," Mim huffs, unaware of how Dylan fared on his taxi ride. "You've got nothing to worry about."

"Unless there's a ban on dogs on this island, I've got as much chance as you do of seeing a ghost," he says.

Mim smiles and leans into his side, mumbling something I don't hear. My gaze has shifted away from my friends, to the figure approaching the far edge of the dock. A lot has changed since last summer. We are in the tropics, and we're no longer new and uncertain about what we're doing. We've had a year to get to know one another, too, ten weeks in person and ten months through correspondence from home.

A lot has changed. And now, the person stepping onto the dock banishes all thoughts of the possible pain this summer's spirits might inflict.

I slide away from the others and try to adopt a casual pace, a task I don't quite manage. I'm quick to reach the end of the dock, where I place my luggage on the wooden boards. The flutter under my skin works itself into a fevered buzz, the way it's wanted to since the moment I started preparing for camp.

"Hi," I say, slightly breathless and probably smiling too much.

Meander appraises me, his expression neutral. But when he speaks, the disinterested façade gives way to a smile as enthusiastic as my own.

"Hey," he says, and that single word promises a summer every bit as delightful as the white sand and blue-green waters suggest.

THE LAST TIME I SAW MEANDER RHOADES IN PERSON, I ASKED FOR HIS email address, hoping we might talk once or twice when we got home.

Which is exactly what happened, at first.

"How was your trip?" he asks. His golden brown curls are perfect despite his insistence they'd be nothing but frizz, even if this is the island's dry season.

"Long," I sigh, stepping around my bag to approach him. "Yours?"

He nods."Long," he agrees, meeting me halfway with a hug.

All those months ago, I was amazed how warm Meander's hand was when he wrote his email address on my palm. Now, I'm not surprised to find that everything about him is warm—his smile, his skin, his mingled scent of sandalwood and sunscreen.

"Did you bring the ketchup crisps?" he asks as he steps back, alluding to our promise of swapping snacks from our respective homelands.

"Yes," I laugh, kicking my backpack. "You better have brought the custard creams."

"Custard creams, Hobnobs, and a pack of cherry bakewells." He smiles, surveying my collection of luggage. "You brought your violin, too. Good."

"Dylan's convinced it'll be swiped before the week's out," I joke, though we both know I'm afraid of the possibility. Last year, our accommodations didn't even meet basic building codes, let alone the high standards I have for keeping my violin well-guarded. But I've secured a dehumidifier, and I plan to check on the instrument after every course. The situation is not ideal, but I couldn't leave my violin at home for another summer. Not after the ache of its absence last year.

"It will be," Dylan says, joining us. He lugs his bags over one shoulder, Mim and Kornelía hanging back a step to keep out of danger's way.

"We'll keep a tight watch," Meander says, his words an assurance I know I can trust.

My relationship with Meander has advanced a lot in the last ten months. After I returned to Canada, I sent an email asking how he fared on his journey home. His reply was short but, after his electronic signature, he inquired about the injury I sustained at the end of the summer. The question was enough to keep me writing. Without noticing how the habit formed, we soon exchanged emails on a weekly basis. I wrote detailed summaries of my life experiences, while he teased me about the length of my messages before sharing much briefer tidbits in return.

Our correspondence quickly became comfortable.

So when a November hiking trip with my family made me ramble for two pages about a spirit I may or may not have felt, I was confident Meander wouldn't be annoyed by my panicked cry for consolation. Still, I didn't expect his equally long and heartfelt response. During our first year of camp, he saw firsthand how easily a ghost drew me under its influence. He understood my fears, and somehow managed to erase them with his words.

Then in January, a bad run-in with a spirit left Meander with a wounded arm. He couldn't type through the pain, but he wanted to talk—and I wanted to listen. So, we connected through video. In an instant, video chatting became the new norm.

Now, Meander glances at Dylan and the girls before his gaze drops to my luggage. Without giving me time to argue, he grabs my duffel bag and heads towards the shore. I pick up my violin and sling my backpack over one shoulder, stepping fast to catch up with his stride. When we reach the soft beach, I rake my fingers through my hair, wishing I'd decided to use my comb before we got off the boat. Meander's curls may be perfect, but my hair is a wind-swept disaster.

"Anything exciting happen yet?" I ask, trying to ignore my hair and focus instead on the positives of my current situation. My feet sink into the white sand, and I take solace in the fact that I'm already wearing my sandals.

"Thankfully, no," he says. He shifts the duffel bag from one hand to the other, and I realize how odd it is to see him without a book. "But I'm sure that will change soon enough," he continues, displeased. "The new Entity campers will be arriving later today."

"Well, if we go into any old buildings for the initiation, let's make sure we stay near an exit," I say.

Meander smiles, nudging my arm as we approach one of the fales. "It's good to see you," he murmurs, drawing a key from his pocket to unlock the door.

When we left Camp Wanagi last summer, Meander and I were nothing more than curious acquaintances. But for the past six months, I've seen his face every day. The ritual has grown more important as it's continued. A subtle yet steady stream has engulfed us, pushing us close and shifting Meander from a possible friend to a sure one. At some point I can't clearly define, it swept him under the current altogether—pulling him down to the bedrock as, quite seriously, the best friend I've ever had.

He pushes open the door to our lodgings, and I pause for a beat to watch him walk inside. After months of communicating from the safe comfort of our bedrooms, finally being here with him is exciting, surreal—and just the slightest bit terrifying. Still, I appreciate that we're reuniting in such a fantastic locale. Under this bright sun, the problems of last summer seem far away. Our wounds have healed, and our fears about the future have, at least momentarily, been subdued.

When Dylan steps up behind me, I cross the threshold and survey our temporary home.

"This is... *nice*," I say, looking around in surprise.

I'd been expecting something old, a house missing parts of the roof or, maybe, an apartment with an unfinished floor. But this summer, we've been given a simple, clean island fale. A small living area with two black sofas connects to a kitchenette, and three doors lead off from the main room. One opens onto a small private courtyard, and the remaining two reveal a bathroom and a white-walled bedroom decorated with the familiar set of black bunks and matching dresser we had in France. I wonder if the Oracle purchases new furniture every year, or if they ship this stuff all over the world. Neither seems economical. Choosing pre-furnished accommodations has to be easier.

"It's great!" Dylan grins, wandering around the living area. "Where are the girls staying?"

Mim and Kornelía have remained on the beach, waiting for us to put away our things before we explore our surroundings.

"A few doors down," Meander says, as Dylan crosses from the kitchenette to the bedroom. "We're self-contained this time around."

"Awesome." Dylan nods. His enthusiasm has been restored to full capacity now he's away from the spirit on the boat. He walks into the bedroom and drops his stuff onto the same bunk he took last year.

Meander places my duffel bag on the bed across from Dylan's, which I guess means everyone's more or less taking up the same places they had before.

"I'm telling you, this is going to be perfect," Dylan says. "I got the unpleasantness out of the way. Now, I'm free to relax."

"Dylan's already seen his first spirit of the summer," I explain to Meander. I place my backpack on the bed and slide my violin case underneath the bunk.

"And it'll be the last, I'm sure," Dylan says.

Meander considers him, shaking his head."Hate to tell you, but the island's full of dogs," he says, leaning against the bunks. He's wearing a white t-shirt, grey cargo shorts, and canvas flip-flops. He bought the outfit last minute when he finally conceded that he couldn't survive the whole summer wearing jeans. He looks good. He's only been here a couple days, but his whole complexion is brightened by the extra hint of pink the sun has lent to his cheeks.

"What do you mean, 'full of dogs'?" Dylan asks, a note of apprehension in his voice. "Like, you've seen a few people walking their poodles?"

"More like packs of stray dogs roaming the streets and the beach," Meander says. "Apparently, they can be aggressive. So be careful if you're going for a run."

Dylan looks like he might slump onto his bed in defeat, but he forces a grin onto his face and grabs some yellow-framed sunglasses out of his suitcase.

"It'll be fine," he says, like he's trying to convince us and not himself. He shoves the suitcase to the back of the bunk, and then slides the glasses onto his face. The sunny color of the plastic is wretched next to the sallow shade of his skin. But the frames do, at least, hide the gray bags under his eyes. "I saw a mini-fridge out there. Is it stocked? I'm freaking thirsty."

Meander nods, and Dylan flashes his teeth in a too-wide smile before bounding out of the room. When he's gone, I turn to Meander, who pushes off the bed frame and sits on my bunk instead.

"Did you have any trouble?" he asks, referring to last year's horrendous flight with the dead man reeking of fish.

"No," I say, moving the duffel bag out of the way so I can sit next to him. "Did you?"

"No." He smirks. "If I did, the whole bloody plane might have crashed."

The likelihood of such an occurrence is troubling. I can picture electrical systems going haywire, luggage falling out of overhead bins and people screaming in the chaos.

Swallowing the disturbing thought, I give Meander a hard stare. "Don't ever let a plane take off until you've done a thorough search of the cabin yourself," I tell him.

He looks like he wants to laugh, but he only nods. "Deal."

Now that we're indoors, I pull my comb from my backpack and sweep my hair to the right in the usual part. Meander watches the routine and, when I'm finished, he kicks my foot.

"So, do I finally get to hear you play?" he asks.

My cheeks warm, serving as a strange reminder that I need to apply sunscreen before we go back outside. The task offers a good excuse to turn away, so he won't notice my embarrassment.

"Absolutely not," I mutter as I unzip my duffel bag.

"You're going to go the whole summer playing the violin without anyone hearing you?" he asks, his tone dubious.

"That's the plan."

I push aside clothing and pull out my toiletries case as Meander releases an amused breath.

"You're ridiculous. People like listening to musicians, you know."

"You've never heard me play," I laugh. "I might be horrible."

I unzip the case and take out some sunscreen. Mom made me pack three bottles. I never knew she was so concerned about my exposure.

"Let me hear you play, and I'll know for sure," Meander counters. His voice is quiet, almost like he's asking a question. The tone throws me off.

I'm glad I've got the sunscreen to focus on while I consider the best way to respond. Meander's questioned me about my music before, and he's tried to get me to play during a couple of our chats. I knew he'd want to hear the violin now that we're together, but I wasn't prepared for him to bring it up so soon.

Every time he asks me to perform, anxiety muddles my head. I'm not afraid of playing my violin in front of people, usually. But for some reason I still haven't quite worked out, I don't want to play in front of Meander. Maybe it's because I know he won't lie if he thinks I'm horrible. I don't play the violin to be praised as a great musician. But I also don't want to be labeled a failure by my closest friend.

Silence falls over us, and I'm relieved when a noise outside the window distracts Meander before I'm forced to answer.

"It's different here," he says, his voice laced with irritation. "Last year, we were secluded in the middle of that damned lake. Now we're surrounded by rowdy people on holiday."

Someone yells something about a missing frisbee, and I can hear the annoyance in Meander's scoffing breath.

I laugh, shaking the bottle of sunscreen before pouring more into my palm. "Am I going to find you hiding in some remote cave off the coast, reading a book by the light of your cell phone?" I ask.

"It's entirely possible." He nods, his hazel eyes more green than brown in the brightness of the room.

"Doesn't sound too bad."

"Okay," I smile, spattering sunscreen over my arms. "Just make sure you tell me where you end up. I'll bring you snacks."

"You ready yet, Cal?" Dylan asks, returning to the room with a water bottle in hand. "I want to say a proper hello to Mim."

"And you need me around for that?" I ask.

Meander smirks as he stands. "Before you do anything, Robbie and Alex will want to know you've arrived," he says.

He waits for me to finish applying the sunscreen before holding a hand out to help me up. I don't need the assistance, but I take it anyway.

"Yeah, I suppose letting the leads know we're here might be a good idea," Dylan admits. "But then I want to see the beach."

He takes a swig of his drink and heads back out the door. Meander turns to follow him, and I fumble for words before he gets too far.

"It's, uh, it's good to see you, too," I say in a rush of breath.

Meander pauses, and I catch the gentle lift of his lips before he turns to lead me out of the room. I trail behind him, smelling of sunscreen and ready to explore the paradise beyond my front door.

*How many people have died on this island?*

In this moment, I don't really care.

THE AFTERNOON SLIDES AWAY. I FEEL LIKE AN EAGER TOURIST WHO HAS just checked in to an oceanside resort. Dylan and I meet with our leads, receiving keys to our fale and a mini-lecture on water safety. Then we say hello to the other five members of Shade.

Sefa looks completely at home at the beach. This year's destination is a lot closer to the climate he's used to in Samoa. Naasir, Reed, and Sabeena are with him, all four lounging lazily under the sun. Lu takes longer to find, and Dylan grumbles about the detour as we shuttle from building to building in an effort to locate her. I keep my mouth shut, even though I agree with Dylan's complaint. Neither of us is close to Lu. When we do find her, she's so engrossed in some online article about the psychology of auras, she doesn't even spare us a glance.

Once we've seen our fellow sector mates, we acquaint ourselves with the island. Between eating a buffet lunch served in what I think is a rustic resort pavilion and walking far up and down the beach with my friends, the hours speed past.

Five o'clock approaches with startling swiftness, marked by the arrival of another water taxi at the dock—this one carrying the newest Oracle recruits.

"What do you think it's like for them?" Kornelía asks as we watch the boat from the beach. "I mean, being dropped off here for their first summer?"

"A hell of a lot better than it was for us," Dylan mutters.

Mim traces her fingers through the sand, making shapes she later wipes away with her palms. "I don't know," she says, her voice thoughtful. "I think this would be worse. It's like a trick. At least when we arrived, it was spooky. There aren't any old houses here."

"Yeah, the old houses are always a nice touch."

I glance behind me to see Robbie approaching. His mohawk is still tall and spiked. This year, its dyed root to tip in a metallic blue I'm sure will be an exact match for his suit, if he ever puts it on. He's been shirtless all day. When I saw him earlier, I was surprised to discover that the tattoo on his neck extends into a long line of text coiling around his collarbone. I haven't been close enough yet to see what it says, but it would be impossible to read the whole thing without circling Robbie at least three times.

"This is your sixth summer at Wanagi," Kornelía muses. She smiles up at our lead, her eyes magnified through the thick lenses of her glasses. "Is it always a big change from year to year?"

"Mhmm." Robbie plops down beside Kornelía and

draws his knees up under his chin. "The Oracle never seems to rest in the same pocket of the world for long. The year before last, we were in the desert. *That* was a boring summer. It was a relief to leave for our final projects."

The taxi stops at the dock, and the new group climbs off the boat. Meander gave in around three and grabbed a book from our room, but he pauses between pages to glance at the distant campers.

"Where'd you go for your final project?" Dylan asks Robbie.

Our lead chuckles. "Good ol' London Town," he grins. "No where better to talk to Victorian ghosts."

The kids exit the taxi and start for the beach. They're too far away to see properly, but it looks like one of them has a stilted walk. Something catches a flash of light from the sun, and I realize it must be a metal crutch.

"Bad luck, that," Meander mumbles, catching the same glint. "Braces are going to be horrid with this sand. Wonder if they broke a foot."

"When I was eight, I fractured my ankle at the beginning of summer," Robbie sighs. "It was hot and I was miserable watching my brothers swimming while I had that itchy cast on. But I guess that wasn't so bad. My second summer at Wanagi, one of the Revenants broke two ribs and shattered his arm after falling out a window while trying to release a ghost."

I pull my knees up and wrap my arms around my legs, my eyes flitting to Meander's right forearm. The wound he suffered from glass slicing his skin during the winter is nothing more than a long, thin scar now, but if the glass had been directed elsewhere, the damage could have been catastrophic. Falling out a window doesn't sound impossible for someone dealing with spirits who feed on anger.

"Speaking of crashes," Dylan says, his crude segue failing to alleviate the unease creeping along my spine, "got anything good cooked up for tonight? Any half-rotted buildings ready to fall on top of us?"

Robbie laughs. "Hopefully not. Mrs. Buxley wasn't pleased we nearly lost half the campers so early in the season. This year they've found a spot more out in the open. You'll see. The other sectors meet for the initiation around eleven thirty, a little while before the new kids."

"We're not expected to participate, right?" Meander asks. He closes his book over one finger and looks at Robbie. "Whatever they're planning for Entity, it's got nothing to do with our talents, yeah?"

"Don't worry," Robbie smiles. "Initiation is all about the new sector. I don't think you'll have any trouble tonight."

"How do you know?" Kornelía asks. "I mean, how do you know other abilities won't interfere?"

"Normally, it doesn't matter if they do." Robbie shrugs. "If an older camper can see the spirit, they stay in the back and let someone younger take center stage." He glances at Meander. "Doesn't always go to plan, but that's why we keep an escape route in place." He stands, grinning as he dusts sand from the backs of his legs. "Last year we got a good test… Did pretty well, too."

"If that's what you call doing pretty well, I'd hate to see a disaster," Dylan says.

"Hey, we all got out, didn't we?" Robbie says.

"That's the difference right there."

He gives us a wave and heads to where Alex and a couple of Wraith campers lounge under an oversized umbrella.

"Anyone else ever wonder if we're always one step away from being killed at this camp?" Dylan asks.

Mim smiles, stretching herself out on her stomach, her red bathing suit and brown legs covered in a fine coat of dusty sand. "At least there aren't any windows to fall out of."

The distant drone of the empty water taxi pulling away from its temporary port distracts our attention until the noise is enveloped by the sound of the waves.

"Do you think Robbie really knows what's in store for tonight?" I ask once the taxi is a speck on the horizon.

"Why wouldn't he?" Mim asks.

I shrug. "Well, it's not up to him to plan it this time."

I remember last year's 'show,' when the Entity campers roused us and took us to the house with the murdered woman and her murderous husband. I wonder which of the Entity campers have returned this year as leads.

"I guess we'll find out tonight," Dylan says. "The initiation will start soon enough. And tomorrow, we've got to pick our courses and act as though we're actually willing to spend the next ten weeks studying our craft. So for now, let's pretend our lives are most definitely not at stake. I'll start by making the first important decision of this trip—what I should eat for dinner. Anyone care to join me in the dining hall— hut—place with food?"

Kornelía smiles. "I'll come."

Her green sundress whips around her as she stands, the fabric wrapping so tight it's easy to see how thin and wispy she is. Dylan puts an arm around her shoulder. With Kornelía's height causing him to crook his arm so high, it must ache if he holds the awkward position for long.

I don't think Mim intended to leave her spot on the beach but, when she sees Dylan's arm around Kornelía, she hops up without bothering to brush herself off.

"I'm starved," she says, nestling into Dylan's side.

I don't know if she's jealous or simply territorial. Whatever the case, Kornelía must sense the danger. She moves away from the couple and glances down at me to see if I'll give her an excuse to keep a few paces back.

"I'm not really hungry," I say in an apologetic tone. We ate a big lunch, and I'm not ready to leave the comfort of the beach yet.

Kornelía sighs, her eyes sliding over to Meander before they peer farther down the beach.

"Oh, there's Sabeena," she says, her face brightening. "I think I'll go and say hello."

"Sure thing. See you later, Korni," Mim says, the smile on her lips a touch too smug. Even Dylan notices. He gives her a sideways stare until she drops the expression and heaves a dramatic sigh. "I'll come and get you in a while, okay?" she adds, and Kornelía nods before heading off.

Meander hasn't said much since our tour of the camp. But when everyone else is gone, he closes his book and places it next to him on the sand. "I feel like that's been my life for the past ten months," he says, picking up an old thread of conversation. "Planning my escapes. I'm thinking I might skip the initiation tonight, just in case."

"You can't miss the entire summer because you don't want to cause trouble," I say.

We've had a few conversations like this over the past six months. After a spirit smashed a pub's dinnerware and Meander had to get stitches because of the glass shard jabbed into his arm, he wanted to stay in his bedroom and forget about school and his job. I spent an entire night convincing him he couldn't become a recluse. Even after he relented and promised to leave his room, I made him show me his homework for a week to prove he hadn't stayed at home all day.

I'm not about to let those efforts go to waste now.

"I know," he says. He rubs his hand along the scar, his eyes trained over the ocean. "But facing spirits as part of a lesson plan is a bit different than ruining Entity's first night."

He's right, and only five minutes ago I was picturing what horrid things could happen if his talent caused a spirit to gain too much control. But the unsure way he speaks, a contradiction to the quiet confidence— or at least indifference—his physical presence almost always evokes, reminds me why I pushed him to return to normal life after the attack. I don't want him living in fear of his own ability.

"We'll stay near the back," I assure him. "If anything starts, I'll leave with you. Okay?"

He doesn't respond, so I lean into his side, pressing my weight against him until he breathes an answer.

"Fine," he sighs, his voice the same mix of appreciation and tired annoyance he used when

I made him present his daily worksheets so I could check the date.

"Good," I smile. I let up on the pressure, but he moves with me so we're still touching. "From what I gather, it won't be a proper initiation if the whole thing doesn't go off the rails anyway."

Meander laughs. "Yeah, you're right. If there weren't a few unpleasant surprises, what kind of summer camp would this be?"

WE DON'T HAVE TO WORRY ABOUT WALLS CRASHING AROUND US, AT any rate. When the Shade sector joins Revenant near midnight, we meet on a stretch of beach fifteen minutes away from our fales. Torches form a circle in the sand, inside which the Entity leads wait for Wraith—this year's oldest campers—to arrive with the new sector.

I met most of the former Entity sector last summer. But when we reach the site of the initiation, I'm still surprised to see a familiar face in the flickering torchlight.

"I didn't know Daniel was returning," I whisper to Meander as we step back from the group, keeping our distance so we don't get stuck in the middle of the crowd when the other campers arrive.

"Maybe you'll finally get your chance to talk to him," Meander says.

I nod, watching my former mentor as he chats with the other Entity lead. I never got to say goodbye to

Daniel last year, or thank him for helping me back to camp after I was concussed by a spirit. We never made plans to keep in touch, so I didn't think I'd have the opportunity to speak with him again.

"Hopefully," I mumble, surveying the army uniform with the medic's band I remember him wearing last year. I could try to talk to him now, but his face is alight with nervous excitement as he waits for the new recruits. I don't want to disturb his concentration. This isn't his first initiation, but it is the first time he's acting in the role of lead. Besides, spots of orange light bob in the distance as the oldest campers lead the youngest to their initiation spot. If I try to talk to Daniel now, our conversation will be cut short anyway.

"Do you feel anything?" Meander asks, the question drawing me out of my thoughts.

I tilt my chin up, feeling for changes in the temperature and listening for a rustle of static between my ears. But the night is warm, and my head is clear. With a relieved smile, I shake my head.

"No," I answer, turning to study Meander's pale face in the uneven light. "Do you?"

He mimics my movement as well as my expression, the lift of his lips so genuine it makes my smile widen.

"Unless they're bringing the spirit with them," he says, glancing at the line of campers heading across the sand. "With our luck, it'll be attached to one of those burning torches."

"If we're attacked by a haunted ball of flame, run for the water," I say.

Meander crosses his arms over his chest. "But what if I can't swim?"

I shrug. "Then I'll drag you along behind me."

My gaze shifts to the procession of light across the sand as the new members of Camp Wanagi approach. When the campers are close enough that I can make out human shapes in the torchlight, Kornelía sidles next to me, her long hair tickling my arm.

"Think this will be as exciting as last year?" she asks.

I didn't expect to find her at the back of the group with us. She'd been with Mim and Dylan near the front of the crowd when we arrived, and I figured she'd want a closer view once the initiation gets underway.

"I guess it depends on what they've got in store," I tell her.

The Wraith sector is in view now, only five of them left. I'm glad everyone from Shade returned this year—arriving to find our sector incomplete would have dampened today's happy mood. I wonder which Wraiths didn't come back for their final summer. More to the point, I'm curious to know what made them change their minds after attending the first three years of camp.

"Do you sense anything, Kornelía?" Meander asks.

She grins, the expression familiar, though she hasn't worn it since my arrival this morning. "Yes," she says in a soft voice.

She doesn't elaborate, but she doesn't need to. Knowing the spirit is already present is enough to prove it's not a spirit Meander or I have to worry about. I exchange a pleased glance with him, then watch Daniel and the other Entity lead, Clarice, turn to face the approaching campers.

The Wraith sector joins the rest of us around the outer circle, while the new Entity campers form a crescent across from everyone else. Their white sweaters, bearing the words *Camp Wanagi* stitched in black and outlined with blue, are bright next to the yellow light surrounding them. They must be boiling under the weight of such heavy material. I didn't even consider wearing my black sweater tonight, a decision made out of foolish confidence I wouldn't need something so warm in this climate—that, or a subconscious hope the warm temperature won't fade.

Seeing the newest Senders-in-training is like looking through a distorted mirror. Seven campers make up the new sector but, just like us, they vary widely in appearance and manner. Some of the campers shrink away from the mass of older teens crowding across from them. Others bounce on their toes, nervous or excited about what's going to happen next. One girl already looks bored of the game. I don't see the kid with the crutches from earlier. I wonder if he or she stayed back in their room to avoid the sand.

"Good evening, Entity," Clarice says as the campers come to a standstill.

"They look young," Kornelía mumbles, studying the new kids. "I know it's only a year, but… They look young."

"They look *naïve*," Meander corrects.

I think Kornelía will tell him he's wrong but, instead, she nods. "You're right," she sighs. "They do."

"Tonight, we're here to welcome you all to Camp Wanagi," Clarice says, eyeing the new campers. She hid her discomfort well while we were waiting for the group to arrive, but the wobble now obvious in her voice makes me certain she's feeling the effects of the spirit.

Daniel stands to the side, more at ease and fixing his

gaze on someone in the middle of the small crowd. I don't know who he is looking at, but I suspect he's waiting to see the reaction of the camper who will be affected by the ghost.

A touch of cold flits across my face, the change so slight I can't tell if it's the caress of a spirit, or simply an island breeze. But then Meander hunches his shoulders, and the whole of Wraith seems to fidget as though they've suddenly been struck with a chill. So, I guess the island's not breezy tonight after all.

Clarice pauses her introduction, takes a shaky breath, and glances at Daniel.

"There's a ghost here with us," Daniel says, picking up the speech. His eyes don't move from the members of Entity. "Would anyone here like to try and interact with it?"

Clarice steps back, a fist pressed to her mouth like she's trying to keep from being sick. I keep waiting for the same feeling to overtake me, for the smell of the air to change, or the clarity of my thoughts to muddle with static. Watching as strange symptoms strike someone else while not experiencing anything myself is surreal, and I wonder if this is how Dylan feels when the rest of us see spirits.

The Entity campers look between themselves, everyone waiting for a volunteer. None of them seem to be in pain. But after an unsure moment, one of them raises a hand.

"I can," a girl says, and Daniel's smile tells me this is who he's been watching.

"Thank you, Isabis," he says as the girl makes her way forward.

She wears a pale yellow head scarf twisted at the

top of her head, leaving a fringe of black visible at the hairline. When she starts forward, her gait is spastic, and I soon see the leg braces covering her calves, ankles, and feet. *She* must have been the one with the crutches we saw on the dock earlier.

"What would you like me to do?" Isabis asks, her words slow and a bit muffled. She waits for Daniel's instructions with an eager expression.

"Whatever you want," Daniel replies.

I would have been confounded by such an open invitation, but the girl only nods and lets her eyes slip closed.

Everyone grows quiet as we wait. The water behind us is loud, the swishing of the waves far nicer to listen to than whining floorboards in a house ready to fall apart.

Isabis's brows furrow in a look of concentration. Her limbs tremble, too, but I think the movement might be involuntary, something related to the leg braces instead of to her talent.

After a pause, she makes a breathy noise and starts to speak in a language I don't recognize.

At first, nothing happens. Isabis waits, scrunching her nose in frustration as the night remains calm. But then she repeats the phrase, this time in a stronger voice that has more effect. Her lips twitch and, slowly, the sand before her feet starts to move. From where I'm standing, it looks as if an invisible finger drags along the ground, drawing a circle in the white grains.

Isabis opens her eyes and watches the circle form. She smiles, satisfied with the result, before she closes her eyes again and continues to concentrate.

"Blow out the fire," she says, this time in English.

The movement of the sand stops. A shorter pause follows, then one of the torches in the circle flickers. The flames sweep to one side before extinguishing.

"What is she doing?" I ask, glancing at Kornelía.

Her eyes are closed as well, but she tilts her head towards me, leaning close. "She's manipulating the spirit," she whispers. "She's making him do what she tells him."

She sounds more concerned than impressed, like she doesn't enjoy the idea of a Sender guiding a spirit's will. But I know what the opposite is like, and this is highly preferable. Not seeing the spirit myself makes it look like Isabis is controlling the elements with her mind. She says a command, and the task is done. Of all the abilities I've encountered, this seems like one of the best.

Isabis continues her demonstration, giving some commands in English and some in the other language she speaks. The spirit, whoever he is, blows out another torch, draws a heart in the sand, and ruffles one girl's dress. A few of the older campers laugh, while most of Entity looks on in confusion, perhaps unaware their sector mate is interacting with a spirit.

Uttering another slow-spoken instruction in the language I can't understand, Isabis convinces the spirit to lift a pile of sand. The grains stream down as if running between unseen fingers. The girl opens her eyes to view the action, looking proud of her accomplishment. She's so interested in what the ghost is doing, she doesn't notice what's happening outside the circle of torches.

Of course, I don't, either. Not until Meander presses a hand to my arm and I look away from the sand to see him staring towards the back of the beach.

"Look at the dogs," he says in a quiet voice.

I follow his gaze to see what has to be fifteen or twenty dogs watching us from the shadows of the night. None of them are sitting or lounging on the beach. They're all standing, lined up like they're waiting for some kind of signal to run. Or attack.

"What the hell," I breathe, as other campers start to notice the menacing sight.

"Are they strays?" someone asks in a hushed voice.

"I've heard they like attacking tourists," a girl mumbles.

"Does anyone have something we can throw at them?"

"We've got the torches. Those should scare them off, right?"

"I don't think they're going to bother us," Kornelía says. She points into the crowd. "Look at Dylan."

Dylan's not watching the dogs. He's pressed into Mim's side, his body hunched in pain. He groans, while Mim rubs his back and looks over his bent head to stare at the dogs along with everyone else.

So much for Dylan's carefree tropical vacation. If he's in pain, it's easy to assume the living dogs aren't the only canines near us. I wonder if he's ever been hit with two spirits on the same day before.

Daniel eyes the dogs, then looks to Clarice. The second Entity lead resembles Dylan, sick, shivering, and not at all aware of the possible impending danger.

"Maybe we should head back," Daniel says, his voice unsure.

Isabis realizes what's going on and tells the spirit to drop the pile of sand he's still holding. The floating grains fall in a dusty cloud but, before they have time to settle, something kicks them back into the air.

"I— No, I said stop," Isabis stammers.

Her eyes are wide as she watches the sand flying before her face. With a panicked flinch, she steps back, losing her balance and stumbling into the girl behind her.

"He did stop," Kornelía says, loud enough for everyone to hear. Last summer, Kornelía kept silent about her ability to see spirits in her mind. I know things have changed for her over the last ten months, like they have for us all. I'm glad she's not afraid to admit she's got the upper hand here. "Something else blew the sand back up."

"Another spirit?" I ask.

Kornelía shakes her head. "I can't see anything," she says. "But there has to be *something* else here."

The sand flies up fast, some of it hitting Isabis in the face. She grunts, trying in vain to issue another command.

I watch the almost automatic motion of the spraying sand before my eyes slide back to Dylan. "Anyone ever see a dog digging in the sand?" I ask.

Kornelía smiles."*Of course,*" she says, sounding happy to have a logical explanation for why she can't see whatever is moving the sand. She shifts into the crowd, slipping between bodies so she can reach Dylan.

"But why are the other dogs here?" Meander asks when she's left us behind.

The living dogs watch, their bodies rigid, as if they're poised to move to some undetermined trigger.

"I don't know," I mutter, my gaze sliding between

Isabis, the pack, and Dylan. "Maybe they sense the canine spirit."

Isabis has regained her footing. Another girl holds onto her shoulder in case she stumbles again. "Stop," she says. The word takes effort, but it has no effect. The sand continues to fly, a depression forming on the beach where the spirit dog must be digging.

Confusion and unease ripple through the crowd. The Entity campers aren't the only ones muttering amongst themselves. Sefa—his bulking muscles larger than they were the last time I saw him, his appearance like that of a club bouncer—takes a nervous step back as he eyes the sight in the distance.

"The dogs are approaching," he says, taking Sabeena's arm and using her as a shield. She rolls her eyes, muttering something before she focuses on the line of dogs padding in our direction.

"Can Dylan do anything?" she asks in a louder voice.

Dylan is out of commission. He struggles to stand against Mim's side and, even if he had his wits about him, he's said before he can't communicate with the spirits he sees. Besides, Dylan's ability is concerned with dead dogs, not living ones. He certainly can't reason with the pack heading towards us.

Which means, if these dogs get vicious, we're all screwed.

"Is this a joke?" one of the Entity campers asks.

I think he's talking about the dogs but, when I glance over, I see he's looking at the sand. No longer is it flying like the spray of a pup preparing to bury a bone. The sand has now formed a solid sheet, stretching up from the ground like a grainy blanket of white.

"Is that the dog, or the human?" Meander asks.

His hand is still on my arm, and I'm glad. The chances of us needing to make a run for it are becoming increasingly likely. If we charge away from danger, I want to make sure he stays close.

"I don't know if it's either," I mumble.

The sand twists, as if a cyclone is brewing within the confines of our circle. Daniel is too preoccupied by the approaching dogs to notice the sand, but Clarice does. She struggles to take control of the situation, her breathing labored as she cautiously steps towards the whirlwind.

"Isabis," she groans, "you need to stop it."

"I-I can't," Isabis says.

She looks at her new lead, her face etched with worry. But then she closes her eyes again and tries to do whatever it is she's supposed to be doing to manipulate the spirit. She speaks in her other language while the sand rises and twists, spraying clods of hard grains. At the same time, the dogs continue their approach, and the campers inch towards the shoreline—everyone afraid to break into a run in case that's what the dogs anticipate.

Dylan raises his head, looking for the first time at the dogs. He glances at the dancing tornado of sand, then he steps closer to the pack. A low growl rumbles from some of the dogs' throats. Mim tries to pull Dylan back, but he takes an unsteady step forward, shaking his head.

"I wouldn't do that if I were you," he says to the dogs.

They look at him and, for a second, it seems like they inexplicably understand what he said. But then one of the dogs rushes forward, and the others follow.

Someone screams, and all the campers turn to run. Meander's hand slides down to mine, and I hold it tight as others push us, everyone stumbling into each other in a spectacularly clumsy effort to get away. Sefa tramples my foot, and one of the Revenant girls crashes into my side. She falls onto the sand, but someone else pulls her up. A couple of campers make it to the shore, splashing into the water in hopes the dogs won't want to get wet.

Isabis remains where she is, as do Daniel, Clarice, and Dylan. Daniel's yelling for the campers not to panic. From what I can glimpse through the scrambling crowd, the other three are watching the sand as it rises like a floating mound and twists into a shape reminiscent of a giant orb.

The dogs are barking now, their growls endless as they echo across the beach. They bound to the edge of the circle before I lose sight of them in the panic. Even though there's no static, my head is full of rushing waves, harsh barks, and piercing screams. Soon I can't make sense of anything except that Meander's grasping my hand and someone is pushing at my back.

Then everything goes dark.

My eyes sting, and it takes a moment to realize I've been assaulted with sand. The panic of being blinded tightens my nerves, until the sparkle of a star in the night sky assures me the sand simply doused the torch flames, leaving us in darkness. Still, without adequate time to adjust, and with my eyes blinking in a furious attempt to dislodge the sand, the blindness is real enough. I trip, tumbling over someone and feeling someone else tumble over me. I can't keep hold of Meander's hand. He's wrenched away from me as raining sand clogs my mouth and sends me into a fit of coughs.

The snarling barks are replaced with subdued whines. The sounds start to fade as someone relights a torch. I squint, my eyes and throat burning while I try to untangle myself from my fellow campers.

"Is everyone okay?" Daniel asks, bringing over the light. His question is met with a quiet cacophony of groans, swears, coughs, and sobs.

When I regain bleary sight, I search for Meander. He's a little ways off, sitting on the beach rubbing his eyes. I struggle out from under a Revenant and crawl over to flop down on the ground beside him.

The dogs are gone. My guess is the spirits are, too. Aside from the racket we're all making, the night is now peaceful.

"You all right?" Meander asks, coughing through the words and pressing a palm to his left eye.

"I've been worse," I say. "You?"

"Yeah," he smirks. "I've been worse, too."

He tilts his head forward and shakes sand from his curls. I watch it fall onto his lap. When he looks back at me—his eyes red from the sand—I start to laugh. He gives me a shove and, when I shove him back, he starts laughing, too.

"Now it feels like Camp Wanagi," I say, and Meander groans, leaning his head on my shoulder.

"And here I thought it might be nice having a normal holiday for a change."

5

When we're back in our fale, each of us takes turns showering the sand off our skin and out of our hair. Then Dylan lectures us as he unpacks his summer clothes.

"The dogs weren't after you," he says, stuffing an array of multi-colored shirts into his dresser drawer.

"Who were they after then? 'Cause it didn't look like they were out for a nice evening stroll," Reed scoffs. He scratches his head, his scalp visible through the buzzed haircut he's sporting this summer. Reed is still pudgy, but he's grown taller since I last saw him. His height, combined with the shorter haircut, makes him look bulky and tough.

"They were after their dead pack member," Dylan sighs.

"But how would they know the dead dog was there?" Reed asks. "Are you saying all dogs are

Senders or something?"

Dylan rolls his eyes."No," he says, but then he shakes his head, his expression less certain. "I don't know why they could see the ghost."

"Isn't that a thing, though?" I ask as I towel dry my hair. "I know it's not the best source of reliable information but, in ghost stories, the dog always knows trouble is coming well before the people do."

"Aren't there cats that, like, know when someone's going to die, too?" Reed adds.

Naasir raises his head, considering Reed's statement with a nod. "Animals are intuitive," he says from his bed.

Out of everyone in Shade, Naasir's the only person who doesn't seem to have changed at all. He looks the same, still tall and broad, his black hair as short as it was last year. He's still quiet and, when he does speak, his voice carries the same deep, sonorous quality I remember. When I first caught sight of him earlier today, he had some kind of centipede crawling over his palm. So, I guess his affection for insects hasn't altered either.

"Yeah, but humans are animals, too," Meander reminds him.

"But only Senders can see spirits," Reed says. "Couldn't that mean other species have Senders as well?" He looks to Dylan as if he's an expert on all things canine.

"No idea," Dylan shrugs, slamming the drawer closed before shoving his empty suitcase underneath his bed. "I only know tonight wasn't typical. Those dogs shouldn't have been able to see that ghost."

"So, how could they?" Reed pushes.

"No idea," Dylan says again. "But it has to have something to do with that girl and her talent. She made the dog able to dig in the sand, and then… she lost control. Gave the dog too much power."

"It was like magic," Reed muses.

He's by far the most interested of us all. I'm curious to know why our night ended in such chaos, but it's past one in the morning, and I'm tired. After the fiasco on the beach, I'm ready to get some rest.

Sefa walks into the room and frowns. "You guys aren't still talking about it, are you?"

"Just because you're scared of dogs doesn't mean we can't talk about them," Reed says.

"I can't believe you never told me you're afraid of dogs," Dylan adds.

Sefa sighs, climbing up to the bed above mine."I'm not," he snaps, before continuing in a milder voice, "I don't like strays, is all."

"What's wrong with strays?" Dylan asks.

Sefa scoffs. "You've only been here a day. We've got packs of strays like this in Samoa, too. You'll see what they're like. I got bit pretty bad when I was a kid. Still have the scar on my arm, though you can't see it unless you're really looking. It was as long as the one Meander's got, at first."

Naasir, Reed, and Dylan glance up at Meander like they didn't realize he has a scar, a lack of notice I'm sure suited him fine. He pretends not to have heard Sefa's remark, but his arm shifts under his blanket when he reaches out to turn the page of his book.

"I wonder if the human ghost had anything to do with the spirit of the dog," I say, deflecting their attention. "They could have been pet and owner when they were alive… Maybe the man died, and that's when the dog became part of the stray pack."

"Maybe," Dylan says. "All I know is that the dog was adding sand to that ball, but she wasn't holding it. The other ghost—the human—must have thrown it at the strays when they got too close."

"Kornelía might know," I say, pulling back my covers and kicking the comforter to the end of the bed. The room is warm, and the thin black sheet will be more than sufficient. "We can ask her in the morning."

A moment of quiet passes as we prepare for bed and, in the silence, I work on forming my own theory as to what happened on the beach. Various ideas scroll through my mind, pieces I'm not sure are even part of the same puzzle. The strays could have wanted to attack their pack mate, angry she died and left them behind. Or the dogs could have been trying to protect her from the spirit of the man. Then again, it could have been pure coincidence that the man and the dog were on the beach together. And while Dylan said all of the dogs were part of the same pack, he could be wrong—the ghost could have been strange and threatening to the living strays, which might be why they freaked out so badly.

Trying to solve the mystery of two spirits I didn't even see proves too much work for my tired brain. Once I've grabbed my phone and unraveled the earbuds, I let the questions of tonight's ghosts fade into the rhythm of Clara Schumann's "Piano Trio Op. 17".

Dylan turns the room's main light out, leaving only the glow from each bunk's reading lamp. Once he's pushed aside his covers and belly flopped onto his bed, Sefa lowers his head over the edge of his upper bunk.

"Hey, you know what?" he says. "This is the first time we've all been in the same room this year." He laughs a little, and the bed creaks as he disappears from view. "It's nice to be back, isn't it? Even if we're someplace different. It's nice to be with you guys again."

A soft chorus of agreement echoes through the room before the quiet returns, and I wonder if Sefa's statement lingers with anyone else like it does with me. He's right. Being here is wonderful, even with my eyes stinging from sand and my nerves prickling with worry that the humming dehumidifier Sefa's already complained about won't be enough to keep my violin from warping. I wouldn't have expected it, but the issues feel minor and unimportant compared to the brilliance of being back at camp. Even the spirits—three in one day, whether I've seen them or not—don't matter. This setting is not as comfortable as my house and my normal routines, but I'm surrounded by familiar company and friends I've missed. In its own way, returning to Camp Wanagi feels like I've come home.

Switching off my reading lamp, I lie on my back and wait for each of the remaining bunk lights to diminish. When only one soft glow remains, I smile and sink into my music more completely, following each pull of the violin and stroke of the piano keys until I fall asleep.

# 6



"WHAT THE HELL IS SENDER STRENGTH AND STAMINA?" REED ASKS, HIS freckled face set in a frown as he stares at his course selection sheet.

When morning came, Robbie collected all ten members of Shade, and took us to the house where the eight sector leads are staying. Alex handed around our course selection sheets when we arrived, and Reed was less than impressed to discover that Basics of Paranormality has been replaced by a different mandatory course.

"Think of it as Camp Wanagi's version of gym class," Robbie says between sips of juice.

Lu's head snaps up, her shortened bob of hair making her look like she's aged three or four years in the past ten months. "You're kidding, right?" she asks, her frown even deeper than Reed's.

"Afraid not," Alex says with a sympathetic smile.

At our end of the long table, Kornelía pushes her

glasses up on her head and squints at the selection sheet. "Why do we need a gym class?" she asks while Mim pulls the glasses down and gives Kornelía a reprimanding look.

"Being a Sender is hard work," Robbie says after downing the rest of his juice.

We shared breakfast with our leads this morning, a full Shade reunion over plates of bacon, eggs, fresh fruit, and some kind of coconut french toast. The ocean is to our backs, the sun is shining through the open windows, and everything smells of fried food and citrus. I'm stuffed, my body is warm, and my brain still fails to grasp the reality of the summer ahead of us. Even after what happened at last night's initiation, it's hard to be apprehensive in a place like this.

"We're not leaping from buildings or anything," Reed grumbles, contesting Robbie's assertion that our job is a difficult one.

"No, but sometimes we do have to run," Robbie responds with a grin. He and Alex didn't come to the initiation, but I'm sure they've heard what occurred.

"And releasing a spirit takes its toll," Alex adds.

"That's right," Robbie nods. "You need to build up your ability to store energy and recover fast. Y'all won't always have a team of people ready to carry you back to your beds after a ghostly encounter."

I brush an invisible strand of hair from my forehead, my fingers gliding over the smooth bit of skin that, ten months ago, was raised and swollen. If I had recovered faster from releasing my first spirit last year, I may have been able to fight the influence of the ghost buried in the woods behind our camp. Gym class would not be my first choice for a climate like this, but I'll gladly break a sweat if it provides me with the skills needed to avoid being manipulated again.

Meander watches the movement of my fingers, a small, almost remorseful smile on his lips. I blame myself for being drawn under that spirit's influence, but Meander thinks my injury is his fault for making the ghost so angry it was able to throw a rock in the first place.

I lower my hand, glad I'm not the only one still feeling guilt over something we apparently can't control.

"This is going to be sweet," Sefa says, excited by the prospect of more exercise in his schedule.

Lu sighs. "This is going to be terrible."

"It's only once a week," Mim reasons.

"Yes, for four hours," Lu snaps.

Evidently, the rivalry between the two girls hasn't diminished in the time they've spent apart. Mim's eyes narrow as she responds to Lu with a derisive snort. "We won't be exercising for four hours straight," she says. "Stop whining."

"No one asked for your input, *Maria*," Lu mutters.

The use of her real name makes Mim's jaw harden with hatred. "No one asked for *yours*, either," she retorts with a murderous glance.

Dylan looks between the girls and, with a tired shake of his head, he turns to Kornelía."What courses are you taking, Korni?" he asks, eyeing her glasses and smiling like he's decided he's fond of them.

"Meditative Communication, Channeling, and Sender Mythos, I think." She taps her pen against the sheet, her mouth twisting up as she considers her choices.

"I think I'm going to try Emotional Entities this year," Mim says, breaking into the discussion without realizing she wasn't already a part of it.

"Don't bother," I say, glancing up at her. "Mr. Bujak is the worst."

"Bujak's not here this summer," Robbie says from the other end of the breakfast table.

"He's not?" Kornelía asks with more interest than I'm able to muster.

"No, he's on assignment," Robbie explains. "Happens sometimes. Ms. Qwick is doing Emotional Entities this year. She's great."

Mim smiles at me. "Well, there you are." She shrugs, marking the course on her sheet and leaving me to feel cheated that I got the bad teacher when the good one was only a summer away.

Before I mope too long over the injustice, Meander kicks my foot under the table. "What are you taking?" he asks, his voice quiet, as if he wishes he didn't have to ask the question in front of everyone else.

"I'm not sure yet," I sigh, looking at the sheet. This year, we're not restricted from taking any of the courses, which means our options are more diverse. "Intro to Communication Techniques, maybe? Sender Mythos sounds like it might be good, too."

Two courses on the list draw my attention each time I glance down the page: Hostage Arts and Resistive Release. But as serious as I am about furthering my studies to make releasing spirits easier—and resist being guided by their will—I'm too chicken to throw myself into the deep end just yet.

"Yeah, Mythos seems like it could be all right." Meander nods, chewing on his lip as he looks at his sheet.

I watch him for a moment, musing over his habit and wondering if he has ever had chapped lips, even in the coldest days of winter. Meander has always been well-groomed, but his appearance has assumed an almost meticulous quality since last year. He fretted about the lack of an iron this summer, genuinely concerned about having wrinkles in his clothes. Even his curls, though abundant, are only ever unruly first thing in the morning—a feat I envy given how neat they remain even though his fingers often run through the strands.

I haven't yet had the nerve to ask whether he might be trying to make up for his scars by keeping himself perfect in other ways. I wouldn't even think of divulging my suspicions, except I wish he knew the scars don't detract from him.

"Are you taking the other history course?" I ask before my thoughts stray too far. Two history courses are on the selection sheet, Ancient and Modern History of Spirits. Last summer, Meander took the Ancient course. He figured if it was offered, he'd take the Modern class this time around.

"Yeah, I think so." He stares at one of the course names for a while, until his eyes flick to the bottom of the sheet and then up to me. "There's Research Methods, too."

He's skipping over the courses he knows he should take, like Hostile Spirits. But I can't very well complain, since I'm doing the same.

"That's probably my third choice, too," I say instead. For a moment, we stare at each other—both of us knowing we're being pathetic, but neither of us willing to state that obvious fact.

"Hey, how come there's no Spirits of the Non-Human?" Dylan asks, his voice so unexpected it makes me jump. Meander smirks, and I look away in embarrassment.

Alex shrugs from her spot next to Robbie."There must not be any campers with that kind of ability this year," she says. With her sundress and messy bun, she looks like a girl on holiday, not a lead for a ghost-hunting summer camp.

Dylan stares at Alex, his eyes wide. "You mean last year's course was only offered because of me?"

"It's possible," Robbie says.

"Whoa," he mutters, looking flattered.

He and Kornelía exchange grins, and he puts his arm around the back of her chair.

"When you've finished picking courses, hand your sheets to us," Alex instructs. "We'll have your timetables ready this afternoon. In the meantime, you're free for the rest of the day."

"Use it," Robbie says, pushing his chair back and propping his feet on the table. "Courses start tomorrow, and your first course is Strength and Stamina. You'll be expected on the beach at six a.m."

Reed nearly chokes on a slice of pineapple."Six?" he splutters. "What happened to courses starting at noon?"

"They do, the rest of the time," Robbie laughs. "But Althea likes the morning sun."

"This is going to be so sweet," Sefa says again.

Lu sighs, Reed coughs, and Meander gives me an amused smile I can't help but return. Whatever our timetables end up looking like, and no matter how useful our courses are, it's good to be with our sector mates again.

Still, my careless attitude disappears after I've handed my sheet to Alex. If Dylan had a class designed just for him, it's possible some of the courses available to us this year have been tailored to our needs. None of the selections mentioned the spirits of murder victims, but the subject could be included in a lesson plan for one of the courses I didn't choose to take.

The others hand in their selections, and I refrain from asking Alex if I can have my sheet back. If a course was necessary, I'd be forced to take it. They wouldn't let me miss something they intended for me to study.

I hope.

"Come on, let's enjoy the day while we've got it," Mim says once all of the sheets have been handed in.

Dylan grabs a last slice of toast, and Sefa downs a glass of water before the ten of us head outside. As we leave the house behind in favor of the busy beach, I push away the nagging worry I've screwed up my summer before I've even stepped foot in a classroom.

# 7

Robbie may have given us warning, but knowing we'll be awakened early doesn't make the next morning easier.

Our Sender Strength and Stamina instructor wastes no time starting her first lesson. At five thirty, she stands in our doorway with a whistle between her lips, its shrieking trill mixing with the huskier key of our startled groans.

"Out of bed, Shade!" she calls, her voice loud and heavy with a Caribbean accent.

"What is going on?" Reed asks in a dreamy voice, like he's still asleep and imagining the whole scene.

"You're getting up," Althea says. She reaches up and pats the top of Reed's head like an affectionate mother. "It's time for your training."

"How are we supposed to train if we're so tired we can't even walk straight?" Dylan asks.

I struggle to open my eyes and focus on the room around me. Althea is a shape in the corner of my vision and, when I turn my gaze to her, it takes a moment before her appearance aligns with the functioning part of my brain. She's going to be leading our 'gym' class, which meant I imagined she'd be compact and fit. But the woman standing in our doorway is large, taller than me and probably three times my weight. She also looks a couple decades older than I expected. Still, the way she laughs at our sluggish response to her wake-up call tells me I'd be an idiot if I didn't prepare for a tough morning.

"You'll be fully awake soon enough," she says, blowing her whistle again in case it hasn't already pierced our ear drums. "Get dressed, get your running shoes on, and get out to the beach. You've got ten minutes."

"Ten minutes?" Sefa balks.

Althea chuckles. "You don't need to look pretty for me. You can clean up after you're covered in sweat and sand."

She leaves the room, and Dylan flops back onto his bed. "What do you think will happen if I stay here all morning?" he asks, burying his face in his pillow.

"She'd likely pick you up and carry you out to the beach herself," Sefa laughs.

He jumps down at the same moment I sit up and nearly kicks me in the face. I flinch back with a groan.

"Throw you in the water for good measure, too," I add in a mumble.

"She might throw us all in the water." Naasir smiles, stretching his arms above his head. "Swimming is good exercise."

"No use talking about it," Sefa yawns. He plucks an outfit from his dresser drawer and heads towards the bathroom. "We're on a timer. I, at least, don't intend to be late."

I let the others grab their things first, waiting until even Dylan's dragged himself out of bed before I fumble with the plug adapter I've brought so I can charge my phone. Once my sleepy fingers have managed to get the plug into the wall, I check to ensure my violin's still where I tucked it under the bed. Then I find an outfit suitable for working out and head for the bathroom line-up.

My sector mates are quick, though I doubt anyone except Sefa manages to leave the fale before our ten minutes are officially up. Althea must have put the fear in us, though. By the time I'm dressed and ready to go, Meander's the only one still inside the fale, his eyes downcast as he sits on one of the sofas in the living area.

"You okay?" I ask, sitting next to him to lace up my sneakers.

He sighs, eyeing my laces for a minute before he stands."Yeah," he says, staring down at his own feet. "It's just… These are my only trainers. They're going to get ruined with sand. I thought I'd be wearing those damned sandals on the beach."

I smirk, tying my second shoe before we walk together to the door."Sand comes off, you know," I remind him.

"Yeah, but it'll be a pain to remove," he mumbles, holding open the door as I step out beside him. "I'll have to use a toothbrush for a good scrubbing."

"Did you bring a spare?" I ask with a laugh.

"Nah. I'll just use Dylan's," he replies, his voice so deadpan, Dylan would be quick to hide his toothbrush if he overheard the remark.

The sun has not yet peeked over the horizon, but the beach is warm when we reach it. We're the last two members of Shade to arrive, although I think we're more awake than at least half our sector mates. The girls don't seem to be enjoying their wake-up call, either. Mim and Lu share similar expressions of exhaustion and matching nests of tangled hair. Sabeena sits cross-legged on the sand, her chin in her hands and her eyes closed. Only Kornelía is bright-eyed when we approach, but even she seems spacey as we pass and I say hello without her noticing.

Once we've assembled, Althea blows her whistle again, the obnoxious noise threatening to give me a headache before the day's even properly begun."Welcome to your second year at Camp Wanagi, Shade," she says, her voice carrying easily over the sound of the waves. "This summer, I will be teaching you the importance of keeping yourself strong and healthy as you train to become a Sender. Every Tuesday, we will meet here for class. You will spend an hour with me, followed by breakfast and a lesson, followed by another hour of hard work."

"Is every week going to be this early?" Sabeena asks, her words drowsy.

"Of course!" Althea smiles, her wide arms resting on her even wider hips. "Today, we'll start off easy. A fitness test, to see where each of your strengths and weaknesses lie."

"Still think this summer's going to be a breeze?" I mutter to Dylan.

He nods his head and stamps his feet to wake himself up."This will be no problem," he assures me.

"She said it herself. We're starting off easy."

Dylan's wrong, of course. Althea's idea of 'easy' is making us all work so hard most of us are ready to pass out before the hour's over. Dylan does okay for a while, his running habit keeping him in good shape. But after lunges, jumping jacks, burpees, sit-ups, and extended planking, even he is flat on the sand moaning that he can't go on.

Althea may be big, but she demonstrates each move, even keeping pace with Sefa, the only one of us who doesn't want to call it quits. When Reed gives her lip, saying she can do knee-high spot runs in his place, she does a full rep without breaking a sweat—then makes him do double what he's been instructed.

The burpees are what get me. Halfway through, my shirt is soaked and my legs are aching. When I slip in the sand on my way into a push-up, I groan and collapse, too tired to attempt getting back up.

"I need food," Dylan mutters after a while. He lies on his back with his arms over his eyes to block out the sun.

"I need coffee," Mim says mid-squat a few feet away.

"You all need to focus," Althea exclaims, her words hard but her eyes mirthful. She surveys the group, all of us slow or stopped, even Sefa panting hard after his latest rep of sit-ups. Then a chuckle bursts from her lips, and she shakes her head.

"Let's go. Breakfast and lesson time. Then it's back outside."

Unlike last year's single château, which housed the entirety of Camp Wanagi, this year we're spread among at least two dozen different buildings. Althea takes us into a small house, the main room half a kitchen and half a lounge. We slump into chairs and sofas while she pours us water and begins preparing breakfast. Watching an instructor cook is weird, but Althea knows what she's doing. She blends smoothies and scrambles eggs, all while talking about the course we've just been introduced to.

"Most of you need some serious training," she says over the sizzling of her pan. "Strength is one of the most important qualities a Sender can possess. Tell me—have you ever had to run from a spirit?"

"No," Lu mumbles.

"Even if we do, we don't have to run far," Mim amends. "Ghosts don't chase us."

"You're lucky, then," Althea smiles.

Meander leans over in his chair and, when he straightens, I see he's snatched a book from the coffee table next to the sofa. I once asked him what kind of books he reads. His response was that he reads everything and, for the next month, he informed me each time he started a new book so I could see he was telling the truth. Classics, crime thrillers, kids' books, romances, even a few textbooks from school. He doesn't care what he's looking at. The way he describes it, he just feels an insatiable need to read.

Now, he flips through the first pages of what looks to be a non-fiction book, possibly taken from the camp library—wherever it's located in the maze of fales, houses, and pavilions. Then he starts to read, probably once he's determined the book is, in fact, printed in English.

"Hey, I know how to run, does that mean I can skip the rest of the course?" Dylan asks, half-serious.

"Alas, there's a bit more to it than that," Althea

laughs. She brings over the first plates of food, and Sabeena and Naasir get up to help with the rest. "You need strength to recover from releasing spirits, and stamina to deal with spirits for extended periods of time. It also never hurts to keep in shape, in case you find yourself in a tight situation."

She places the plates on the square coffee table before our sofa and rolls up the sleeves of her blue running jacket.

"What do you mean, tight situation?" Sabeena asks.

Althea reaches forward and grabs the book out of Meander's grasp. His eyes flash with annoyance, but his expression changes when he notices the jagged scar running from the inside of her wrist all the way to her elbow.

"Ever been trapped under a cabinet after a mischievous spirit played a trick on you?" she asks, her gaze lingering on his.

"Did that really happen?" Sabeena asks.

Althea nods, humming her agreement as she turns and heads back to the kitchen.

Meander's chest rises and falls before he reaches forward to select two plates from the table, one of which he hands to me. I'm starving, and I don't have the self-restraint not to dig into the food the instant my fork is in hand.

"Pace yourself," he smirks.

I shake my head, swallowing a mouthful of scrambled eggs, pausing only long enough to answer before I devour more. "I don't care if I get a stomach ache later."

"I'm going to gloat when you inevitably get a stomach ache later," he teases, taking a more reserved bite.

"Miss Althea..." Sabeena begins.

"Just Althea, no Miss," Althea replies.

"Oh, right. Sorry." Sabeena sweeps matted hair from her forehead and takes a green smoothie from the counter. "Althea," she corrects, "what is your talent?"

"I deal with what you might call poltergeists," Althea says, far more straightforward than the other instructors I've met at Camp Wanagi. "Ghosts who deal with their annoyance, frustration, or fear by acting out against the living."

Sabeena opens her mouth to ask more questions, but Althea cuts her off. "We have the whole summer to talk about me," she says. "Right now, eat your food. I'll do the talking, and we'll discuss what we're going to accomplish in our time together."

For the next two hours, Althea does talk. She tells us more about why we need to develop our strength, and she goes over the types of fitness we'll do. The course agenda includes a lot of running, with some swimming and even climbing in the summer's second half. She details situations for when each type of fitness would be useful, too. Some of her examples relate to things that have happened to her. Other times, she speaks to one of us—like when she tells Reed he'd better learn how to swim if he plans on working with spirits who have drowned.

If our first hours are any indication, Sender Strength and Stamina is going to be a tough course. But this part—eating breakfast and sharing stories of when it would have been handy to have super speed or stronger muscles—is nice. Camp Wanagi is not new anymore, and this morning helps to emphasize that. This isn't a course meant to introduce unfamiliar concepts. We're talking about the dangers many of us have already faced, while exploring what we may encounter in the future as our talents continue to develop.

After the two hours indoors are over, however, it's back out into the heat. Althea sets us running, giving us directions on how to make a loop that should take around forty-five minutes to complete at a steady jogging pace.

We start off together, the ten of us running in a tight group, but soon we find ourselves separating. Lu is the slowest, and she falls back within the first fifteen minutes. Then the dogs arrive. Another pack of ragged strays, six in total, run towards us as soon as we're in sight.

Sefa halts, backing away with panic in his eyes when the first dog barks. Sabeena and Naasir soon join him, running in the opposite direction. I'm prepared to stop as well, but Dylan heads out in front of us, and the dogs swarm around him, running at his side. They don't snap at his ankles or sniff at his pockets looking for food. Dylan's confused at first, the sudden appearance of the pack startling him, but he doesn't stop. When he figures out they're not about to attack, he gives us a grin and adjusts his speed so he and the six mutts keep an easy pace together.

I don't think Dylan had a clue he'd have so much company on this island. But the sight is amusing and, when I glance at Kornelía, we both start to laugh.

Mim isn't such a fan, though. "I'm not running behind a bunch of filthy dogs," she huffs, hands on her hips even while she jogs.

"Don't let Dylan hear you say that," Kornelía whispers.

Mim scoffs. "I don't care if he does. Let's cut up here." She points to an approaching road and starts to veer towards it. "We've been running long enough. We can head back early."

"I…" Kornelía watches Dylan running further and further ahead, the dogs urging him into a faster speed. He's leaving us behind, but that doesn't make her slow down. "I want to keep running," she says, her words tired but determined. "Althea is right. We need to build our strength, and I think I can do this. I want to finish the loop."

Mim rolls her eyes and turns to the rest of us. "Do you three have any problem stopping early?" she asks.

Within a step I've slowed to a walk, leaning over and resting my arms on my thighs as I come to a full stop. "Not the slightest," I pant, blinking sweat out of my eyes.

"I didn't think anyone would ever ask," Meander mutters, stopping beside me.

Mim smiles, patting Reed on the back as he, too, stops running. Sweat drips from his chin, and his whole face is red. He doesn't say anything, only drags breath in and lets out a few wheezing coughs. Mim considers him, giving him another, more forceful pat before she looks around.

We've passed the street she suggested turning onto but, instead of going back, she nods in the direction of the beach.

"Let's go near the water," she offers. "The breeze might be cool."

We walk along the unfamiliar beach—this part of the island well away from our camp's base—until we find shade under a canopy of foliage. The water is only a few feet away, and a large, luxury house behind us makes for an impressive backdrop to this hidden slice of Vava'u.

"I feel like I'm going to throw up," I say, slumping onto the sand.

"Saying 'I told you so' seems way too easy," Meander says. He sits next to me and wipes a hand across his forehead, his nose scrunching in distaste when his fingers come away slick with sweat. "Besides, I feel like I'm going to throw up, too."

"Some start to summer, eh?" I mumble, dropping my head to my knees to keep the queasy dizziness at bay.

"You should tell Rose," Meander says. "It'll make her feel better about ballet camp."

I laugh, my stomach swelling as I give him a sideways glance. My sister asked if she could attend dance camp this year, and Mom enrolled her in ballet, though what she actually wanted to do was hip hop.

I told Meander about her complaints weeks ago. I didn't think he'd remember.

"I wish we were somewhere less... Interesting," Mim grumbles. She and Reed sit a couple spaces away from us, his legs out in front of him and her chin resting on her knees. "There are too many distractions here. I wanted this summer to be serious. Everyone else seems intent on wasting time."

I don't ask if *everyone* refers to *anyone other than Dylan*. The summer doesn't seem to be going well for the pair. Dylan's beach vacation may not be as carefree as he planned. And Mim, apparently, wants a boring landscape where she can study without vacation threatening to engulf her academic pursuits.

"At least there's a lot of water here," Reed says with a shrug. "I didn't even think I was going to come back until the invitation came. I figure, if I'm ever going to encounter more than the one ghost I saw as a kid, this is a good place to do it, right?"

"One of the many pleasures to be found beachside," Meander says.

He rubs the scar on his arm, and I sit up straight, my vision swinging a little with the motion.

"Does it still hurt?" I ask, focusing on the ground until the spin stops.

When I look up again, he's shrugging, a finger tracing the maroon-pink line. "Sometimes," he says.

My eyes stray to his face, to the old scar along his jaw. "Does the other one?"

Meander pauses, his eyes darting to me before they return to his arm. "No, not anymore," he mumbles.

He shifts, squirming like his shirt is bothering him. If it's as heavy with sweat as mine, it'll be sticking to his skin and making him cringe.

His fingers run the length of the scar again before he glances up, first to meet my gaze, then past me to the house behind us. He frowns, a curious expression drawing his brows together.

"Cal, that house there…"

I look behind my shoulder to the expansive structure built on stilts and backing into a dense cluster of trees. The bamboo exterior and thatched roof are classic examples of island architecture, while the wide, modern-style windows offer what must be spectacular ocean views.

"It's nice, isn't it? Have to be rich to live somewhere like that," I muse.

When I turn back to Meander, he's still staring at the house.

"Yeah." He nods, squinting. "But, um… Are we being watched?"

I follow his gaze up to one of the high windows, where a white, gauzy curtain hangs behind the windowpane. The curtain billows, and the movement reveals an undefined flicker that may or may not be a face staring in our direction.

A chill runs over my skin. Part of it is the unnerving possibility of being spied on. But another part—a bigger part—is realizing I'm still dizzy, sick, and now the slightest bit cold, which leaves me wondering if the eyes in that possible hazy face are living or dead.

"I don't see anything," Mim says, craning her neck to look up at the house. Her tone is unburdened, and it more or less confirms my uneasy suspicions.

"Nevertheless, maybe we should head back to camp," I say, staggering to my feet.

Meander's gaze lingers a few seconds longer before he stands to follow me and the others back to the main road.

COMPARED TO LAST YEAR, THE FACT THAT IT TOOK THREE DAYS TO SEE MY first spirit of the summer is a blessing—especially since the house it occupied wasn't related to our camp. Having a ghost nearby is unpleasant, but it's a situation I'm used to. Even with the sighting, my worries vanish by the time we return to where Althea waits on the beach. Even the memory of the spirit's watching eyes washes off along with the sweat and sand when I shower before lunch. By the end of the day, the eerie moment has slipped from my mind altogether.

The remainder of the week is busy enough to keep my thoughts far away from the billowing curtain in the window. While the first few days of camp were vastly different from last year, once Tuesday fades away, the rest of the week takes on a more familiar routine. My timetable is once again spread over four days. On Wednesday, I have Sender Mythos from twelve until four, Thursday is Introduction to Communication Techniques from four until eight, and Friday is Research Methods from twelve until four again.

I don't have any courses with Dylan this year, aside from fitness. Mim and Kornelía are both in Sender Mythos, and Meander is in Mythos as well as Research Methods. I'm the only member of Shade in Introduction to Communication Techniques, though. I guess everyone who wanted to take it got this course last summer. Still, I'm lucky I didn't have any conflicts in my schedule. Mim had to switch one course, and Naasir had to change two in order to make their timetables work. I wonder how many campers had to switch their schedules around last year.

Typical classroom introductions, course agendas, current assignments, and hints at future projects fill the rest of our first week. Friday feels especially comfortable. Mr. Olenev—my first-year Basics of Gadgetry instructor—is teaching Research Methods this summer, and I've got Meander to keep me company.

I'm quick to fall into the week's groove. The habitual pattern is so complete I'm not even surprised when Daniel finds me in the library on Saturday afternoon.

"I was wondering when I'd see you," my former mentor says. He waves to someone at the back of the library before sidetracking to approach the table where I'm taking notes for my first Communications assignment.

I pull out my earbuds, thinking I've forgotten a mentoring session until I remember he's no longer working with me. "Hey, Daniel." I smile, clearing a spot on the table so he can sit across from me without a pile of books blocking his sight. "I saw you at the initiation. I didn't know you were going to come back as a lead."

Daniel hovers behind the chair, looking indecisive. He must have a meeting scheduled with someone else—whoever he waved at when I first caught sight of him. But after a beat of hesitation he sits down, glancing at the books and picking up one at random.

"Didn't know I was, either," he laughs. He flips through the book, a volume on recorded cases of conversations held with spirits, before placing it back on the table. "I thought my years at Camp Wanagi were through."

I turn off my music and slide my phone into my shorts pocket, intrigued by his response."So, uh, why *are* you here?" I ask.

Daniel crosses his arms and lays them on the table. I didn't notice last year, but he looks different without the beige army uniform. His black hair is not obscured by a cap, his blue eyes not shaded under its brim. During the initiation, Daniel was in charge, commanding but nervous at the same time. The person sitting across from me now is more mellow. He still feels like a mentor, too. I suspect he'll always seem more confident and far wiser than I am, even if he's only a few years my senior.

"Last August, I finished my final project earlier than I expected," he says, the words smooth and rhythmic, like a storyteller relating a well-rehearsed tale. "I was disappointed, to be honest. I planned everything out, and everything went according to plan."

He laughs, shaking his head. "Talk about being

ungrateful. I suppose I imagined it would take extra work because it was my last camp-related spirit. When it didn't, I had nothing else to do except go back to France and wait out the remaining week. During those final days, I felt rather sorry for myself. I thought I hadn't chosen the right spirit, and that I'd wasted my time."

Daniel never faltered when talking about his path as a Sender or his plans for his final project. Hearing him confess those uncertainties now is strangely unsettling. I have to remind myself that, cordial as we are, I'm not truly Daniel's friend. Maybe he shared his fears with some of his sector mates, and kept his worries away while mentoring the new kid.

"One night, the few of us in Entity who were still at camp were in the library," he continues. "We were talking about what we planned to do after the summer was over. I had nothing to say because I had no clue. Then your friend found us."

"*My* friend?" I wasn't expecting to be a part of this tale. I flounder, trying to make sense of his meaning until I realize he must be talking about the night the spirit attacked me in the woods behind the château. "You mean Meander?"

"Yeah, him. We were sitting in the library, and there was a loud noise in the corridor. I think he was so tired he slipped down the bottom half of the steps. He came stumbling into the library, struggling to stay awake, but coherent enough to tell us you needed help."

Daniel leans back in his chair with a sigh. "One minute, I didn't know what I would do with my time now that my four years at Camp Wanagi were finished. The next, I had a mission. In the end, I didn't even do anything except stand watch while Ada ran back to get others to help carry you inside. But that whole night changed something in me. You needed help, and I liked being able to offer my assistance. I enjoyed being a mentor, and I thought, perhaps, I could mentor some other kids, too. So, I decided to spend a little longer at Camp Wanagi. Mentoring. Helping."

"Wow," I mutter.

My memory is fuzzy on the details of that night. I foolishly dug into the earth and released a spirit from its prison. But trying to recollect the specifics feels like reconstructing a dream. I do remember Daniel and Ada arriving, and Meander absorbing the spirit's anger until it was forced to cross over. Having some of the other details filled in, like how we got back to our beds after the spirit was released, is interesting. So is hearing that Meander fell down the stairs trying to find help.

I smirk to myself, wondering if he even remembers.

"Thank you, by the way," I say, blinking back to the present. "I never got to say so last year."

Daniel smiles. "You're welcome." He nods. "Thanks for getting yourself into such a spot. If you hadn't, I wouldn't be here."

"Happy to help," I say, letting out a breathy laugh.

"How has the first week of camp been?" he asks, glancing at the journal I've been using for my assignment. "Any noteworthy occurrences? Aside from the initiation, of course."

"And the two days it took to shake off all the sand?" I add. "Nothing much. It's been pretty quiet so far."

He nods, staring at the notebook for a moment before he gazes up at my face, and my forehead. Then he nods a second time and leans across the table."Want to change that?" he asks.

By the low, serious way he speaks, I'm certain he's not simply making small talk."W-What did you have in mind?" I stammer, unsure of how else to respond.

I'm not eager to throw myself into a dangerous situation. But I didn't enroll in the courses I should have taken this summer, and I've ignored what I think I saw in the house on the beach. Being here is pointless if I'm going to hide from every potential spiritual encounter.

"We're taking a boat over to another island tonight," Daniel explains. "There's a spirit we think might make a good case for the new campers. But we need to see if we can establish contact, to learn a bit more in order to match it with the right Entity talent. You should come along."

"Really?"

I'm pleased he's made the offer. We might be in a different setting, coconut palms visible through the library's window and the chatter of vacationers on the beach audible beyond the door, but sitting across from Daniel makes me feel like I'm once again unable to even fathom approaching spirits on purpose. Knowing he considers me mature and experienced enough to take this trip is flattering, even if I'm not sure I actually want to go.

"Why not?" Daniel asks. "It's always good to have a variety of Senders around. We don't know what this ghost's story is. We don't even know if it's real or a local myth. Hopefully we'll get the answer tonight."

My stomach constricts as if I've notched a belt too tight. I'm not one to puff up my chest and pretend I'm the bravest person in the room. The idea of confronting an unknown spirit terrifies me, but I push the fear away, forcing a smile to cover my quaking thoughts.

"Yeah, that sounds like…" I stop, unable to go so far as saying it sounds fun.

"Interesting, perhaps?" Daniel offers.

I laugh. "Yeah, interesting."

"Should be," he agrees. "I'm glad you're going to come along. We'll be leaving from the dock around eleven. Sound good?" He stands up as I scribble the time in the corner of my notebook. "Oh, and don't let the weather fool you. Dress warm. Just in case."

"Right," I nod, circling the time and adding a note to bring a sweater.

"I've got to go, so I'll let you get back to your work," Daniel says, turning from the table. "See you tonight, Cal."

He gives me a wave as he makes his way to the back of the library. When he's gone, I try to continue working, but thinking about what I'll be doing tonight makes it hard to focus. Half an hour later, I give up and leave, my knowledge on spirit communications still scarce.

Meander, Kornelía, and Reed are in the living area when I return to the fale. Although the houses are separated—one for the girls and one for the guys—the main room of each house is open to everyone.

Kornelía glances up from her sketchpad when I walk in, her glasses on the floor next to where she's sitting cross-legged in front of the coffee table. I step over Reed's legs and sit down next to Meander. Neither one of them looks up at me.

"How'd the essay writing go?" Kornelía asks.

"It was going okay, but I got interrupted by Daniel," I say. She looks confused, so I amend my explanation. "My mentor from last year is now one of the Entity leads. He saw me in the library, and we started talking."

Meander raises his head, his stare unfocused for a few seconds before he blinks out of his daze and realizes who is sitting next to him. "Aren't you supposed to be writing an essay?" he asks.

I smile, dropping my backpack to the floor by my feet. "You have got to be the easiest pickpocketing target," I tell him. "You don't notice anything when you're reading."

"Lucky I don't have any money to steal, then," he sighs, folding down the corner of his page and shutting the book. "How come you're back so early?"

"I saw Daniel," I say.

Reed shifts in his seat, his head drooping forward in sleep. The graphic novel he was reading slides off his lap onto the cushion seat next to him.

"Did you get to talk to him about last summer?" Meander asks.

"Yeah," I say. I'll relate the whole conversation at some point but, right now, I've got a different topic on my mind. "He invited me to go spirit seeking tonight."

"Really?" Kornelía asks, sounding interested.

I nod. "He and some others are looking for a spirit that's supposed to be on a nearby island. They want to try and make contact, to see whether it might be useable for the new campers' final project."

"Is it a murder victim?" Meander asks. His tone is weird, like he's not sure if what I'm saying is good or bad.

"They don't know." I shrug. "That's why Daniel suggested I come along. In case it is." Meander's expression is hard to read, but I don't give it time to settle into a more distinguishable emotion. "Why don't you come?" I say, nudging his knee with my own. "You're way more useful than I am."

His eyes widen with surprise—an expression that is followed by a pleased smile that slips into a worried frown in the space of three seconds. "Thanks for the offer," he says. "But I don't want a spirit sighting this early in the summer."

I nod, biting back a retort. Meander's been hiding from spirits for the last ten months. His efforts haven't been entirely successful, but he's tucked himself away from the dead—and the living—as much as possible.

I know why he's afraid. I've been hiding, too. When Mrs. Buxley told me to stay away from spirits at the end of last summer, she erased everything I learned about dealing with the dead. My paranoia about possession grew, culminating in a panic attack in November, when a sudden dip in temperature had me convinced a spirit was going to force me over a steep ledge. I'm better now. But I'm still careful, and I've handled my unavoidable ghost encounters badly.

I know it's been worse for Meander. But now that we're here, I'm ready to enter the fray again. At least, I'm ready to try.

I want Meander to try, too, but I also don't want to push him if he's not prepared. Nor do I want to piss him off by telling him I understand what he's going through. Fear I get. But I've never been stabbed by a glass-wielding spirit, so I can't assure him our worries are the same.

The front door bangs open, and my thoughts are cut short by the arrival of Dylan and Mim. Reed startles awake, grimacing as he wipes drool from his chin.

"Good, you're here," Mim says, gazing at Kornelía. She gives Dylan's side a squeeze before joining Kornelía on the floor. "We're going to explore the beach tonight," she declares happily.

"Explore the beach?" Kornelía says, sounding weary. She hasn't spent a lot of time lounging in the sun. My guess is she's not too big on the tropical climate.

"Yeah," Mim says, oblivious to her friend's disinterest. "See what's around, maybe do a bit of late-night swimming..." She glances at Dylan with a suggestive smirk that makes Kornelía's whole face go pink.

"Oh, well I..." she starts, and her unease makes me realize I was a jerk for not offering her the chance to escape Mim's clutches.

"She's coming with me tonight," I say before Mim can interrupt.

Mim gazes at me, her brows furrowed."Coming where with you?" she asks.

Kornelía's eyes brighten in relief, and she mouths a 'thank you' over Mim's shoulder.

"We're going to look for a spirit with the Entity leads," I explain.

Mim arches one eyebrow in confusion, as if none of that sentence made any sense. But Dylan crosses the living area, his hand sliding across Kornelía's hair as he passes.

"Cool," he says, grabbing a soda from the mini-fridge in our kitchenette. "Let us know if you find something."

"Of course we will." Kornelía smiles, her mood so suddenly perky she doesn't even hesitate to put her glasses back on.

WHEN KORNELÍA AND I MEET THE OTHERS, THE MOON IS BRIGHT. BUT BY the time we reach the nearby island, clouds have rolled in to block its light. Water laps against the boat's side, the waves choppy even though the engine's no longer running as we glide onto the shore. When we disembark on wet sand, the sky is so dark I can barely make out our surroundings.

"Good night to see spirits," Clarice says, studying the clouds above us. "You know, that's the question people ask me the most. Why are ghosts only seen in the dark?"

She smiles at me and Kornelía, while Daniel, the boat driver, and one of the Revenant leads named Gianna unload equipment.

"It always surprises me how many people think ghosts aren't around during the daytime," she continues. "Like they sleep until sunset or something. No one thinks about the fact they're simply easier to distinguish in the dark and easier to hear in the quiet of night."

"Some people don't think much about anything," Kornelía sighs as she stares over the empty beach. Despite passing on Daniel's warning to bring heavy layers, she wears only a white dress, the thin material fluttering in the breeze. She didn't even bother to put on shoes.

"How far away is the house?" I ask, following Kornelía's gaze. The coastline looks similar to the one by our camp in the low illumination of the boat's light.

"Not far," Clarice says. "Less than half a mile beyond the beach, I think."

The captain of the small motor boat stays with his vessel while the five of us walk to the main road. Clarice and Gianna have flashlights but, once we're off the beach, there are enough lights in the passing buildings to guide us.

"What will you do to try and make contact?" Kornelía asks.

"We'll set up cameras and readers," Daniel says. "But Clarice is hoping to primarily use dowsing rods."

I glance at Daniel, surprised. Mr. Olenev mentioned dowsing rods last summer, but we never got into much detail about their use. I know they're a method for spirit communication, but I've never seen how they work.

We turn up a side street and approach a house with a well-tended front garden and a set of painted paving stones leading to a decorative, wrought-iron screen door.

"Is this it?" Gianna asks as we stop in front of the small home.

Daniel nods, pulling a set of keys from his pocket. "Should be," he says, walking up the path. "The Oracle convinced the owners to vacate while we investigate. They're gone until next week."

"But what if we find something and need to visit the house again?" Gianna asks.

He shrugs. "We'll have to convince them to take another trip."

Daniel unlocks the front door and we walk inside. Making our way from one room to the next, we talk about the ghost we're trying to see.

"We think it's a man," Clarice says, her fingers trailing along different objects as we pass.

"How do you know?" I ask. "I mean, how does the Oracle even get word of hauntings like this?"

We move through a bedroom into its adjoining bathroom, and Clarice pushes open the shower curtain, gripping the purple linen in her fist before letting it fall back against the liner.

"I'm not an expert," she says, moving to the sink and opening a trinket box on the counter before continuing forward. "But I don't think it's as complicated as I used to believe. There are scouts, people who travel around gathering stories of hauntings and the people who claim to experience them. A lot of the time, I think the Oracle finds out by chance."

"They don't have some kind of database?" Kornelía asks. "I mean, they must keep records of hauntings."

"Sure, for the one's they're familiar with." Clarice laughs. "But the Oracle is small, and hauntings are numerous. I don't think they intuitively know everywhere that's haunted. So, sometimes they have to rely on local interest and pure dumb luck. A Sender will be somewhere and feel a spirit or hear local tales of it. That's how they found this place, anyway. Someone was on vacation and heard some stories. So, here we are."

We walk into the kitchen, and Daniel drops a bag of equipment on the table. "This is where the bulk of the activity has been reported," he says.

Clarice wanders the room, her fingertips gliding over canisters and tea towels. The air has a slight chill to it, as well as a vague smell of gasoline. The windows in the kitchen look old, though, and there's a gas stove about three feet from where I'm standing, which could explain the unpleasant scent. My head isn't fuzzy, at any rate, and my stomach is settled. If there is a spirit here, it's not one I'm going to see.

Clarice rests her hand on the stove top as she nods. "Let's set up," she says.

She joins Daniel at the table, while my eyes linger on the stove, wondering if anyone else can smell the gasoline.

"Do you sense anything?" I whisper to Kornelía.

She stands in the doorway, her eyes closed. She doesn't have her glasses on. I think she left them back at camp. "I'm not sure," she says after a moment, her lips pressed into a thin line. "No one is here right now. But there's definitely a presence in this house."

"We'll see if we can draw it out." Clarice smiles. She's wearing her white Entity sweater and black running shorts, the same outfit she wore to the initiation. Daniel has his uniform on again, and Gianna keeps playing with a long scarf wrapped several times around her neck. I glance at Kornelía's bare feet, white dress, and spectacle-free face. Her appearance is purposeful, as is everyone else's.

Except for mine. I didn't plan my outfit before leaving camp. I don't feel attached to the red zip-up hoodie I've dropped in the corner of the room, or the blue board shorts I happen to be wearing today. Last year, Robbie explained that Senders collect trinkets, clothing, and sometimes entire personas to help them deal with spirits. Dylan still thinks the notion is nonsense—his theory is that Senders who choose specific ghost-hunting attire only do so because everyone else is dressing up.

I don't believe the people around me are wearing costumes just for kicks. But I can't fathom how something as simple as an article of clothing could make dealing with spirits easier. Unless it was a bodysuit impervious to cold. But the idea of donning a parka and long johns every time I plan on seeing spirits isn't appealing, even if it would keep some of the chill at bay. So, maybe Dylan is right. Perhaps the idea of collections *is* nonsense.

At least for some of us.

Clarice sets the dowsing rods on top of the stove while she helps set up the cameras and voice recorder. Daniel hands me a thermal reader, and I give him a reading of the room before we start, indicating a drop in temperature near the stove and the coolness of the air close to the tiled floor. He does his own reading with an electromagnetic field meter, which doesn't detect anything unusual. While we call out measurements, Gianna sits at the kitchen table, scratching notes on a yellow pad of lined paper.

"Are we good?" Clarice asks once our readings are taken and the cameras are ready to record.

After noting everyone's approval, she picks up the dowsing rods and holds them out before her, her elbows tucked tight against her sides, the rods unmoving in her fists. She waits for Daniel to make some introductory remarks, stating the date and the names of everyone present, before she takes over.

Clarice stands with her back to the stove. Guessing where a spirit might show up is never easy, but I hadn't expected to do this in a kitchen. Meander's absence is probably a good thing, after all. I doubt it would take much for Clarice's sweater to catch fire if that stove suddenly flicked to life.

"We are here tonight to communicate with the spirit who resides in this house," she says, her voice low, almost a mumble. "If you will talk to us, please give us a sign for 'yes'."

She waits, the room silent as everybody watches the rods. Slowly, the copper sticks turn towards each other until they join in a straight line running between her two fists. I can't tell whether the spirit created the movement, or if Clarice's hands twitched and caused the swing. Being skeptical in the midst of something I know to be real is hypocritical, but no one else in the room seems excited, either. Clarice even sighs as she moves the rods straight again.

"Ask for a 'no' sign next," Gianna prompts.

Clarice gives her an annoyed glance before focusing on the rods once more. "I will," she says, then, in a lower voice, continues, "Will you now give us a sign for 'no'?"

Another pause ensues, the wait a few seconds longer, before the right rod turns outward while the left remains still.

"Okay," Clarice says, resetting the rods again. "Now, let's talk."

For the next ten minutes, Clarice asks a series of 'yes' or 'no' questions, vague prompts meant to determine if the spirit is male, if it is sad, if it misses its family, if it knows it is dead. The rods respond accordingly, offering a good mix of positive and negative responses. But it's impossible to tell, without one of us seeing the spirit, if the rods are actually working.

"I can't get a good sense," Clarice admits halfway through the questions. "I'm not sure if the spirit's answering, or if my mind's making up answers for me."

This must be what it's like for non-Senders, people who travel to local haunting grounds and create setups in an effort to catch sight of a ghost. I'm not sure why anyone would choose to do so much work for such an inconclusive response. At least when I see a murder victim, there's no doubt what I'm up against. Dowsing rods would be useless when I could just talk to the spirit face to misty, half-formed face.

After the eighth or ninth question, Kornelía's back tenses. She whips her head around, eyes shut tight as she faces the dark hallway beyond the kitchen.

"Is there something in the other room?" I ask in a whisper.

Kornelía pads to the doorway. Her head tilts to one side, and she turns in a slow circle, her arms out to keep her balance.

"I... don't know," she says. She opens her eyes, the tawny shade of her irises dark in the dim shine of Gianna's flashlight. "I mean... There's a spirit here. I know there is. But I can't see him. I keep having the feeling that…" She looks behind her, her long hair sweeping with the flare of her dress.

"Do you feel something?" Clarice asks, lowering the dowsing rods.

Daniel focuses one of the cameras on Kornelía, and Gianna turns her chair so she can see what's going on.

Kornelía takes deep breaths, like she's working to calm herself down. She closes her eyes and does another turn, moving slowly at first, then twirling fast as a frenzied ballerina. A sound somewhere between a whimper and a growl issues from her throat as her eyes snap open.

"He's here," she says, looking between us until her gaze settles on me. Her expression is unfamiliar, one I've never seen before.

She's scared.

"He's here," she says again, her voice strained and squeaking. "But I can't see him. I think… He's following me. I… I think he's standing right behind my back."

# 10

My eyes stray to the empty space behind Kornelía, and I tense against an uneasy shiver, wondering if there's a spirit staring back at me.

"Why do you think someone's behind you?" Gianna asks.

No one questioned what our talents were when we tagged along on this trip. Daniel knows mine, of course, but they might not have any idea what Kornelía is capable of.

"She can see spirits in her mind," I say before Kornelía has the chance to downplay her ability.

She gives me an indecisive glance, but she doesn't argue with what I've said. Nodding, she hugs her arms around her middle.

"He's close," she explains. Her shoulders hunch and she wriggles forward like she's trying to shirk away from unwanted attention. "If I move quick enough, I think I catch a flash of something. But I can't see him.

Why would he stay behind me?"

"Could be playing a trick," Clarice says, as Daniel brings over one of the readers to measure the air behind Kornelía's back. "Or hiding. Maybe he just fancies you. It's impossible to say."

"Not impossible," Kornelía mumbles. "We'd figure it out if I could see him."

"There's an electromagnetic spike here," Daniel says. He passes his hand through the area. "It's cold as well. Cal, can I see the thermal reader?"

I pass over the reader, amused he's being so methodical. Kornelía's assertion of a spirit close at hand is proof enough for me. Still, Daniel calls out the temperature range, and Gianna notes it in her book. They might be required to be thorough since they're on a scouting mission. Or maybe they enjoy plotting everything out.

"What should we do?" I ask.

I look to Daniel. He sighs, checks his readers, then glances across the room to Clarice. "You could use the rods over here," he suggests. "Stand behind her and place them right in front of him."

Kornelía doesn't appear to like the idea. She stares at the floor, her eyes huge with dismay. I can't blame her. The thought of standing still while a dead man hovers behind me is incredibly creepy.

"Okay, sure," Clarice agrees. She walks over to Kornelía, standing a pace away so she can hold the dowsing rods an inch from Kornelía's back.

"You all right with this?" I ask.

Kornelía glances at me, looking like she's about to say no. But then she nods, her arms still hugged to her as Clarice begins a new line of questioning.

"Are you the spirit residing in this house?" she asks.

The right rod swings outward, causing Gianna to tap her pen against the paper, unsure of what to put down.

"That's a 'no'," she says.

"Definitely wasn't me," Clarice replies, straightening the rod and shuffling closer. She plants her feet shoulder-width apart as if she's bearing down in preparation for a fight. "It's going to be like that then, is it?" she asks, before repeating her initial question. "Are you the spirit residing in this house?"

The rod swings outward again, and Clarice sighs, straightening it in her grasp once more.

"Maybe it got the signals mixed up," Gianna offers.

Daniel shakes his head. He walks back to the table, replacing the readers before scratching his chin in thought. "It's answering wrong on purpose," he says.

"I agree," Clarice nods. She holds the rods still and takes a deep breath. "We know you're playing a game. We'd like you to stop. Answer honestly, please. Are you a male spirit?"

The rod swings outward again.

"He's saying 'no'," Gianna says.

"It's a man. With very masculine energy," Kornelía argues.

"He's lying," Clarice says.

"Or he's mixed up the signals," Gianna suggests again. "Why don't you try re-establishing the signs?"

Clarice doesn't think it'll do any good, but she agrees to the plan anyway.

"Let's start over," she says. "Please give me a sign for 'yes'." The rods turn together, just like they did the first time she made this request. Clarice watches the movement with a frown. "And a sign for 'no'?" she asks. Before she's even straightened the rods, the right one turns outward.

"Okay. So he's lying," Gianna acquiesces. She drops the pen on the pad of paper and leans back against her chair. "Now what?"

Clarice isn't ready to give up her questioning yet. "Are you a female spirit?" she asks. The rod turns outward, as I think we all suspected it would. Daniel huffs through his nose while Clarice continues. "Is there another spirit residing in this house?" Another 'no'. Clarice grunts. "Are you going to answer 'no' for everything we ask?"

I almost smile when the rods turn inward, indicating a positive response. I would, if Kornelía wasn't so uncomfortable.

"This is pointless," Gianna says.

"At least we've established contact," Daniel offers. "We know there's a spirit. And we know it's a male. That's something."

"Not enough to be useful for the campers," Clarice argues. She drops the dowsing rods and steps back. "He still behind you?" she asks Kornelía, who nods.

"Yes," she says, her voice meek.

"Should we go, then?" Gianna asks. "I don't think we're going to find out anything else. Not if he's uncooperative."

"Wait." Kornelía straightens her back, looking around the room. "If… if I could just get a look at him, I could tell you more." Her eyes find their way to me, and an apologetic expression curves her features.

"What?" I ask in a tight voice.

"If I can get someone between us," she begins,

"there'll be enough distance for me to have a look."

I gape at her. "Unless the spirit just stands in the same place as me," I say, tamping down a shudder. I don't want the spirit *literally* stepping on my toes.

"That might work," Clarice says, more enthusiastic than I am. "Spirits don't like to occupy the same space as the living. Living and dead energy don't play well together. It's like… like sticking your hand into a fire. Possible, yes. But it's not something you're going to do for the fun of it. There are consequences."

Kornelía smiles at me, and I sigh, beckoning her over.

"Thanks, Cal," she says.

She closes her eyes and inches sideways towards me, grabbing my arm, then feeling her way across my stomach to my far side. Her back glides against my chest as she moves into place. Cold snakes through the back of my shirt, coiling up my spine and making me wish I'd put on my sweater instead of leaving it in a heap on the floor. The hairs on my neck bristle, and the smell of gasoline wafts over me, the scent faint but distinct enough I'd think it was Kornelía's perfume if the smell were sweeter.

The cold proof of the spirit lingering behind me is enough to make me unexpectedly claustrophobic. My breathing is shallow, my view obscured by the back of Kornelía's head. The addition of cool pressure, like a breeze directed at my spine, makes me want to jerk away. I clench my fists to resist the urge.

"He's behind me," I say, swallowing the nagging question of what happens when a spirit doesn't care about the consequences of putting his hand in the fire of living energy. My muscles are stiff as I wait, ready to dart sideways if the ghost starts to worm his way into my skin.

"Okay." Kornelía inhales as she reaches a hand back to grasp my arm. She turns her head, slowly enough she doesn't have to move the rest of her body. The jerky way she twists one centimeter at a time, combined with her closed eyes and the dim light of Gianna's flashlight, makes the whole scene feel like a horror movie.

I try not to stare at Kornelía as she turns. But she's so close, it's hard to avoid it. When her neck's strained as far back as I think it can go, her expression changes, her face taking on a look of shock.

"Can you see him?" I mumble.

She nods, her fingers trembling against my arm. I hold my free hand over hers, letting her know she's not alone.

"He's... middle-aged," she says. She speaks in a monotone, like she's working hard to suppress any hint of emotion. "Tongan. Missing most of his teeth." She grimaces and swallows, her nails digging into my flesh. "He's... got a mark on his face. A burn, maybe? Along his right cheek." She pauses and swallows a second time. "He's got beady eyes, and he's balding."

Her fingers squeeze so tight I flinch. With a sharp gasp of breath, her eyes snap open and she jumps away from me.

"What is it?" Daniel asks, panicked by her intense reaction.

She shakes her head, but the first note of a quiet sob slips from her throat before she can stop it. "It's nothing," she says with a strained laugh. "He's... being inappropriate. Trying to scare me."

Even as she says the words, the chill on my back spreads, cutting across my right shoulder like a hand reaching forward. A draft sweeps along my side, creeping forward until it ruffles Kornelía's hair. She jolts to the side, biting back another sob. When the edge of her dress crinkles, she snatches the fabric like she's pulling it away from invasive hands before she rushes out of the room.

We watch her go. Then we survey each other in silence.

"I think we're done here," Clarice says after a moment.

Daniel nods. "Go see her, Cal. We'll pack everything up."

I don't offer to stay and help. Pausing only long enough to grab my sweater, I rush out of the kitchen and through the living room to reach the front door. Kornelía is outside, crouching on the far side of the street.

"Are you okay?" I call, bounding down the steps and across the road.

She throws her head back with a huff. "My first chance to really be useful, and I get scared like a child," she says with annoyance.

"No one blames you for getting freaked out," I say, trying to appease her. "Hell, I got freaked out, and I couldn't even see anything."

She smiles, raking her fingers through her long hair as she stands. "I shouldn't have left," she sighs. "But I've never seen a spirit like that before."

"It's okay," I say. "You *were* useful. We got a lot of information." I pause, considering the way her hand trembles as it comes to rest by her side. "What did he do?" I ask, keeping my voice as neutral as possible.

"He was being… inappropriate," she says again. She lets out a long breath and looks down at the ground. "*Lewd*, you would call it. He was trying to scare me. It shouldn't have worked. But, I mean… I wasn't expecting it."

Her eyes are wide with uncertainty when she glances up again. "My talent has changed so much, Cal," she says, a sudden rush to her speech, as if she's confessing a secret. "I used to sense when a ghost was nearby and, if I was lucky, I could cling onto a few details about the entity. Now, when I close my eyes, I see spirits more clearly, like misty forms of living people. But even though I can still tell when a place is haunted, unless I focus on the images inside my head, I can't gather details anymore."

She stares at the house, her expression almost remorseful. "And with *this* ghost… I couldn't see him at all while he was behind me. The Oracle told us our abilities would develop, but no one warned us they could change altogether. How can we learn to utilize our talents if they keep morphing into something new? What if my ability is completely different by the time I turn sixteen?"

Kornelía is the youngest member of Shade. She won't be fifteen until November, which means her sixteenth birthday won't occur until after she attends camp next summer. Our talents develop at their own pace, and it's not like a wave of newfound power will sweep us away the moment we blow out our sixteenth birthday candles. But from what I've gleaned over the last year, sixteen *is* special. Our talents will reach their maturity in the months—or weeks—surrounding our birthdates, and most of us will return to Camp Wanagi next year with at least an inkling of what the full extent of our abilities are.

Still, despite the changes she's already experienced—huge advances spurred by her arrival at camp last year—Kornelía is the only one of my friends who has never expressed frustration over her talent. She has always been grateful for the gift of seeing spirits, and it's obvious even now, as she stares at me with anger in her questioning gaze, she's uncomfortable admitting her concerns.

"Maybe your talent—" I start, but she doesn't give me time to fumble through a response.

"I'm okay. I only… I hope they don't give him to the new campers," she says, glancing again at the house as she brings the topic to a quick close. "I'll be okay. I'm only bothered because I've never seen a spirit act so… so *rude.*"

Across the street, the leads exit the house, their appearance perfectly aligned with her final word. I watch Daniel lock the front door, knowing Kornelía won't let our conversation continue with company nearby.

"Some people are jerks." I shrug in answer to her latest remark. "Some spirits are, too." My hand brushes the spot on my head where the rock hit, before my eyes stray back to Kornelía. A slash of red on her elbow catches my notice. "What happened?"

She lifts her arm, giving me a better view of a slanted cut welling with blood. "Tripped on my way out and caught my arm on the porch railing." She grins, pointing to her slightly squinted eyes. "Couldn't see where I was going."

Once the others have joined us on the far side of the road, we head back in silence. I expect they'll press Kornelía for further details, but no one says a word as we return to the boat. The leads must be eager to discuss the night's findings, but they're cautious around Kornelía, afraid they'll frighten her again. She stares over the water as we make our way back, and I watch the others around me, wondering what will come of tonight's events.

When I get back to my fale, I use the light of my phone to guide me into the dark room where the others have all gone to bed. I dig out my pajamas, and slip off my shoes before I hear rustling behind me.

"How did it go?"

I turn towards the sleepy voice to see Meander peeking out from beneath a mound of blankets that must make a sweltering cocoon in this heat. His hair is mussed, and there's a pink spot on one cheek from where he's been sleeping. I'm sure he'd cringe if he noticed his disheveled state. But I'm glad his defenses are down, that his brain is too tired to panic about his appearance.

"It was fine," I mumble, tilting the light up to see him better. "It wasn't a murder victim."

"That's good," Meander says, rubbing his eyes.

"Kornelía had a rough go, though," I sigh. "Think she got her first taste of an unpleasant spiritual encounter."

More sheets rustle, this time from below us. I glance down to see Dylan sitting up, his hair matted over his eyes. "Is she okay?" he asks, his words slurred.

"She's fine," I assure him before another noise causes all three of us to look across the room.

"Will you guys shut up?" Reed says, rolling over. "I'm trying to sleep."

"Sorry Reed," I mutter, flicking off my light.

Dylan drops back against his bunk, and I give Meander a last smile before heading to the bathroom to get ready for bed.

KORNELÍA SPENDS THE NEXT WEEK AND A HALF WORKING ON HER SKETCH of the spirit from the other island. She draws several drafts, crumpling the first designs in annoyance, claiming they don't capture his likeness. Seeking out whatever shaded areas of the beach she can, she sits on a towel and watches the waves whenever she pauses to think about what to detail next.

She won't let me see—one thing that hasn't changed since last summer—but the glimpses I do get are of a leering stranger with empty eyes and a partially distorted face.

Dylan hovers over her, asking her if she's okay long after she's recovered. Mim doesn't like it, but she stops short of telling Dylan to quit paying attention to another girl. Instead, she throws herself into her coursework. Last year, she was quick to volunteer as leader of our group's final project, and it would seem she plans to continue that trend.

"I never realized how many spirits refuse to leave, even after their business has been completed," she says one evening while we sit at the table in the boys' kitchenette. She scans over her notes from the Resistive Release course she wasn't afraid to enroll in, mouthing the words as she reads. "You would think—'hey, here's the answer to the question that's kept me around, now off I go!'" she continues as she turns the page. "But no. Some spirits stay around, even after."

"Sometimes they don't even have unfinished business," I say absently, scrolling through an email from my mom. She's written a lengthy message about the camping trip the family is going on as soon as Rose finishes ballet camp. The family vacation they're not waiting to take with me.

I read the letter a second time, then sigh and close it. When I look up at Mim, she's staring out the open window. The beach was too noisy for Kornelía this afternoon, so she set up in the courtyard behind the fale. Now, she swings in the oversized hammock while Dylan sits on a chair across from her, laughing at something she said.

I lean across Mim and grab a magazine someone left on the small kitchen table.

"No, sometimes they don't," she says, distracted by my movement. She looks back at her notes, sweeping her black bangs away from her eyes. "There is so much… What's the word? *Opportunity*. Sender's have such a lot of opportunity."

"Opportunity?" I place the magazine back on the table without opening it.

Mim glances at me, her brown eyes bright."Yes," she says, smiling. "So much opportunity to do something great."

"I didn't know you had so much ambition," I say.

Mim shrugs, her eyes straying back to Kornelía and Dylan. "I didn't come here to spend my summer sitting on the beach," she mutters. "Last year, I failed my attempt to lead our group. This time, I'm going to do better. And I want to achieve something beyond a normal release."

"Are any releases normal?" I ask.

Mim doesn't respond. Her attention has been drawn to noises outside, this time from the front of the fale. I follow her gaze, and turn to see Sabeena entering the living area with the new camper, Isabis, behind her.

"I'll get you a cloth," Sabeena says, sounding apologetic.

Isabis smiles, her movements more confident now she's off the sand and has the use of her forearm crutches. "It's no problem," she tells Sabeena, her slow words amused. "Only a bit of sand."

"What happened?" Mim asks.

Sabeena starts, turning to see who spoke before walking into the kitchenette to grab a cloth and soak it in water.

"Naasir's stupid bugs started crawling on my legs," she says, shuddering. "I tried to kick them off, and ended up spraying sand into Isabis's face."

"No problem," Isabis repeats. "I'm only a *little* blind now."

"I'm so sorry," Sabeena moans, wringing out the cloth.

Dylan and Kornelía must have heard the commotion. They come into the fale together, and Mim is quick to reach for Dylan's hand, pulling him over to stand next to her. Kornelía pretends not to notice. She walks by us and makes her way to one of the sofas.

"What's going on?" Dylan asks, rubbing Mim's shoulder.

"Nothing important," she sighs. She gives him a dreamy smile as she leans into his touch.

I fight the urge to roll my eyes, busying myself instead with moving over to stand behind Kornelía.

"Meander's history course finishes in ten minutes, so I'm going to meet him for dinner," I say, leaning over her shoulder. "Want to come?"

She hugs her sketchpad tight to her chest before I have a chance to see what she's drawing. I *do* roll my eyes when she looks over her shoulder, but she ignores me in favor of glancing at Dylan and Mim.

"Yeah, sure," she says, closing her book and laying it on the coffee table before she stands.

"We'll come with you," Sabeena says. She takes the cloth back from Isabis, whose purple, flower-printed headscarf is still covered with a fine sheen of sand. "I've got to get back to the boys. I'm sure Sefa will have eaten half of my dinner by the time we return."

Mim and Dylan remain cuddling by the table while the rest of us clear out of the fale. Outside, Kornelía and I walk a few paces ahead of Isabis and Sabeena.

"I'm sure you're sick of this question given how many times Dylan's asked it, but how are you doing?" I ask as we walk along the road. A cluster of Wraiths pass us as they chase a rouge volley ball.

Kornelía lets out an amused breath. "I'm okay," she says, twisting her hair into a bun as she walks. "I just want to move on from it. Find another spirit I can maybe be more helpful with."

"I know of a ghost," Isabis says from behind us. We both turn, stopping so she and Sabeena can catch up. "There's that guy from the beach, of course. But he's been claimed. I know of another one, though. At least, I think I do."

"You're not sure?" Kornelía asks.

Isabis doesn't stop when she reaches us. She keeps up her rhythm, and we fall in at her side.

"I never know for sure," she says between steps. "I can't see them."

Sabeena looks as surprised by this information as we are. "But our first night here. You were the one to—"

"I can interact with them," Isabis clarifies before Sabeena finishes her sentence. "But I can't *see* them." She laughs, the sound like a heavy, winded breath. "I grew up thinking I was telekinetic. Sometimes I got this feeling—like I could move things if I concentrated hard enough. And usually when I concentrated, I *did* move things. But it wasn't my mind. Turns out I can make ghosts do things—if I concentrate."

"That's incredible!" Sabeena exclaims.

"That's awful," Kornelía mutters at the same time, her softer tone buried under Sabeena's strong voice.

"Can you make them do anything?" Sabeena asks, oblivious to Kornelía's remark.

Isabis laughs again. "No. When the ghost is too powerful, I can't control them. And even when I do control them... I can't make them do anything big. I tried ordering a ghost to cross over once. Didn't work."

"You haven't fully developed yet, though," Sabeena muses. "Your talent might grow stronger."

Isabis sighs, like this is something she's been told before. "I don't care if it does," she admits.

She pauses, resting for a moment on her crutches as she tries to catch her breath. I wonder if she's keeping a faster pace than normal so as not to slow us down.

"Why not?" Sabeena asks, stopping beside her until Isabis is ready to move again.

"I don't want to spend my life flying around the world, hunting ghosts," she says. "It's exhausting. I like being at home—not living out of a suitcase. Besides," she adds with a smile, "do you know how annoying airport security is with crutches?"

Kornelía's head tilts to one side in consideration."So, why did you come here this summer?" she asks.

"To learn," Isabis says. "I want to be a para-psychologist. Heavy emphasis on the psychologist part. I want to help others like me. Kids who think they have mental powers when really they're interacting with ghosts."

A niggle of annoyance acts as a pinching reminder I've come across yet another person who's brand new here and already has their future mapped out. Last year, I arrived at Camp Wanagi not knowing if I'd even return for a second summer. By the time I went home to Canada, I knew I'd come back to enhance my skills and learn how to protect myself against a spirit's guiding will. But that doesn't mean I know what I want for my future.

I'm amazed by the vast range of reasons people have for coming to this camp. But it would be nice if I could determine my own reasons as well.

We reach the spot on the beach where Naasir, Sefa, and Reed lounge on plastic recliner chairs. Sabeena and Isabis start to veer away from the main road, Isabis easing off her crutches and slowing her pace as she steps onto the soft sand.

"You said you knew about a spirit," Kornelía says as Reed gets up to help Isabis into a chair.

"There's a house a ways up," she says, pointing in the opposite direction to where we're going. "It's like a treehouse or something."

"That big place by the beach?" I ask, remembering the house we stopped near during our first morning with Althea.

Isabis nods. "I was walking by there the other day, and I got the feeling… The sensation I get when a ghost is close by. I'm sure it was coming from the house."

"I've been there, too," I say, turning to Kornelía. "She's right. It might be haunted."

"We should check it out," Kornelía says. Her smile is enthusiastic, bordering on excited. "Maybe we could go tonight."

"Could we come?" Sabeena asks, gesturing between herself and Isabis.

Kornelía shrugs. "You're the one who told me about it," she says, looking at the Entity camper. "You're welcome to come. We can meet at the boys' fale at midnight."

Sabeena nods, like all this has been planned for ages and isn't something they've cooked up in the last sixty seconds. "You're coming, too, right?" Sabeena asks, and it takes a second to realize she's talking to me.

"Oh, I-I guess," I stammer, thinking of the house and the eyes almost lost amongst the billowing curtain inside.

Venturing back to the treehouse in the middle of the night doesn't sound like a marvelous plan. Especially when one member of the group is a camper I don't know, a girl who isn't capable of running if things get too intense. But Isabis doesn't seem concerned about the trip, so I guess I shouldn't be, either.

"Sure, I'll come," I say with firmer resolve.

And with any luck, I won't regret my decision in the morning.

"I DON'T THINK WE SHOULD GO," MEANDER SAYS, PACING OUTSIDE THE FALE as we wait for Kornelía and the other girls to show up.

When I agreed to risk venturing back to the treehouse tonight, I also decided that, if I was risking it, Meander was, too. I've at least been on one excursion this summer, while he's done nothing. I know he's nervous about what we might see. But I can't let his summer dwindle away anymore than I can let the weeks slide past myself.

I grab his arm to stop him from circling back and forth. "We're going," I say.

He halts in front of me, frowning.

"It'll be fine," I add, doing my best to convince him with an easy smile. "We won't be inside the house. We're just going to check out the property… to confirm it's haunted. This is mainly for Kornelía, anyway. You don't have to get anywhere near the spirit. At least, not *yet*."

He almost looked like he might calm down, but the end of my sentence makes him glare. "Not *ever* would be the better alternative," he grumbles.

He shoves his hands into the front pocket of his black Camp Wanagi sweater, and I smirk, giving his shoe a kick when I notice the girls approaching.

"Come on, they're here," I say. "You don't have time to try and sweet talk your way out of it now."

He breathes a quiet laugh, his eyes catching mine in the bright darkness of the star-spotted night. "If I'd known I could sweet talk my way out of it, I would have been *far* more charming," he teases.

The words tingle across my skin, little sparks of heat that flare and diminish before I can even begin to fathom where they came from.

Sabeena's voice breaks the momentary silence, forcing my eyes to leave Meander's. "You two ready?" she asks, waving from where the girls have stopped on the path.

Meander sighs, turning on his heel with one final, fleeting glance at me. "Let's get this over with," he mutters, grabbing my arm and pulling me alongside him. I smile, following his movement with a bounce in my step I wouldn't have expected given our destination.

Sabeena carries a flashlight as we make our slow trek, but she leaves it off. The moon's shine and the lights from nearby fales are enough to keep us on route. Music blasts in the distance and, closer to us, the occasional happy shriek punctuates a chorus of laughter. Last summer we were isolated from everything, separated from our neighbors by a large piece of land and a lake. But this year, we seem to be part of a massive resort-owned property. Certain buildings have been converted for our use, but fales on the far side of the premises are inhabited by vacationing Non-Senders.

Of course, even our own camp mates are enjoying the escape while they can. Earlier this evening, Sefa organized a Shade versus Revenant soccer match on the beach. I'm not sure who won. About halfway through, all the players ended up in the water and, at some point, the ball drifted out to sea while Mim prevented Dylan from paddling after it.

The five of us would look ridiculous to anyone who caught us walking by. We move with slow determination, and three of us wear heavy sweaters despite the heat. Isabis and Kornelía, at least, dressed in keeping with the island temperature. Isabis's blouse matches the flower print of the head scarf she's been wearing all day, and Kornelía is in her white dress again.

"Shouldn't you be wearing shoes?" Meander remarks at one point, noticing that Kornelía's feet are bare.

She shrugs, glancing down at her feet while she walks. "My shoes are too heavy," she says.

Like that makes any sense.

Meander gives me a dubious sideways glance, and I try not to laugh.

The noises of normal life eventually fade as we leave the main road and start down a dirt path that winds towards the treehouse. I'm disoriented trying to plot how we made it onto what must be a private beach at the house's rear the last time we were here. From the front, the landscape looks totally different than the day we ran in this area.

Plants, trees, and flowers edge the dirt road, the growth so thick I don't think a car could make it through without whacking greenery on both sides. We take our time as we walk the path, careful to listen for oncoming traffic, since it's impossible to see what's up ahead. Once we're through the narrowest section, the road opens into a wide patch of packed earth as the treehouse comes into view.

"Whoa, this house is huge," Sabeena says after we've crossed the empty plot of land resembling a parking lot. She flicks on her flashlight, shining it up at the house's front.

"Keep your light down," Kornelía scolds in a hushed voice. "Someone might be at home."

The house is dark and there are no cars in sight, suggesting the property is empty. Still, Sabeena lowers the light, shining it at the ground instead.

"So, what do we do now?" I ask, surveying the house. The bamboo slats and thatched roof are odd companions to the impressive, sleek wooden staircase that curves around the tree trunk and up to the home's verandah-style porch.

"We need to find out if there's a spirit inside," Kornelía says. She turns to Isabis, who stands a step behind the rest of us. "You said you felt it when you were near the house. How near were you?"

"No closer than this," Isabis replies. "We were up on the main road. Someone wanted to see where the dirt path led but, when we reached the house, we turned back."

"Do you feel the spirit now?" Sabeena asks.

Isabis closes her eyes, and we all stare at her, waiting

for her response. When she opens them again, she doesn't seem the slightest bit surprised to find us watching. "No, I don't feel anything," she says.

Kornelía frowns, and Sabeena sighs, swinging her light beam back up at the house. "Well, this was a waste," she mutters.

She shines the beam into the black windows. No movement or shifting curtains can be seen. No eyes watching from the darkness, either. But there are more windows on the other side of the house. Before I'm willing to let go of what I may have seen after our run, we need to investigate further.

"We should go around back," I suggest.

Kornelía smiles. "That's a good plan, Cal."

Sabeena nods, focusing the flashlight over the expanse of packed dirt at the tree's side until it lands on what looks like a set of steps heading down to the beach. The girls start forward, but Meander and I linger behind.

"You're determined to get us in trouble, aren't you?" he asks.

If this were last summer, I'd think he was angry. Now that I know him so much better, I'm quick to register the amusement in his voice.

"I just want to make sure there's nothing worth checking out," I say, my tone over-sweet.

"You're *such* a good student." He sweeps his arm out indicating for me to lead the way as we continue on to the uneven, half-dirt and half-stone steps.

"These stairs look pretty steep," Sabeena says when we catch up to the others. She gives Isabis an uncertain glance, and the Entity camper sighs.

"I'll stay here," she offers, planting herself a little

ways from the top of the stairs. "If anyone comes home, I'll shout."

"But you're the one who can feel if a spirit's close," Kornelía says.

"Uh, so can you," I remind her.

Kornelía opens her mouth to answer, then ducks her head to cover her blush. "Right, I know," she says with an embarrassed laugh. "Isabis is just the one who felt something before. I thought she might be able to feel the ghost while it's still too far away for me to sense."

"Let's see what the rest of us can find," I suggest. "If we don't sense anything, we'll come up with a new plan. Maybe return some other time. There's another way to reach the back of the house, via the beach."

"Do you want me to stay with you?" Sabeena asks Isabis.

She shakes her head, smiling.

"I'm a big girl," she says, ignoring Sabeena's attempt to give her the flashlight, "and I'm not afraid of the dark."

She looks up at the house, watching the windows for movement, while the rest of us walk down the stone steps to the private beach. This side of the house is cooler. It's becoming a running gag this year that I can never tell whether the coolness is from the sea breeze or something dead drawing warmth from the air around us.

Kornelía walks close to the house, near enough she needs to crane her neck to see the upper windows.

"Do you feel cold?" Sabeena whispers. She wraps her arms around her stomach, shivering under her sweater.

"Yeah, it's getting a bit chilly." Meander nods, his

eyes fixed on the high curtained window.

"There is a spirit here." Kornelía smiles, gazing back at us. "Up there. I can't quite make out if it's a girl or a boy, but it's a child."

"Of course," Sabeena says. She sniffs and rubs her nose. "The child must have been sick."

A damp chill seeps into my pores at the same moment a sickly sweet smell of overpowering vanilla wafts down from the house.

"Must have been murdered, too," I add.

"Must still be angry about it," Meander concludes.

He points at the window, where the billowing curtain cannot shield us from a pair of eyes that are definitely looking our way. Meander glances at me and I, in turn, look at Sabeena. She shifts her eyes to Kornelía, who begins to laugh.

"That's a useful start." She doesn't shiver or scrunch her nose at the smell. If anything, she looks amused by the state of our mild discomfort.

"So, what now?" Sabeena asks. She watches the window, her eyes squinted and one hand rubbing her temple. "Should we investigate further?"

"How?" I ask. "We don't have access to the house."

"We might," Kornelía says. Her eyes roam the dark windows. "There doesn't seem to be anyone at home."

"Are you suggesting we break in?" Meander asks. He crosses his arms over his chest, his eyes narrowing with suspicion.

Kornelía fails to notice his obvious disapproval. Her gaze returns to the high window as she shrugs. "Why not?" she says, her voice coy. "How often does it happen four Senders feel the same presence at the same time?"

"Five Senders, if you count Isabis," Sabeena corrects. "And I suppose it *is* pretty special. Last year, I was the only one who saw our group's ghost."

Four members of our group saw the spirit of Isabelle Levasseur last summer but, since three of those four people are here now, mentioning it is pointless. Still, generally speaking, it must be uncommon for five Senders to happen across a spirit like this. Certain members of the Oracle have abilities that are incompatible with other Senders'. Sabeena sees children, Sefa sees the elderly, and Lu and Naasir don't see spirits at all.

Kornelía's oddball reasoning does not, however, mean her proposal is a good one. After her unsettling encounter with the man on the nearby island, I know she's desperate to find joy in helping spirits again. But suggesting we sneak inside someone's house just to get a better look at a ghost is preposterous.

"Breaking in is illegal," I remind her.

She's not paying attention, though. She's looking for a way up, surveying the house above us with thoughtful consideration. "If we return to the front and take that staircase up—the one that wraps around the tree trunk—I think the porch extends all the way to the back. Then we can boost someone up to the window."

"Shouldn't we wait until we have some equipment or something?" Sabeena asks, her voice wavering between nervous agitation and intrigue. "We have nothing to document what happens."

"We're not doing it to document," Kornelía retorts. "We're doing it to help the child trapped in this house. Who needs equipment? I mean, we can all sense the spirit, so we don't need to measure the temperature in the room or use metal rods to communicate."

Sabeena looks at Meander and me, her long black hair draped across one shoulder. "She has a point," she says, convinced.

Meander heaves another sigh. "If we do this tonight, I'm taking the rest of the summer off," he says, knowing full well I dragged him on this escapade to force him into some spiritual interaction.

"You've got it," I agree.

We head back to the stone steps along the side of the house where Isabis is still standing guard. As we ascend to the dirt path, she eyes us with curiosity and impatience, like she has something she wants to say.

"There's a spirit in the house," Sabeena tells her before she has a chance to speak. "We're going to try to get inside."

"I don't think that's wise…" Isabis starts.

Kornelía cuts her off, walking by without stopping to chat. "We need to try," she says, her footsteps so light she almost looks like she's floating.

"You don't have to try *right now*," Isabis argues.

"We won't take long," Sabeena promises.

Isabis watches the girls with a frown. "It's not about how long you're inside. It's—" She stops when Sabeena walks off without letting her finish. For a few seconds, her expression clouds with indecision. Then she huffs. "Fine, go on then," she seethes, barely sparing Meander and I a glance. "But I'm heading back to the road."

"Okay," Sabeena calls over her shoulder. "Do you want the flashlight?"

"No," Isabis sighs. "I don't need it."

"Are you sure you'll be okay?" Meander asks.

Isabis smiles. "I'm not the one you have to worry about," she says, nodding to where Kornelía and Sabeena have started up the porch's wooden staircase.

Isabis starts back along the dirt path, her steps uneven but confident. We watch her for a moment, then turn towards the house as Kornelía beckons us to hurry. The stairway is easy to climb and, in a matter of seconds, we're on the wood porch that wraps around the entire property.

"This place is stunning," Sabeena says, peering through one of the first storey windows. "I wonder what it looks like inside."

"Apparently, we'll find out soon enough," Meander mutters.

The porch is wide and sturdy, resting on high stilts. Even once we've passed the point where the stone steps veer down to the beach, we remain on level ground. Once we've made it to the back, the cold returns, stronger now and accompanied by a sweetness vile enough Sabeena holds a hand against her nose. No static pops in my head yet. Still, my stomach twists with slight unease.

The rear of the house has no first-storey windows, so our only option is to try one of several panes higher up. The biggest windows halfway up the house's exterior are closer to our reach, but they look like decorative glasswork meant solely to showcase the view. I suspect if we got close, we'd find they don't open. One other window is available to us—the one we stared at before making the decision to enter the house. But to reach the haunted room, we first have to scale the wall.

"Who's going up?" Meander asks, standing against the cedar porch railing.

"I can do it," Kornelía offers.

Sabeena shakes her head. "You're wearing a dress," she says.

Kornelía looks down, then glances up at Sabeena like she doesn't understand what wearing a dress has to do with her ability to climb. But Sabeena shakes her head again, her expression stern.

"You're not going up."

"All right," Kornelía sighs. She walks over and takes the flashlight out of Sabeena's hand. "Then you have to go."

"I will," the other girl agrees. She presses my shoulder as she walks by, which I guess means I'm giving the boost.

Following her over, I brace against the wall of the house while Kornelía and Meander help Sabeena climb onto my back. She straddles my shoulders and reaches upwards, but she's not close enough to grab the windowsill.

"You'll have to stand," Kornelía says.

Sabeena groans. "I can see that, but I don't know how to do it!"

"Cal, you'll have to crouch down," Meander instructs. "Then she can stand on your shoulders and you can raise her up."

I do, staggering under the added weight until I drop heavily onto my knees. The pain of the landing makes me wince, but I try to keep still as Sabeena readjusts her position. Once her feet are planted on my shoulders, I grip her ankles and struggle to stand.

"I don't think I'm strong enough for this," I grumble

through gritted teeth.

"Clearly we need to stop bunking off during our fitness runs," Meander laughs.

"Shut up, I'm not that heavy," Sabeena says, pressing her palms to the side of the house as I rise up. "There, that's high enough!" she calls after a few painful seconds have passed. "The window's locked, though. If I just..."

She gasps, swaying backwards. I grip her as tight as I can, throwing her weight forward so she falls against the wall.

"Sorry," she mumbles. "The spirit's here. It's a..." she takes a few deep breaths, like she's swallowing sickness. "A little girl."

"Do you think there's a way in?" Kornelía asks.

"No, there's not. Only—Oh!"

Sabeena flails back again and, this time, the movement's too forceful to counter. She topples off my shoulders, falling onto Kornelía while I stumble back into Meander.

"Are you okay?" I ask, kneeling down to help her up.

"I'm all right," she says, waving me away as she scrambles onto her knees and hurries back to her feet. "But we have to go. *Now.*"

"Why?" Kornelía asks.

Sabeena pulls her up and points to the window."Because of that," she says.

I follow the direction of Sabeena's finger until my eyes reach the window. Yellow light illuminates the distinctly living face of a startled woman staring out at us.

"Oh, shit," Meander mutters. He looks over the

porch railing, and sighs. "No time to run back to the stairs. We'll have to jump."

"Are you crazy?" I ask, staring over the railing to the beach below. The drop must be at least ten feet.

"We can still make it around to the front," Sabeena says.

Kornelía shakes her head and, when I face the house again, my gaze is drawn to two people staring at us. One of them disappears. Probably to track us down.

"Someone's coming," I say. "I don't think we can make it back out front in time."

"Then we've got to go over the rail," Meander suggests again.

"Can we make it?" Sabeena asks, peering over the edge. "It's far."

"Let's all discuss the distance for a while, yeah?" Meander says in annoyance. He stares at the ground, then pulls himself up. "I'll check it out."

I just have time to see the tightening of his forearm muscles before he swings his legs over the wood railing and drops onto the distant sand. Panic swells in my chest, and I grip the railing as I look down to see him land. His whole body is still for a beat before he shifts to wipe sand off his legs.

"I'm still alive!" he calls. "Now, *come on!*"

I press my head to the railing, huffing with relief. When I lift my eyes again, it's to see Sabeena following Meander. She drops over the side, and I wait for Kornelía to do the same before I push myself over.

The drop is quick and, in a second's time, I land. Pain sizzles through my ankle. "Damn it," I growl.

Meander helps me up, and I stagger a couple of steps before I catch my footing.

"Are you okay?" he asks.

"Yeah, yeah, I'm fine," I say, limping forward.

The sound of someone opening the house's front door makes us jump, and I motion for the others to keep moving. We take the beach route, the girls running ahead, and Meander holding back to keep pace with my pathetic limping. When we circle around to the main road, Isabis is waiting for us, looking like she's about to laugh.

"Get a fright, did you?" she asks.

"The house… It wasn't—" Sabeena begins.

"Empty?" Isabis finishes. "I know. That's what I was trying to tell you. While you were all on the beach, I saw someone walking around upstairs."

Sabeena gapes. "You what?"

"I know I talk slow," Isabis says, her smile smug. "But next time, maybe listen?"

Meander chuckles, while Sabeena gives a solemn nod. "Yes, all right," she concedes. "Lesson learned. Now let's get out of here, before those people catch up to us."

The next morning, Kornelía sits in the living area of the boys' fale. Dylan yawns beside her on the sofa. I sit on the other couch, my leg stretched out on the cushions and an ice pack on my swollen ankle.

"You said people live there, right?" Dylan asks in a groggy mumble.

He didn't need to get up so early but, when Kornelía knocked on our door first thing this morning, he dragged himself out of bed so he could spend time with her without Mim nearby. I don't know what's going on between the three of them. But while I'm curious about where everyone's loyalties lie, I'm not going to start a brawl by nosing around for more information.

Kornelía nods in response to Dylan's question. "Yes, someone was there," she says, pulling her legs up under her.

"Then doesn't that mean you're at a dead end?" Dylan asks.

"No," Kornelía says, her voice determined.

Meander joins us from the kitchenette, handing me a mug of tea before he walks around the sofa. Lifting my leg, he slides onto the seat beside me and lets my foot drop into his lap, sipping his own drink as he peels back the ice pack to ascertain the condition of my puffy skin.

"It's fine," I mumble, embarrassed I got injured on such a spirit-light outing. "Just a little sprain."

"We need to find a way to get inside the house," Kornelía continues, drawing our attention back to her. "That's the only way we'll be successful."

"Yeah, but there are people *living* in the house," I say. "Which is the problem, remember?"

Kornelía sighs, leaning back against the sofa.

"Maybe you can watch the house," Dylan suggests. "You know, wait and see when the people go out."

"So we can what...? Break in while they're out to dinner?" I laugh. Or start to laugh, until I notice Kornelía's considering gaze. "You can't be serious."

"It's not like we're going to steal anything," she protests. "Besides, we were planning to break in last night when we thought no one was home."

"I never pegged you for a criminal." Dylan smiles, looking almost proud.

Kornelía shifts her legs into a crossed position."It's for a good cause," she mutters.

"And if we get caught?" Meander asks. "Think the Oracle will like finding out half a sector broke into a private property *for a good cause*?"

"We could alert the Oracle," I say, glancing at him.

"Tell Robbie and Alex, or someone like Althea. That's what we're supposed to do in a situation like this."

Kornelía taps her foot as she weighs my words. Then she gives a reluctant nod. "Yes, all right," she agrees, though she doesn't sound happy about the decision.

"While the camp's looking into it, we can still research the house," Meander adds. "Try to find out who owns it—who used to own it—see if there are any stories about a young girl being murdered."

"That's true," Kornelía says with a hopeful smile. "We can do all the prep work while we wait for permission. Then when we get it—"

"*If* you get it," Dylan interjects.

Kornelía ignores him. "Then we'll have an easier time figuring out what she needs to move on."

"We'll search the property listings," Meander says, not bothering to indicate who the other half of 'we' is, "and you can look for the girl."

"Sabeena will want to help, too." Kornelía nods. "Isabis as well, I imagine. Between the five of us, it shouldn't take long to get some answers. It can't, in a place as small as this."

"Listen to you," Dylan scoffs, running both hands through his bedraggled hair. He hasn't been spiking it like he did last summer. More often than not, this year's look is a shaggy mess. "We're only a couple weeks in, and you've got yourself a project. What happened to a lazy summer in paradise?"

"You were the only one planning on total relaxation." Kornelía smiles. "The rest of us came here to work."

"You've got your priorities all wrong, darling," Dylan laments.

"There's nothing wrong with my priorities,"

Kornelía says. "And don't you think it's time you were a little more serious? You've hardly been at ease while we've been here."

Dylan squirms, put off by the suggestion he should be thinking about the dogs surrounding him on this island, both living and dead. He rubs his head again, then stands in one quick, popping motion. "You tackle as many ghosts as you want," he says, sounding annoyed. "But leave me out of it."

"You were never a part of it to begin with," Kornelía grumbles.

Dylan glowers at her, and I turn my attention to Meander while they stare each other down.

"Why'd you stick us with researching the property instead of the spirit?" I ask.

Meander shrugs through a sip of tea. "Figured she'd be happier with that arrangement. Anything to stop her waking us so bloody early to complain."

"I'm sitting right here," Kornelía says.

He offers her a cheery smile complete with a salute of his mug. "So you are," he says, downing the rest of his still-steaming tea before extracting himself from beneath my foot. "I'm going to shower. You keep ice on that until I'm back."

"Yes, sir." I smirk and give him a salute of my own.

On his way around the sofa, Meander's hand grazes the back of my head. For a terrible moment, I think he's going to ruffle my hair—an aggravating habit several of my relatives maintain despite knowing how irksome I find it. But then his fingers still and, after a beat of hesitation, he flicks my neck instead.

"Ow… Way to add to my injuries!" I call after him as he disappears into the bedroom.

I shake my head, so pleased by his intuitive guess, I can't keep from smiling as I rub my neck. Turning my sights to the living area once more, I'm surprised to find only Kornelía looking back at me. Dylan is gone. I'm not sure how he managed to leave the room without me noticing.

"Meander's taking good care of you," she says, amusement dancing in her eyes.

"He feels guilty." I shrug. "It was his idea to jump over the railing."

Kornelía tilts her head to one side, her eyebrows arched, as if she doesn't believe my explanation. But after a pause, she shakes her head.

"I'm sorry you hurt your ankle," she sighs. "We were a bit stupid last night, weren't we?"

"It's not a big deal," I assure her. "We shouldn't have assumed the house was empty. Or, uh, tried to break in. But at least we confirmed there *is* a spirit there."

"Yes." She nods, then sighs. "It's odd, though. I know Sabeena said it was a girl, but I couldn't get a distinct idea of her. Usually I can tell more about a spirit than that."

"We were outside," I offer. "Maybe we were too far away. I don't think we were fully feeling her from the far side of that window."

"That doesn't matter, though," Kornelía says. "At least, it doesn't for me. Or, it never used to. I used to be able to sense things from far off. Now, I'm having trouble sensing spirits close by. And then there's the fear. I've never felt it before, the fear I had with that man on the other island. Last summer we were new, so I didn't know what to expect from the Oracle. This time, I thought I did. But so far, Camp Wanagi is not going as planned."

"Yeah, I get that," I say.

I don't feel the same way she does, at least not totally. I'm annoyed I didn't dive into my studies like I promised myself I would. But we're still early in the summer, and already I've ventured to seek spirits twice. Besides, unlike Kornelía's unplanned experience with fear, the fears I prepared to face this summer have, so far, been non-existent. Before I left home, I worried that when I got face to face with Meander, we'd be awkward again—a hard reality after months of easy correspondence. But being close to him is more natural than I could have hoped. Talking to him in person makes me feel like we've always communicated this way, as if none of our previous chats took place with a computer screen between us.

My worries haven't revolved much around spirits lately. But still, I understand where Kornelía's coming from. If nothing else, I see the same uncertainties in Dylan, even if he won't admit them. He wasn't expecting an onslaught of nearby strays. As much as he likes dogs, I think the living packs following him on his frequent runs are a new experience.

"I shouldn't complain," Kornelía says after a moment, pushing her hair behind her shoulders as she lets out a decided breath. "It's a challenge—and I've never backed down from a challenge. I only hope the Oracle doesn't take too long getting things sorted once we tell them what we found."

"They won't," Dylan says, reappearing in a pair of black running shorts and an orange shirt with a jack o'lantern design on the front.

"Little early for Halloween, isn't it?" I ask.

Dylan shrugs. "I figure if we're going to be around ghosts all the time, I might as well embrace my inner Halloween fanatic year-round."

Kornelía looks like she wants to say something about spirits not being fodder for a holiday, but instead she stands, touching Dylan's arm on her way to the front door. "I'm going to have some breakfast," she says. "You want to walk with me before your run?"

"Of course," Dylan says with a grin. He turns to me, noting my ice pack and appearing not at all sorry I can't leave the sofa to join them. "Later, Cal."

I give them a wave as they exit the fale, then I relax on the sofa to enjoy the sea breeze through the open window while I drink my tea. The distant sound of the shore mingles with the not-so-distant rush of the shower, and the shine of the morning sun is so peaceful, not even my throbbing ankle can dampen the tranquility of the moment.

Any instant of quietude in the whirlwind of events at this camp is strange. There were interludes like this last year as well, seconds of bliss punctuating the chaos. I'm glad those moments haven't changed. I don't feel them at home, even when I've gone a good stretch without a spirit making me ache and shiver. I don't know why the calm comes to me here. But I won't let it go without appreciating it as well as I can.

I take another sip of tea and watch the light play on the coffee table until Meander's finished his shower and my other roommates wake up to disturb the peace.

"HERE, I NIPPED THIS FROM THE BEACH THIS MORNING. "EIGHT DAYS AFTER
our disastrous night at the treehouse, I sit down
next to Meander in one of the four vacation homes
that have been converted into classrooms for the
duration of camp. Mr. Olenev will be here shortly
to start our Research Methods course. But for now, I
have a moment to hand over the paperback I found
half-buried in the sand this morning, after I gave up
running with Dylan and his dogs.

Meander eyes the book, then takes it with a quiet
laugh. "You're stealing presents for me now?"

"Someone left it." I shrug. "Thought it'd be more
use to you than the waves. Have you read it?"

The book is a mystery thriller, forgotten by someone
too busy enjoying another facet of their vacation.

Meander turns the paperback over and reads the
cover blurb. "Nope, haven't read it," he says, glancing
up at me with a smile. "That's the thing about books.

There are always new ones to read. Thanks."

His eyes rest on mine for a beat longer than a normal glance warrants, an odd habit I never realized I missed until I arrived on this island three and a half weeks ago. Even when we talked over video, our gazes never lingered—the effect isn't the same over such a long distance.

"Think we'll get outside today?" I ask, turning before the stare stretches too long, even for us.

Mr. Olenev has always been good about giving us hands-on experience, but researching is more of an indoor activity. Today the sky is overcast, and a storm is set to roll in this afternoon. Hanging out by the water on a day like this wouldn't be ideal but, knowing our instructor, he might consider the unpleasant weather a perfect excuse to kick us all outside.

"Who knows," Meander says, already reading the first page of his new book.

I pull it from his grasp, and he scowls with fake indignation. "I knew I shouldn't have given this to you until after class," I say.

"The course hasn't even started yet," he reminds me.

At his words, the classroom's screen door creaks open. I grin, and Meander rolls his eyes before we both turn to see Robbie unexpectedly entering the room.

"Hey, y'all!" he calls as he perches on the edge of the instructor's desk.

"What are you doing here?" I ask.

Robbie swings his legs against the bottom of the desk like an energetic schoolkid.

"Your instructor has been called away," he says. "So, they've let me take charge."

"You're a Shade lead, aren't you?" Ralli, one of the familiar Revenants, asks.

"I sure am," Robbie says. He looks gleeful. I'd be worried he was going to make us do something tedious-bordering-on-sadistic, if I didn't know him better. His elated smile, combined with his tall hair and formal blue suit, is unnerving.

"Robbie's my name," he continues, staring around the room. "Robbie Quillin. And for today, y'all are lucky enough to have me as your instructor."

Shuffling noises ripple through the room as kids swivel their heads towards Meander and me. We're the only Shades in this class, which means everyone is looking to us to gage whether having Robbie in charge really is lucky or not.

"What are we doing, then?" Meander asks, his words clipped with annoyance as he makes a show of ignoring the glances. He sinks into his seat, crossing his arms over his chest and eyeing the mystery book on the table. I slide it to my far side, out of reach.

"I am so glad you asked, Mr. Rhoades," Robbie says, the use of a surname strange on his tongue. "Today, we're going on a little excursion. Follow me, guys and gals. Leave your stuff—but grab some water. It's friggin' hot outside."

Robbie hops down and heads out of the room. After a few seconds of mumbling uncertainty, everyone gets up to follow. Despite the grey sky, it's hot and muggy outside. A fine sheen of sweat glistens on Robbie's face, and he wipes his brow with the back of his hand.

"Do you have to wear the suit?" I ask as we crowd around him. "It's not exactly appropriate weather for it."

"Official duties call for official attire." Robbie smiles, straightening the jacket before wiping his forehead again. "Would be nice if they let us wear shorts, though," he admits.

When everyone is standing close enough for his liking, Robbie pulls out three folded squares of paper and holds them up for us to see.

"What are those?" one of the Entity girls asks.

Our Research Methods course is small, with only seven students in total: two Shades, two Revenants, and three Entity campers. No one from Wraith has enrolled.

"Your assignment," Robbie says, beckoning us closer so he doesn't have to raise his voice over the hammering of a nearby construction site. "Today, you're going to use my favorite form of research to determine the history behind some local areas of interest."

"Like, tourist spots?" one boy asks. He sounds dubious. "What does that have to do with hunting ghosts?"

"If you're going to use research to learn about spirits, you need to know which methods are most worthwhile," Robbie explains. "You're familiar with how to find books, and Mr. Olenev's been teaching you tricks for tracing records using genealogy sites and visits to local archives. And if he's back in time, I believe next week you'll start the ever-useful lesson on tools for helping you translate languages you don't know. But sometimes, you can't beat today's gem of a method… talking to the locals."

"How is that research?" Ralli asks, and Robbie grins.

"People are great," he says, slowing his speech so it's smooth and languid. "They love to talk. Sure, they'll tell you all kinds of wild stories, but fiction is founded from truth. Talk to enough people and you'll start to get an idea of what's truly going on."

He flicks his wrist, and the pieces of paper fan out like a lackluster deck of cards.

"Is that really what we're doing?" the Entity girl asks. "Talking to people?"

"Sure is," Robbie replies. "I have three pieces of paper here. Each piece lists a different place. All three locations are tourist destinations. *But*, all three have other stories surrounding them, too. Separate into teams—two couples and a trio, I suppose—and each team will tackle one location. Find out whatever you can by talking to the people who live here. We'll meet back thirty minutes before the course is over, so we can talk about what y'all have found."

Robbie holds out the papers, and I grab one of the sheets at random. Ralli grabs a second, and the Entity girl grabs the third. As usual, we're uninventive in choosing our teams—each sector sticks together.

"I'd tell you not to cheat," Robbie says as we're preparing to depart, "but I doubt you'd find anything on a computer, anyway. Lots of stories make it online. But, in my experience, most of the best stay local."

We head off, all of us taking different routes though we don't yet know which way we're supposed to be going. Meander and I walk a few paces down the beach before we stop so I can unfold the paper.

Robbie's handwriting is crooked but legible. "Swallow's Cave," I read. "Looks like there *is* a cave nearby after all."

Meander gazes out to sea as if he'll be able to spot the cave against the horizon. Then he peers at the slanted handwriting on the sheet. "Might as well get going," he says. He glances around and makes the arbitrary decision to keep moving in the direction we started.

We cross a paved courtyard and turn up the main road beyond the resort. From there, our walk isn't far. Meander leads us to the first commercial bit of beach he can find, where a few locals stand around talking at the edge of a short dock.

"Excuse me," Meander calls, waving to get the men's attention. "Do you know where we can find Swallow's Cave?"

"About fifteen minutes that way." One of the men nods, pointing along the shore.

"Thanks," Meander says, starting to turn away.

"You can't reach it by land," another man adds. "You'll need a boat." He sweeps his arm back, showcasing the worn collection of small boats bobbing in the water. Meander surveys them as well, then glances at me, his brow quirked in question.

"We're supposed to find out about it, not visit it ourselves," I laugh.

His pale lips lift into a mischievous smirk I know I can't argue with."We could do both," he suggests. "We've got more than three hours. If the cave's fifteen minutes away, it'll be no problem getting there and back in time. We won't go inside… We'll drive past and then turn around. We can talk to the locals once we've returned."

I wasn't under the delusion we'd spend our allotted time hounding people on the street to get as many details as possible. But the idea of renting a boat and visiting the place is not what I envisioned.

I am, however, happy to make a change of plans. "I

guess we're going on a boat ride, then," I smile.

Meander saunters forward to pick our ride. He negotiates like a pro, and I'm not sure whether I'm shocked to hear his hard back-and-forth with the boatmen, or if I never doubted he possessed this skill. He reasons that a short trip for an unplanned journey is worth a discount, particularly since he's certain the men aren't running a registered business. The men grumble, exchanging words in the Tongan language that don't sound friendly. But, in the end, they concede to offer us a lower price.

When it comes to payment, I step in, saying a silent thanks I have the proper currency in my wallet.

"It was my idea," Meander argues, his shoulders tensing at my offer to pay.

I've come to know a lot about Meander. Like the fact that he lives with a single parent who doesn't have a high-earning career, and doesn't care to give her son any of the income she does make. Meander works part-time in a cemetery, weeding, mowing, and clearing away dead flowers left at graves. But he doesn't make much, and the money he does have he uses for practical things like clothes—not for spur of the moment adventures like boat rentals for exploring caves.

He's not pleased that I keep his arm from his pocket, but I don't back down from my offer. "You got us the price," I say, pulling out my wallet. "I'll pay it."

Meander crosses his arms over his chest and sighs as I hand over the fee. Then we load onto a blue rowboat with an outboard motor. I expect the owner to climb aboard with us. But once we're seated, he revs the motor and pushes the boat out into the water—the two of us the only occupants onboard.

"**Do you know how to drive a boat?**" I ask as the men and the dock—drift out of sight.

"Not a clue." Meander smiles, leaning over the rowboat's edge to watch the water streaming away.

"Oh, great," I groan. "We're going to be lost at sea, aren't we?"

"It's highly possible," Meander agrees.

He splashes water at me, his calf sliding against mine from across the vessel's narrow interior. I'm now wondering if any of the men at the dock are the actual owner of the boat we just took—since I'm sure it's not exactly legal for us to be driving this watercraft sans permit. I should probably be regretting our rash decision. But despite the incoming storm, the waters are calm, and the shore is in view. As I splash Meander back, droplets of water glimmering on his sun-pinked cheeks as he laughs, the thought of panicking evaporates into the muggy air.

He's a liar, at least partially. He does know how to manage the boat. Meander lives near the coast, so it's not far-fetched to assume he's been on a few boats in his lifetime. Of course, being him, he's probably picked up the know-how from reading a series of boating manuals.

We pull a couple of ragged lifejackets from under one seat and slide them on. Then Meander guides the motor, and our boat cuts across the waves, rounding bends until the sandy shoreline gives way to rock. Tall formations of grey and green loom before us. A forest tops the cliffs that stretch down to the clear turquoise water rolling against its sides.

We don't intend to enter the cave. But, when the boat nears the break in the rock, the entrance is so wide it doesn't seem dangerous for us to venture farther in. Meander kills the motor and guides the tiller as we glide between the tall cliffs on either side. I expect the landscape to be dark, but Swallow's Cave isn't a true cave at all—at least not near its opening. A gap in the rock formation high above our heads creates a large pocket of open air. Despite the sky's heavy cover of cloud, light streams through the branches of the uppermost trees.

"Yep. I could read here," Meander says, his voice content as he cranes his neck for a better view.

Light plays on the water, turning it from black to blue, the brighter spots revealing schools of shadowy fish darting around the edges of our boat. Above us, plant life grows on various stone ledges, dotting the grey with leafy green. The open ocean rocks against the sides of the cave, the entrance like a giant keyhole shining with the brilliance from the other side.

I pull off the lifejacket so I can twist to take in the full extent of our surroundings. Meander does the same, and I move to the other side of the boat, sliding beside him to watch the water drifting through the rock opening.

"I thought it'd be a dark hole," I mumble. "This is incredible."

Meander smiles. "And you wanted to spend our afternoon chatting with strangers."

We're quiet for a moment. Meander looks up as I observe the fish circling in the deep water. I'll have to thank Robbie for his fantastic lesson plan. When we received our invitations to camp two months ago, Meander and I joked about how Tonga would end up being far worse than our dreary abode in France. But even while we speculated what horrors might await us, this is the kind of setting I imagined. Water, light, and the two of us by ourselves, no chance of interruption from sector mates wanting to play ball or hunt for ghosts.

I've pictured many variations of this scene over the last couple months. But only now that the moment has become reality do I realize that, in all the fantasies I conjured, none of my other friends were ever present. I smile to myself, until the thought repeats, sending my lips into a troubled frown. Every daydream I've had of enjoying the blissful Tongan sun has involved me and a single other person—the only friend I've ever cared enough about to include in my perfect moment.

When Meander shifts, his leg pressing against mine on the small bench seat, I swallow a shock of heat. Then I raise my eyes to find him watching me.

"When I left camp last year, I didn't honestly believe

I'd be back," he confesses.

I struggle to control my thoughts and focus on what he said. "What made you change your mind?"

I wasn't sure I'd come back until I was coerced into digging up a grave in the middle of the night. If absorbing a spirit's entire energy source wasn't enough to convince Meander he had more to learn from the Oracle, I'm curious to know what was.

He shrugs, his fingers straying to the hem of his shorts. He picks at the threading in the fabric until he catches the movement and forces his fingers to rest flat.

"I suppose part of me wants to see if I can figure out why I've got such a messed up ability," he admits as he peers around the cave.

"And the rest of you?" I prod when he doesn't volunteer the information.

He stares into a recessed landing in the rock as I ask the question. But, once the words are out, he turns to me with a quizzical glint in his eyes.

"To see you," he says, like the answer's obvious.

I must look surprised. Meander smiles, the expression almost shy, before he goes back to gazing into the depths of the cave.

I should do the same, but I'm unable to keep from studying his profile in the grey light of the overcast day. My throat is dry, and I wish I'd listened to Robbie's advice about bringing water with us. Unscrewing the cap of a plastic bottle would give me something to do, at least. Drinking would stop me from staring at Meander like an idiot, watching him in stunned panic that swept over me so fast I'd assume a spirit was nearby, if I wasn't so warm.

Four months ago, my sister Rose learned what the word 'oblivious' means. She likes to use it to describe me, and her taunts are accurate more often I'd ever admit. I'm slow to catch onto things. Thoughts work their way through my mind at a more leisurely pace than the average person. When it comes to spirits, I'm occasionally on the mark. But among the living, I tend to straggle a beat or two behind everyone else.

Still, I never realized how terrible I am at recognizing my own feelings. Because for as long as I've known Meander is my friend—someone I look forward to talking to everyday, someone I couldn't wait to see in person this summer—I didn't expect a simple visit to a cave would rock me so hard it feels like the whole boat is capsizing.

One brilliant, terrifying moment is all it's taken for a hundred little pieces to tumble into place. And in the achingly long seconds I've been stuck here, unable to stop examining each detail of Meander's face, a new picture has sketched itself in my mind. Not just the two of us alone in this cave. The two of us alone in this cave, with my lips on his.

Rose would be giddy. I'm so damned oblivious, I never even knew I was desperate to kiss my best friend.

I work to take normal breaths as I reel with the fantasy and sway with the truth of how this sudden longing shouldn't feel sudden at all. Old moments tick through my head, highlighting details that, at the time, I never noticed on a conscious level. Things like my overwhelming joy of touching Meander—of smelling him—when we first arrived on the island. Or the way I always watch his mouth when he smiles.

And the habit I've formed of waiting for everyone else to fall asleep so I know that, for a moment, the two of us are alone.

Not to mention that imagining our lips locked feels less like an outrageous dream and more like something I've pictured before, a desire I've unknowingly harbored for a long time.

Hell, my obliviousness has made *me* giddy. In a *what on earth am I supposed to do now?* kind of way.

Meander looks at me, and the world settles into one of those rare, Hollywood instances when the universe seems to be urging a monumental scene into existence. Here we are, sitting next to each other, our bodies touching and our eyes locked. We're alone in a cozy boat, floating in a picturesque cave on a beautiful, tropical island.

The moment is begging to come alive.

So, of course, I say, "We shouldn't take too long in here," proud I don't stutter each syllable or crumble into a swooning mess. "There's supposed to be a storm coming."

"Yeah, you're right," Meander sighs, admiring the view a final few seconds before grabbing his lifejacket and starting the motor. "We should make some attempt to find out the story of this place, anyway. And that guy will try to charge us more money if we don't get the boat back in time."

"Hey, at least we found your reading cave," I say, my voice a convincing charade of ease.

He guides us around and heads back through the opening, the lapping cave water fading into the louder rush of the boat speeding through open waves.

"If you ever can't find me, you're safe to assume this

is where I've gone." Meander smirks.

I smile, trying not to let my gaze linger on his face as my heart pounds against my ribcage. The clouds above us are billowing and dark, and I feign interest in their ominous shapes as the cave and its perfect moment fall behind.

# 16

I NEVER EXPECTED I'D BE A GOOD ACTOR. BUT, AS WE LEAVE THE CAVE, I manage to act believably normal. Being weird is not an option. A jittery, standoffish disposition would put Meander on guard, and I can't risk him prying for information. I need to understand what's going on before I start freaking out about him also being in the know.

"Do you think anyone will be there when we bring the boat back?" I ask, part of the ongoing stream of conversation I force myself to keep up.

Meander looks surprised."Why wouldn't they be?" he asks as the rock cliffs end and the sandy white beach comes back into view.

"That guy sent us out in a boat without any sort of paperwork. He didn't even make sure we were wearing lifejackets. There's a decent chance he sent us off in someone else's boat. Maybe he's got a vendetta against one of the local fishermen."

"The thought hadn't occurred to me," Meander says with a laugh. "But now that you mention it, let's hope we don't return to find some stranger screaming at us."

"If there is, we can always go on the run," I offer, patting the side of the rowboat. "You've proven to be an excellent driver... I'm sure nothing would go wrong if we ventured out to sea."

We joke about our "stolen" boat the rest of the way to the dock. But while the easy topic stops me from falling back into a state of shock, I can't disregard the epiphany that now leads me to dwell on all of Meander's inane perfections. Whenever he turns to check the boat's progress, I revel in the way his hair shines pure gold under each momentary streak of sun. And while we discuss how far we could get before our small motor ran out of fuel, I'm overwhelmed with the peculiar knowledge that I'm probably the only person in this kingdom who knows his bottom teeth are crooked—the crowded incisors only visible when I'm close and he's laughing at something I've said.

The boat is hot. Even after we've docked—the original group of men still there to help us disembark—the heat stays, boiling and sticky against my skin. I'm glad the mugginess gives us something else to talk about, even if Meander keeps pushing back his hair, revealing the small freckle next to his left ear I've seen but never *noticed* until this afternoon.

Once on dry land, we make a half-assed attempt to complete our assignment by talking to the men on the dock as well as a girl cleaning tables inside the main pavilion of our resort. A few quick questions lead us to discover that the cave's supposed to be haunted. I didn't feel anything while we were there. Although to be fair, I was too busy dismantling my whole universe to have given a spirit much notice. Still, the resort waitress tells us stories of boats tipping and wailing noises whipping amongst the wind. Things that should have registered even in my distracted state.

Robbie might not think our research is detailed enough for a three hour expedition. But when everyone reassembles, the three Entity kids use the last thirty minutes of the course to recount their findings without giving the other teams a chance to talk. I'm happy when class is over, but I don't have the opportunity to sneak off by myself to cool down and think. Kornelía waits for us outside our classroom, bugging us for updates on the treehouse we still haven't bothered to look into.

"We've been busy." Meander shrugs, opening the book I brought him from the beach.

Kornelía sighs, plucking the novel from between his fingers. "You have not," she says, eyeing us both. "The two of you are as bad as Dylan. We're here to work, not to laze about fl—" She stops, perhaps noticing the way my eyes are widening with worry she's about to accuse us of *flirting*. "Flustered at the very suggestion of an assignment," she continues after a pause. She arches her eyebrows, staring us down.

"I'm sorry we've been slacking off," I mumble, trying to hide my possibly unfounded panic. "We'll work on the project soon."

She considers me, looking unconvinced that I'll heed her scolding. But then she hands me the book she took from Meander and leaves us in favor of questioning Robbie about why we haven't yet received permission to access the house.

The evening continues in the same manner, people flitting in and out as we return to our fale and leave for dinner. I maintain my calm pretence as best I can, figuring I'll head to bed early and spend a while with my earbuds in and my eyes closed for a bit of peace.

But I don't last that long.

Around eight-thirty, Dylan asks if we want to watch a movie. I say yes, thinking the film might be a good distraction from my thoughts. But by nine, the movie has failed to do anything except draw my attention to some of the room's other occupants. Dylan sits with one arm around Mim and his other hand on Kornelía's ankle. I'm not sure the latter even notices, as she's ignoring the movie in favor of coursework. Still, the three of them are too cozy, especially since it shouldn't be the *three* of them at all. The closeness and comfort puts me on edge. When Meander shifts next to me, his arm resting against mine after he turns the page of his book, I can't keep still any longer.

He glances up when I stand, a question in his eyes.

"I think I'm going to play my violin," I say, which earns me a surprised smile entirely too sweet for my nerves. We're more than three weeks into camp now and, although I've checked on its condition and made sure it stayed safe, I haven't played my instrument yet. I haven't needed to, until now. "I'll go outside," I say with a shrug I hope he doesn't take as a brush-off. "So I won't disturb anyone."

"Okay." He nods, and I pretend not to notice his disappointment as I walk into the bedroom, grab my case, and step into the night.

The beach is busy, and the distant rumble of thunder

suggests the storm that's been brewing all day may soon make landfall. An outdoor venue isn't the best plan after all, so I walk among the fales of our camp, peering through the windows of each to see which one might work. The other half of Shade is in the girls' fale, three of them playing cards while the other two sit on a sofa arguing and laughing in turns. The dining hall is locked. I check various classroom buildings, but find they're closed to me as well.

The only place open but empty is the library, which is not the best place to shake Meander from my thoughts. But that's not my aim tonight. At least not totally.

*So, I guess this will have to do.*

I place the case on a table and pull out my violin. The polished wood gleams under the library lights. The smell of rosin and wood polish have an immediate soothing effect as my fingers glide over the fingerboard and the strings vibrate beneath my touch. I smile, drawing out the bow and preparing it for play. Then I use the opened case as a makeshift stand to prop up some folded pieces of music.

The resonance of the first note feels like stepping out of the cold into a house warmed by a blazing hearth. I start with scales and a bit of Brahms' "Lullaby." I almost always begin my practice with this piece. The gentle notes were the first I ever memorized. I learned the piece to commemorate Rose's birth—not because I couldn't wait for her arrival, but because I resented her existence (or at least my suspicions for *why* she existed). I allowed my bitter guilt to manifest in the soft tune I played for her every night until she was four or five months old.

The sheet music, when I get to it, is Ernst's Grand Caprice on Schubert's "Der Erlkönig." The work is challenging, but I don't worry about achieving technical perfection. I've played the violin since I was five, studying at home and taking years of private lessons. But despite my teachers' insistence the violin is meant to be performed in public, I've never been interested in competition. Someday, I'd like to join an orchestra but, even then, the battle for chairs isn't something I want to bother with. My life is troublesome enough without the stress of striving to be a star performer.

I slide the bow across the strings, slipping into the music. Notes flow through my brain, sweeping away everything else, and I welcome the tranquil numbness. For ten or fifteen minutes, I don't stop, wavering between *presto* and *adagio*, *piano* and *fortissimo*. Eventually, my eyes slip closed and I drift away from the black marks on the page to play a composition of my own.

The escape is, momentarily, complete. But when my bow rests against the strings and the world around me becomes quiet once more, my eyes blink open to find the library bright and colorful, the bookshelves an instant reminder of why I came here in the first place.

With a sigh, I drop the violin to my side and survey my surroundings. The recently-constructed shelves are like towers of a castle I'm about to invade. I size them up, consider their immensity, then lay my violin in its case before I slide into the nearest seat to plan my attack.

"Okay," I mumble, holding onto as much of the calm as I can.

Snapping the black case closed, I trace the clasps with my finger while I let myself delve into the thoughts I've been keeping at bay since this afternoon. I dig through the memories that struck me earlier, trying to understand where this new desire came from and wondering if I've ever experienced a hint of these feelings before.

As soon as the question's asked, the answer seems ridiculously obvious. *Yes.* Or, more precisely—*of course*. I'm not far from responding with a simple *well, duh*. The moments are so easy to pull from my mind, I'm convinced they have always been floating on the surface, waiting for me to come by and scoop them up.

One Monday in March, Meander brightened my day by telling me about a piece of cake he'd had at work because he loves sweets but rarely eats any that are homemade. Near the end of April, when I was sick, he texted me flu remedies he'd read in who knows how many different books—everything from common sense calls for medicine and rest to outrageous rituals for bloodletting and using live frogs to aid a bad cough.

With a swell of anguish, I remember the night a few weeks before camp began when Meander's mother was on a bender. He was planning to stay out all night to keep out of her way. I didn't think twice about clearing my evening to keep him company. We talked for five hours until his mom passed out near four a.m. and he was able to sneak inside to go to bed.

Slumping back in my chair, I rub my temples. I don't know when things changed between us, if they ever changed at all. Meander has always intrigued me. Even when he was hardly more than a stranger, I was drawn to his side and determined to break through his silent exterior. Maybe there was never an instant when things started to change, only a series of moments when things stacked together, constructing a staircase meant to take me to the next, inevitable level of our relationship.

Now I've ascended. But that doesn't mean I have the slightest idea where I'm supposed to go next.

My hands are shaking when I bring them down to my lap, and shivers wrack my limbs even though I'm not cold. I guess it's because I'm scared—less about these new-not-new feelings than about what they mean for the two of us. A picture of this afternoon comes into focus, and I let myself imagine what would have happened if we'd kissed. The thought makes my shivering worse, and I'm glad no one's here to witness it. Despite my quaking limbs, an idiotic smile has taken control of my lips.

But then I close off the image, pulling the smile down with it. I won't be able to act natural if I imagine us kissing every time I look at Meander. He can't suspect what I'm feeling, not until I know if he might feel the same way.

"Oh, hell," I mutter, an avalanche of new questions cascading over me.

Oblivious I may be, but I'm not so dim I don't already know that Meander cares about me. When we parted last year, I wasn't sure if we were friends, or if I was just another person in a sea of faces to him. Even once we started emailing, I was never *sure*. Not until the night in January when he showed me what the ghost in the pub did to his arm. Only when I realized he'd chosen to spend that night talking to *me*, telling me what happened and divulging his fears—all while swallowing medication and grimacing with the fresh pain—did I understand.

Meander cares about me, and I don't want to jeopardize that. So, I can't risk it. Not yet. I'd rather deal with these feelings on my own than press myself on him and force him into retreat.

I sigh, retrieving my violin and playing another few bars of random music, a soft melody not unlike the piece from Brahms. The notes smooth the wrinkles out of my day, the bow an iron I run forward and back against my uncertainties until they are tamed. And, when they are, I play a little longer, simply to enjoy the music.

When I get back to the fale, the movie is still on. My absence cut through most of the plot, but I'm able to tuck my instrument away and slip back onto the sofa in time to catch the final act.

"Feeling better?" Meander asks as I drop onto the couch.

I look at him nestled in the corner of the sofa, a too-heavy blanket over his lap and the book I gave him earlier open on the arm rest. One golden curl hangs across his left eye as he watches me, patiently waiting for a response. He looks the same as he did before I left to play, the same as he did before this day began. He hasn't changed, but the way I see him has. Studying him now is like hearing a familiar symphony live for the first time.

"I'm not sure," I admit, my voice low.

I settle beside him and turn to the movie, a peculiar amusement thrumming through my mind. This summer, my biggest fear was having my life uprooted by ghosts.

Suddenly, the dead don't seem so terrifying.

# 17



Eyes fixed on the lines of my notebook, I hold my breath for a beat and try to ignore the press of fingers on my shoulder before I glance at Meander. He leans over the back of my chair, no longer a safe distance across the library where he's supposed to be working on one of the computers.

"What's up?" I ask, twisting away from his touch as I stand to follow him to his computer station.

Nearly a week has passed since I played my violin to the empty chairs and full pages within this library. The time has been short, but it feels like I've been living with a weight on my chest for months. Pretending nothing has changed between Meander and I hasn't been quite as easy as I expected. Mostly because I never realized how much he touches me—or how often I've been in the habit of touching him.

"I figured I'd look up that treehouse," he says as we

cross the room. "Kornelía's expecting an answer from Robbie by tonight about accessing the place."

When we reach the computer, he drags a chair from the nearest table so I can slide in next to him. I do my best to avoid touching my leg to his as I sit and wait for him to explain why a vacation rental website is on the screen.

"Find anything interesting?" I ask.

He sweeps hair from his eyes and moves his hand to the mouse. "I'm not sure it's *interesting* so much as it's... *something*." He scrolls through a selection of houses until he lands on the fifth listing—the treehouse. "Turns out it's a vacation property, which could explain why it's taken so long for the Oracle to approach the owners. They rent it out like a hotel."

He clicks through the photos of the house. One stylish room after another flits across the screen. Then he glances at me.

"Good find." My fingers twitch, almost reaching to take over the mouse, and I ball my hand into a fist to keep them still. "Which room do you think we were looking at?"

"There are three bedrooms," Meander says, backtracking through the images until he lands on the correct ones. "Since we *visited* the place after midnight, I figure there's a good chance the people in that room were in bed. Which would mean it's one of these."

We study the three rooms, guessing by the layout which one most likely houses the spirit. The house is nice inside, everything clean and bright with white walls, tiled floors, and sleek steel fixtures. I can see why it's being rented as a hotel. I wouldn't say no to staying there. If it didn't come with a ghost, of course.

"I feel bad for the people who were there when we tried to get inside," I admit, glancing between the images. "They were probably having a nice vacation until a gang tried to break into their home. We're lucky we got out of that scrape scot-free."

"We didn't, though," Meander says. "At least, you didn't. You got hurt."

I smile. "It was *nothing*," I tell him for about the hundredth time.

It's been two weeks since I sprained my ankle, an injury that healed after a couple days of rest and was back to full strength by the time our next Strength and Stamina course came around. Which was for the best. Meander told Althea I was wounded in an attempt to get me—and, by extension, himself—out of the fitness portion of our fitness course. Althea had none of it and, if I'd still been in actual pain, the day would have been its own kind of hell.

"Your ankle could have ended up in a worse state," Meander says. "You shouldn't have jumped that far."

"You jumped down first," I remind him.

He runs his teeth along his bottom lip, clicking on random photos of the house. "That's different," he mumbles.

"Why, because I'm a klutz? Or because you think it's no big deal if *you're* the one getting hurt?"

He doesn't respond, which means I've called out what he's really thinking.

"I'm glad you weren't hurt," I say. "You've had enough injuries. Besides, you did *tell* us to follow you."

Meander shakes his head before turning over his arm to examine his latest scar. My reaction is automatic.

Before I can stop myself, my fingers glide over the raised skin that is still a deep shade of maroon-pink. Meander doesn't flinch or make an attempt to stop what I'm doing. I trace the scar, struggling to keep my hand steady as I try not to overthink his lack of reaction.

The heavy drop of a book startles us, and my hand snakes back to my lap. We look over to see Mim leaning down, her hands pressed against the cover of a thick, old book.

"I have a question for you," she says to Meander. Her words sound annoyed and heavily accented, like she's fed-up speaking English and is only doing so because she knows he won't understand her otherwise. Her black hair is greasy and her eyes are sunken. My guess is she hasn't been sleeping much. Even from this distance I can smell the coffee on her breath.

"Yeah?" Meander says, noting her harried appearance before focusing his gaze on the book.

"Do you know any Latin?" Mim asks. If anyone at camp was going to know Latin offhand, I suppose Meander would be a good bet. But the way she asks it—her words strained and hopeful—makes me laugh out loud.

"Sorry, no," Meander says, sounding perplexed.

Mim groans, slumping into the chair of the neighboring computer station. "You were my only chance," she sighs, staring at the book like she wants to tear it in two.

"Why did you think I'd know Latin?" he asks, taking the book from the table.

The title is not written in English, and I make an easy guess it's a Latin tomb. I'm surprised it's even here. I know Wanagi campers come from all over the world but, multilingual or not, I doubt many of them can translate Latin text.

"You're English," Mim says, slumping back in her chair. "And, you know, you read. All the time."

"We're a small country, but there are a lot of us," Meander says, flipping through the foreign pages. "Not all of us are intellectuals with a penchant for dead languages."

"What is a *pen… penchant*?" Mim asks.

"Not really helping your cause," I mutter to Meander with a smirk.

He smiles at me before shaking his head. "A strong partiality. A *keen interest*," he clarifies. "Why do you need to read Latin, anyway?"

"I'm trying to plan an exorcism ritual," she says.

My eyes widen as I process her words. "An exorcism?" I repeat, half-convinced I misheard.

Mim nods, taking the book back from Meander and dropping it into her lap. "For my Resistive Release course," she explains with a tired smile. "Last week, we learned about exorcism. A fascinating subject. Forcing spirits who won't move on to do so. Did you know there could be an exorcism on this island soon? One of the ghosts here won't leave. Dozens of Senders have attempted to get it to move on, but it refuses. The Oracle's ready to give up. After camp is over, they might come and perform an exorcism."

Her eyes are bright with interest. I don't think I've ever seen her look so intrigued by a spirit.

"So, you're doing a paper on exorcism?" Meander asks.

"Yes." Mim nods. "I've been working on it for days.

I've got most of the ritual planned out, but the Latin phrases are defeating me."

"You could try an online translator," I suggest.

Mim looks at the computer, her gaze suspicious. "I hadn't considered that," she mumbles. She places the book back on the tabletop and shifts to face the computer screen.

"I don't know how well they work," I say with a shrug, watching as she logs on. "But you can try."

Mim opens an internet tab and finds a translator that will convert Latin into Spanish. She types a phrase for translation and smiles when she reads the converted text.

"It works!" she says with a laugh. "Well, it maybe works. I don't know how perfect these translations are. But I can check them against a different translator later." She pats the top of her book before leaving the computer station.

"She's really thrown herself into her coursework," Meander says when she's out of earshot. He closes the vacation rental website and logs off the computer. "Think maybe she's getting a bit obsessed?"

"That, or she's trying to distract herself from something else," I say.

Before he has a chance to respond, Mim returns with her notebook and a sharpened pencil. "If I hurry, I can get most of the phrases translated before Reed shows up," she sighs, more to herself than to us.

"You're meeting Reed?" I ask, one eyebrow quirked. I didn't realize she and Reed talked outside of course time.

Mim glances at us with a small snort. "He told me he spent three weeks sitting on the beach, waiting to see a ghost in the water." She grins. "When he figured out he wasn't going to spot anything out there, he decided he wanted to be tutored instead. As if knowing more about ghosts will make him more likely to see them or something."

She shakes her head and turns back to the computer. "Sabeena and I are taking turns. Today, I'm teaching him how to find local hauntings for when he gets home."

"Isn't this the kind of stuff he should be learning from our instructors?" I ask.

"Try telling him that," Mim sighs.

Meander nudges my knee and nods to where Reed is walking through the library door and peering around as if he's already trying to spot his tutor. "Looks like your student is early," he says.

Mim glances up with another sigh, and Meander gives her a look of mild pity as he stands from his station to give the two of them space.

I follow him back to the table where I'd been working on an assignment before he showed me the pictures of the treehouse. He watches as I collect my things, then we head outside.

"You could be right," he says once we're back in the sun. "About Mim trying to keep distracted. People are useless, aren't they? Instead of talking to one another, they keep everything to themselves and let secrets fester until everyone's screwed over."

My stomach tightens as I wonder if he's talking about me. Then I wonder if I'm simply being an overzealous idiot who should force his feelings back into his subconscious—at least then I'd be able to enjoy Meander's company without examining every detail of our co-existence.

"Then again, Mim was like this last year, too," I say, remembering Mim's aloofness as she became more engrossed in last summer's final project. "This might be how she is when she gets involved in an assignment."

"A lot of people seem to get like that while they're here," Meander says. "I don't get it. Kind of feels like I'm missing part of the equation."

"You're not alone," I sigh.

He looks at me like I've stated the obvious. "I know." He smiles, his lovely eyes bright in the sun. "Do you need to work on your paper more, or do you want to go into town for some lunch?"

My lips press together, and I stare at the unending stretch of beach so I can, for a brief moment, avoid looking at him. "I was thinking I might play my violin for a while," I mumble, trying hard to sound nonchalant.

"You've been playing a fair bit this past week," Meander says. "Should I be worried?"

I glance at him, pleased to see the concern in his expression. "I've missed playing." I shrug, settling on a half-lie. He frowns, and I scramble for a way to make him less suspicious. "But, uh, we can get dinner later."

"Yeah, sure," he says, his words measured. He knows he's not getting the truth. I'll have to find a better excuse so he doesn't think I'm avoiding him on purpose.

Even if I am.

"We could go for a boat ride as well," he offers after a pause.

My heart hammers so hard it rivals the thuds from

the construction site outside of our Research Methods course. I'm surprised my ribs don't break under the strain. I don't know if he's serious. Considering our first boat trip was something I'm sure the Oracle would disapprove of, risking it again is not a good idea. But over the last five days there have been a few moments like this, when Meander says or does something to make me question whether his feelings might actually match my own. Right now, he may have nothing more than a casual night in mind. But, to many people, dinner and a boat trip for two would sound like a date.

*A date.* Is that even possible? I can easily imagine us sailing off into the sunset. But would Meander be driving somewhere with romance in mind? If we ended up in that cave again… Would I be able to suppress my longing a second time?

Would he want me to?

My uncertainty keeps me from divulging the truth of how I feel about Meander. But I can't turn down what could be an offer to explore those feelings together.

"Well, you *are* a master boatswain," I say, nodding my agreement.

Meander smirks. "Don't you mean captain?"

"Whatever," I laugh. "You're the master, not me." I falter, pausing for a moment before I work up the nerve—or maybe just the stupidity—to add, "We could go back to the cave."

He smiles, reaching up to run a hand through his curls as he looks over the water. "You sure you don't want to go now?" he asks. "I could bring a book, and you could bring your violin. I promise I won't listen."

I force another laugh, the suggestion simultaneously

tempting and terrible. Given my hopes for why he's so eager to spend time with me, I'm almost willing to take him up on the offer. But the note of genuine interest in his tone reminds me how much the idea of practicing the violin in front of him bothers me. He may be joking about me taking my instrument out to the cave, but he's serious about listening to me play. Perhaps this, too, should excite me, but my nerves get the better of me and I only hunch in retreat.

"You're never going to give up on hearing me play, are you?" I ask, keeping my voice light.

"Nope." Meander steps closer to me, his arm nudging against mine as we walk. "But I won't listen, I promise," he repeats.

"I'm sure sound won't carry at all in a *cave*," I say.

"Caves are notoriously soundproof," he argues.

I nod like what he's said is obviously true, then stare at the ground until he sighs. "You play, and I'll meet you later," he says. When I look up, he's stepped away from me, prepared to head in a different direction.

"Okay," I mutter. I stamp my foot against the ground and let a long breath whistle through my lips. "I *will* let you listen sometime."

I give him my most appeasing smile, begging him not to be disappointed. I don't know why he's so interested to hear me play and, until recently, I didn't fully understand why I'm so nervous about letting him. The idea should be thrilling, another bond to bring us closer. But one realization has made others shuffle into place. My violin is my safe haven, and I'm afraid letting him listen will strip away its walls.

He shakes his head, clearing away his own thoughts, whatever they may be. "Before the summer is over?"

he asks, looking unconvinced.

"Before the summer is over," I agree, making the words a promise to both him and myself. I eye him for a moment, then pull my gaze away before I lose myself in his stare. "You'll finally hear me play and think I'm terrible," I add.

"If you can play "Twinkle, Twinkle, Little Star," I'll be impressed," he says.

I smirk. "What about a lullaby?"

"Like I said. Impressed. So get practicing, and I'll see you later, yeah?"

He moves toward the dining hall, possibly for lunch but, more likely, for tea before he finds somewhere quiet to read. I watch him go, studying the way he walks. He steps with an odd mix of confidence and invisibility, like he's not afraid of attention—just doesn't want to bother with it.

The knot in my stomach twists hard as I turn away. I scold myself for being so damned timid. Then I skulk towards the momentary comfort of my violin.

DREAD AND GLEE FIGHT FOR TOP BILLING AS I SPEND THE REST OF THE DAY
preparing for our dinner and boat ride to the cave.
I can't decide which emotion has the lead under my
nervous skin, but it doesn't end up mattering. As
we're making our way outside, my throat tight with
apprehensive excitement while we talk about where
in town we should stop for food, Kornelía steps in to
shatter our plans.

"Robbie said he'll be here soon with an answer
about the treehouse," she says, ushering us into the
fale without bothering to ask where we were headed.

"So, tell us the answer when we return," Meander
says, unimpressed that she's more or less shoved him
back inside.

"You're a part of this," Kornelía scolds. "If we get
the okay to investigate, it means we need to start
planning. Which means I need you here. Both of you."

"What about Sabeena and Isabis?" I ask, dropping

onto one of the sofas. "They're not here."

"They will be," she assures us.

Meander looks like he's ready to push her out of the way, and I spend too long wondering if it's because he was looking forward to food and quiet, or because he was excited to be alone with me. When he glances back to where I sit on the sofa, I swallow my anxious hope and offer him a sympathetic smile.

He resigns himself to slumping down beside me, arms crossed tight over his chest. "This better not take long," he mumbles.

Kornelía beams in triumph before she disappears to find the others. While she's gone, Meander tries to convince me to sneak out the back, beyond the small courtyard with the swinging hammock. By the time I realize he's serious, and the thrill of escaping into the night starts to sound like an irresistible temptation, Kornelía has returned. The remaining members of our makeshift group are not with her, but she does have pizza and a container full of salad. I'm not sure where the food came from but, regardless of its origins, the arrival of a meal signifies she plans on more than a few minutes of conversation.

I try to pretend I don't notice Meander eyeing me, but the tactic doesn't work. When Kornelía drops the food onto the table and heads outside again, an amused smile twitches at the edge of my lips, spreading until I'm forced to laugh.

"This wasn't my idea," I say, happy to know the food hasn't appeased him.

I'm annoyed we can't be alone but relieved I can enjoy Meander's company without obsessing over where the night is headed. Being next to him on the sofa, his body close to mine as he sulks, is difficult enough. But at least I won't worry about divulging my secret if Kornelía spends the evening rambling about dead people.

"Yes, but you didn't knock her down and make a run for it," he counters.

I laugh again, sliding my hand against his knee as I lean forward to grab a slice of pizza. He doesn't worm away from my touch or look at me funny when I sit up straight.

"At least we get free food," I say, my fingers lingering, waiting to see what his reaction might be. He only looks at my pizza, and then at my face, his expression still moody. "If we finish up in time, we can still get the boat," I add.

"If she doesn't keep us here for a twenty-four hour study-a-thon," he says, reaching for his own slice while my hand slides back to my side.

"There's a better chance she'll want to try breaking into the house again," I say. "In which case, we'll *have* to run for it."

"Nice, who brought pizza?"

Dylan bounces through the front door, a notebook in one hand and an impossibly tacky, gold, sleeveless shirt hanging almost to his knees.

"It's not for you," Kornelía says, entering behind him and making him jump.

"Way to give a guy a heart attack," he says, cradling his notebook to his chest.

Kornelía rolls her eyes and walks around him, approaching the coffee table. "We're having a group meeting," she says. She pulls free a slice of pizza and brings it to him. "And you're not in the group. So, take your free food and leave."

Dylan gives her an offended look while he grabs the pizza and takes a bite. Kornelía grins, and he grins too, his teeth flashing while he chews.

"Wanna hang later?" he asks, backing away as he speaks.

"We'll see," Kornelía says, her voice brisk, like she's too busy with more important matters to decide if she's got time to waste with him.

Sabeena and Isabis step into the fale, and Dylan gives them a quick wave before disappearing into the bedroom.

"Are we late?" Sabeena asks.

"No, Robbie's not here yet," Kornelía says.

Isabis looks over her shoulder before she makes her way into the room. "No, but I think he's on his way."

I glance out the window, and spot Robbie's spiky hair bobbing through the air as he approaches the fale.

"Good," Kornelía smiles. She settles on the tile floor without grabbing any food.

Sabeena brings plates and cutlery from the kitchenette. She serves herself and Isabis salad while Robbie introduces himself to the Entity camper for the first time.

"What did you find out, Robbie?" Kornelía asks after a couple minutes, too impatient to let him get to the news in his own time.

Our lead leans next to the window, one leg back so his foot's pressed against the wall. With his hands in his pockets and an unhappy expression on his face, he looks like a stereotypical scowling punk.

"Nothing good, I'm afraid," he sighs, directing his gaze at Kornelía. "We got in touch with the owners, telling them who we are and why we want to access the house. They weren't interested in accommodating us... Which isn't an unusual reaction. The Oracle has mediators for such occasions, to help convince property owners we're not a bunch of looneys or crooks with an elaborate scheme to rob them. But our efforts didn't pan out. The owners of that treehouse don't want us involved. They won't give us permission to go inside."

Kornelía crumples, her whole body tightening like a flower closing its petals. The whispering glide and fearless determination she's displayed this summer vanishes in an instant, and the meek girl I knew last year returns.

"Sorry, Kornelía," I mutter, wishing she didn't look so defeated.

Sabeena holds up a forkful of salad, using it to point at Robbie. "Isn't there anything we can do?" she asks.

"Without their permission, we're out of luck." Robbie shrugs.

Kornelía raises her head. "What if we do it without their permission?" she asks, the words cautious but imbued with quiet enthusiasm.

Robbie looks surprised. I suspect mostly because the idea is coming from her. "We can't break the law." He smiles, his tone more encouraging than his words.

"No, but..." Kornelía huffs in frustration. "There has to be a way we can go inside without them knowing."

Pressure tightens on my knee, and my face flushes when I realize Meander's fingers are pressing against the hem of my shorts. "There might be a way," he mumbles, turning to me for confirmation.

I have no idea what he's talking about, until I

remember the website he showed me this afternoon in the library. I nod and, when he continues to look at me, I realize he's waiting for me to take over the explanation.

"The house is used as a vacation rental," I tell the others.

"How does that help us?" Sabeena asks.

"If we rented the house, we wouldn't be breaking the law," Isabis says, placing her plate of half-eaten salad on the end table beside the sofa.

"We wouldn't have to break in, either." Sabeena nods.

Robbie laughs. "You were entertaining that plan, were you?" he asks, amused.

Sabeena purses her lips, but Kornelía starts talking before she has time to admit what we attempted during our first visit to the house.

"We could rent it for one day, and then we'd have lots of time to work," she says. She smiles at me before shifting her grin to Meander. "Thanks for discovering that."

"Wait a minute," Robbie says, holding up a hand to stop us talking. "If y'all were to book the house for a night, that'd be swell. The owners wouldn't have to know a thing, and you'd be there under legal terms."

"Yes, and then we could—" Kornelía begins.

"*However*," Robbie continues, cutting her off, "if you plan to rent the house, you might be in need of something I'm not sure any of you have." He looks at us, turning his hand palm up and shrugging one shoulder. "A credit card."

Kornelía groans, her long legs sliding down until they're straight out in front of her.

"A minor setback," Sabeena says, more confident than Kornelía. "Robbie, if we can figure that piece out, can we do this as our final project for the summer?"

Robbie's eyes flick to Isabis, and he shrugs again.

"The four of you can, sure," he agrees. "I'd have to check for Isabis. Sectors usually stick together. Considering the circumstances, though, I bet Buxley would allow it." He surveys the group, raising his hand to scratch his chin. "But first, you need to find a way to make the reservation."

The room grows silent as everyone tries to think up the answer to our sizeable dilemma. But when no one offers a solution, Meander stands and walks to the kitchenette.

"I can use my brother's card," he says, his back to us as he pulls a bottle of water from the fridge. He unscrews the cap and leans over the counter. "He won't have a problem with it."

I quirk an eyebrow, stunned at the suggestion. A couple months ago, one of our conversations turned to the expense of long distance texting. Which is when I learned Meander's half-brother Liam, who is older and lives in London, has an arrangement with him regarding credit card use. Liam is in charge of Meander's phone account, and Meander gives him the money needed to cover each month's bill. But the agreement extends beyond that, to any out of the ordinary purchases requiring credit.

Their mother can't be relied upon, so the brothers rely on each other, and I know Meander doesn't use the arrangement lightly. I can't believe he'd do it for the sake of a rental he'd be hard-pressed to explain.

"Really?" Kornelía asks, her eyes brightening as her

hope returns.

Meander nods, staying behind the counter to drink his water and avoid my gaze.

"Good thinking," Robbie says, sounding impressed. He nods as he pushes off the wall. "Let me know when you have a receipt, and I'll make sure you're reimbursed the cost. We'll keep the details of this plan to ourselves, though. No need to let the instructors know quite yet." He pauses, considering something. Then he smiles. "If you want to get results, sometimes you need to be creative. Seriously, folks. Good thinking. I think you're going to make a great team. Proud of you, Shade."

Isabis looks annoyed not to be included but, in Robbie's defense, he doesn't know she's the one who told Kornelía about the house in the first place. Still, she fixes him with an aggravated stare while he turns and leaves us alone to work on the details of our plan.

We watch his retreating figure through the window. Then Meander sighs and returns to the living area.

"That's so cool of you to book the house for us," Sabeena says.

"I'm not booking anything," he replies, sitting next to me and taking another swig of water.

Kornelía crawls onto her knees, her elbows resting on the coffee table. "What do you mean, you're not booking it?" she asks, panic creeping into her voice. "You *just* told us you would."

"Do you honestly think a house as nice as that would be available for booking on such short notice?" he asks, a logical detail I failed to consider.

"We can still check," Kornelía says, not wanting to admit defeat again.

Meander shakes his head. "The rental website states the property is fully booked," he says. "No vacancies for the rest of the summer."

I wonder if he looked this up before he showed me the website earlier, or if he's lying to avoid putting the room on his brother's card.

"Why'd you tell him we could book it, then?" Kornelía asks, anger flashing across her face.

"So he'd be okay with us doing something," Meander says.

He waits a beat, wondering if anyone will pick up on his idea. No one does, and I'm glad I'm not the only clueless one here.

"We need the house for a single night," he explains. "Well, we'd only be booking it for a night, anyway. Even without a vacancy, we might still be able to get a night inside."

"How?" I ask.

Meander's eyes are hesitant, but his smile is sly—a warning that I'm not going to like what he has to say. "We'll have to break in," he admits.

"What? I thought we were done with that," Sabeena huffs. She places her salad plate on the coffee table and takes a slice of pizza. "And it didn't work so well the last time, if you recall."

"It'll work a lot better if we know the place is empty first," Meander says. "With hotels, people check-out in the morning and new occupants arrive in the afternoon. But it's different with a personal house. The owners need to assess it for damage and get it cleaned up. Even if they don't do it themselves, they need to pay someone else to come in. We're not talking a basic turndown service. They have to clean and tidy a full house, and that takes time."

"So, while one group might check-out in the morning," Isabis says, the first to understand his meaning, "the next set might not check-in until the following day."

"Exactly," Meander nods. "Giving us a night alone, as long as we know when there's a gap."

"Well, how do we know that?" Sabeena asks. "The website won't show availability if they want it closed for cleaning."

"We'll watch it," Kornelía says, smiling. "We can take turns."

"We don't have all day to spend watching a house," Sabeena argues.

"Could we install a camera or something?" I ask. Sabeena looks appalled by the idea, but I forge ahead, anyway. "Breaking in isn't legal, so what's a hidden camera going to hurt?"

"Does the camp have a camera we could borrow?" Isabis asks.

"Maybe," Kornelía says, her voice unsure. "But even if we get a camera, we need to make sure it's safe and well-hidden. We also need to make sure we've got enough battery life."

"The equipment here is meant to be used around spirits," Meander says. "I'm pretty sure they use high-quality batteries."

"Good point." Kornelía nods. "Okay, then this might work. We can station the camera in the foliage outside the house and direct it at the front drive. That way we'll be able to see whenever someone comes or goes. If we review the footage each evening, we'll have a clear idea when people leave the house with all their luggage, and whether someone's been by to clean."

"We'll have to make up an excuse for why we need the equipment," Sabeena says. "They're not going to give us an extended loan without asking questions first."

Kornelía turns her gaze to me, a too-innocent smile on her lips. "Robbie told me Mrs. Buxley's in charge of those kinds of arrangements. And she likes you."

I scoff. "She doesn't like me any more than she does anyone else," I say. Mrs. Buxley teaches our Sender Mythos course, but I don't think I've talked to her since our first week. "Sabeena, you've worked with her more closely than I have. Last year, you and Naasir were always going to her for advice."

"Yes, which is why I can't ask her for this," Sabeena says. "She knows I'm not interested in technology. I ranted to her last year about why video cameras are a waste of the Oracle's resources. She'll be too suspicious if I request the use of a camera."

"She *does* like you, Cal," Kornelía says, "you and Meander. She's got a soft spot for the two of you, after you were nearly killed on camp grounds."

"You nearly got killed?" Isabis asks.

Kornelía keeps talking overtop of her. "You've shown an interest in the gadgets," she continues. "And, you're a lot easier to talk to than Meander is." She offers him a quick glance. "No offense," she adds.

Meander shrugs, not arguing the point.

"Okay, I'll talk to her," I mumble, slumping back against my seat. "We need an excuse, though. She won't give us equipment without a reason."

"That's not a problem," Kornelía says, relieved. "We've got all night to plan."

Meander deflates at her assumption we're all going to stick around. When he mimics my slump into the sofa cushions, I allow myself the tiny pleasure of settling closer to him.

I'm annoyed we'll miss our boat trip, too. But more than that, I'm pleased he's more disappointed about it than I am.

I DON'T SEE MRS. BUXLEY UNTIL A WEEK AFTER OUR GROUP MEETING. Sender Mythos is on Wednesday, and we attended the course only hours before deciding I should ask her permission to borrow a camera. Kornelía was frustrated I didn't make a stronger effort to seek her out during the ensuing week. But I'm not happy about lying to her face, so I don't feel guilty taking my time.

The course comes again soon enough, bringing with it a frenzied debate about what we've learned so far this summer. Sender Mythos is my largest course—in addition to seven members of Shade, there are four members of Revenant and a Wraith lead acting as a teaching assistant. I'm not shocked Mythos is such a popular course. In essence, the entire purpose of this class is to determine *why* Senders are able to see spirits.

Each week we've covered one major school of theories to explain our abilities. We've talked about scientific theories, religious theories, non-religious spiritualist theories, and theories of coincidence. Since we're now over the halfway point of the summer, Mrs. Buxley is guiding a class-wide debate about what we've covered before we move on to more unusual ideas.

We're supposed to be having a structured discussion of what we think is the most logical explanation for why our talents exist. Instead, the class is full of loud voices shooting off rapid-fire arguments.

"It's genetics," Anna, a Revenant girl, says.

"If it was genetics, they'd be able to pinpoint it," Lu argues. "We'd know we had an abnormal chromosome or something."

"There hasn't been enough research," Anna protests. "But the answer is there. It has to be."

"No, it doesn't," Ralli says. "I think it's in our heads, anyway. The chemical makeup of our brain is different. It allows us to see beyond the normal world."

"But that doesn't explain why we all engage with ghosts in different ways," Sabeena says. "Our connections are personal."

"So, you think it has something to do with independent experience?" Lu asks.

"Yes, I do," Sabeena nods. "I think it relates to our past lives. We were afflicted so strongly by our demises, we've retained impressions which allow us to see others who died in a similar way."

"Wait, does that mean I was murdered in a past life?" I ask.

"Yes!" Sabeena exclaims.

"And now he's back to seek revenge," a Revenant named Connor says in a dark voice.

Sabeena rolls her eyes. "*No.* He's back to help release

others who died like he did. Others who have shared the same tragic fate."

"I don't know how I feel about that," I mutter.

"It's bollocks," Meander smirks. "Who'd ever want to murder you?"

I pretend to make a note on my paper so he won't notice how big my smile is.

"What if we were all spirits freed by Senders?" Carrigan, the last Revenant in the course, suggests.

Sabeena sits up straight, her pencil tapping against her notebook. "I hadn't considered that before," she says. "I like it."

"But then where did the first Senders come from?" Kornelía asks. "Besides, it doesn't explain people like me. I don't see a specific type of spirit."

Lu scoffs. "It's nonsense," she says. "There are no such things as past lives."

"I don't think we're meant to know," Ralli says, expanding on his previous explanation. "Our brains are wired the way they are for a reason. I believe we're chosen to do this."

On the far side of the room, Mim crosses herself, the movement of her finger so slight it's hardly noticeable.

"Oh, *please*," Connor moans. "I've never heard of "chosen" ghost-hunters."

"Not ghost-hunters," Ralli says. "Spirit… releasers? We're meant to help them, not hunt them down like game."

"Not all of us can release spirits, though," Kornelía says again, sounding exhausted. "Some of us can only assist. And some of us can't even do that."

"Not everyone has a nice ability, either," I add. "If we're *chosen*, why is seeing a spirit so awful?"

"It's not," Carrigan says. Several pointed stares turn in her direction, and she shrinks into her seat. "It's not, for everyone. But you're right. We're all different, which supports the past life theory. If we were chosen to do this, we wouldn't have such uneven abilities."

"I see auras," Lu counters, her voice oozing sarcasm. "What does that say about my past life?"

"There are no such things as past lives," Anna says, agreeing with Lu. "And we're not *chosen*. It's in our genes."

"Maybe it's not any of those things," Sefa says, his tone almost meek. "Maybe it's just… random."

"Or maybe people with bad abilities are being more thoroughly tested," Ralli says. "Or punished."

The words crackle against my skin like the coarse sand that pelted us our first night here. "No," I snap. "No one's being *punished*."

"Or maybe we're *all* being punished," Carrigan says in a mocking voice. "Maybe it's a *demon* giving us powers."

"I think we've made a good start," Mrs. Buxley interjects. She stands, bringing the argument to a close with her commanding voice. "You've seen how varied the theories explaining our existence can be. As varied as the beliefs surrounding just about every facet of life and death. The truth is, we don't know why some people are able to see spirits, while others cannot. We can only research, theorize, and form our own beliefs to support the talents we possess."

She walks around the room, her heels clicking against the tiled floor. "During the second half of this course, we'll talk in further detail about how these theories co-exist and overlap," she continues. She holds a pen in her right hand, tapping it against her left palm as she talks. "But right now, I want you all to partner up with someone who does *not* share your views on the subject. Together, you will write a paper, due next Wednesday, on how your views *could* co-exist. And if you find such a co-existence impossible, you'd better have a clear explanation of why."

Meander and I share a glance to confirm we'll work together. We don't hold the same beliefs—at least not totally. He thinks it's random chance we're like this. I'm not thoroughly convinced of anything, but I'm leaning more in a scientific direction. Maybe, as Ralli initially suggested, it *is* the wiring of our brains, a connection most people don't have that allows us to unlock a greater realm of sight. I wouldn't stake my life on the theory but, other than simply calling it *magic*, there isn't another reasoning I find fitting.

"Because you're an odd number," Mrs. Buxley continues, "we'll have one group of three." She smiles as she returns to her desk. "Now partner up. And *not* with the person you're sitting next to."

A collective groan resonates around the room, everyone annoyed Mrs. Buxley has caught on that, five weeks in, we're all sitting next to the people we're most comfortable with.

"Bloody group work," Meander grumbles, folding his arms onto the table and slumping forward.

He makes no attempt to get out of his seat, so I do, patting him on the back before I survey the room. Kornelía has moved to work with Sefa and Carrigan, which means Mim is now sitting by herself. I don't know what her views on our talents are, but it's worth finding out if we'll make an acceptable team.

I walk across the room and slide into the seat usually occupied by Kornelía. Lu has moved to stand behind my chair, talking as she pulls the seat back so she can sit next to Meander. He looks at her for a moment, then searches me out, his eyes so full of panic I struggle not to laugh.

"Poor boy," Mim says, watching the scene as well. "Lu won't shut up until he's admitted her idea is the only plausible one."

"Lucky for him, I don't think he has any moral qualms about lying to make her be quiet."

We both smirk at him, and he, in turn, looks at us as if it's our fault he's been put in this situation. When Lu actually *snaps* her fingers to make him look back at her, he tightens his jaw and faces forward once more.

Mim snorts and picks up a pen so she can take notes. "This assignment is pointless," she says, her jovial expression falling into a tired frown. "No one's going to change their beliefs in a week. Not if they have any conviction in them."

"I think the point is to get us working together," I say. I glance at our instructor. Her hair is greyer than it used to be, but her manner is as poised as it was when we first met her at the beginning of last summer. "That's a big theme with Mrs. Buxley."

"I suppose." Mim slides the fingers of her free hand through her hair. The black and pink strands fan out before they drop straight back against her neck. "So, what do you believe?"

I tell her my half-formed theory, and she nods in a way I know means she doesn't agree. Which is good, I guess. At least for the purposes of this paper.

"What about you?" I ask once I finish talking.

Mim shifts in her seat, twisting the wooden beads of the necklace she keeps tucked into her shirt. "I think there's a purpose," she says, the words careful. She pauses as if she's picking through thoughts, her lips forming the beginning of three different phrases before she lands on the one she wants to say. "I don't think it's in our brains. I think it's something else. Something bigger."

Mim crossed herself when religion came into the discussion earlier. I've never heard her talk about it much, but I know she likes churches. And angels. Maybe she's trying to hide a deeper value set.

"So, how do we combine our beliefs?" I ask.

"Who cares," Mim sighs, gazing around the room.

I let my eyes wander, too, my foot tapping a slow tempo as I take stock of how the other teams are faring. Carrigan makes notes for her group's essay, while everyone else works together, a couple campers arguing but most chatting amiably.

Mrs. Buxley is conversing as well, a friendly smile on her face as she talks with her assistant, Dimitri. My courses didn't have any assistants or teaching substitutes last summer. But the practice makes sense. The Oracle must be training leads to teach future Wanagi campers.

After a minute, Mim shifts in her seat so she's closer to me. "Listen," she says, her voice quiet, almost conspiratorial. "I've got something more important to work on. Are you busy tonight?"

"Uh, not really," I say, put off by her sudden change of tone.

"Good," she says. "We're going to have a late night hangout on the dock. Just us."

"Just… us?" I ask, pointing between her and me.

Mim rolls her eyes. "No, not *just us*," she says. "Just the group. The original five."

"The original…" My eyes sweep over the room, past Kornelía and over to Meander sitting slumped in his chair while Lu writes and talks at the same time. "Five?" I ask, looking back at Mim.

She sees the direction of my stare and nods. "Five," she agrees. "Kornelía already knows, and I'll tell Dylan after we're done here. You can tell Meander. We'll meet at midnight. Okay?"

"Yeah, sure. But why—"

"I'll explain tonight," Mim says, cutting me off with a sharp look. "For now, let's work on our paper. I'm sure we can make up something."

She bends her head over her notebook, ready to fake an answer. I stare at her black-pink hair, wondering what she's gotten herself into—and why she wants to drag the rest of us along.

# 20



AFTER SENDER MYTHOS IS OVER, I LIE TO MRS. BUXLEY ABOUT WANTING A camera for a multi-night study of the beach outside our fale. With as much enthusiasm as I can fake, I explain my plan to capture orbs of light and particles of dust on video, in an effort to understand why laypersons often mistake these natural occurrences for glimpses of the spiritual world. The lie is weak, and I feel like an idiot trying to pass it off as genuine. But Mrs. Buxley grants her permission—even if she does look suspicious when she tells me where I can pick up the camera.

Once I retrieve the camera from the camp's equipment library, I join the other members of this summer's project group so we can start setting up. We test the camera's features, and work out a schedule for switching the memory cards and analyzing each day's footage. Then we take it to the treehouse.

Kornelía keeps watch by the main road, and Isabis

stands near the house to inform us when the camera is hidden from view. She calls out instructions, while Meander does his best to camouflage the camera and its stand with greenery.

"This is ridiculous," he says, ducking low to fix the leaves at the base of the tripod.

"I'd rather be ridiculous and safe than risk the camera getting stolen," Sabeena sighs, taking two steps to the right before giving him an approving nod. "I can't see it from here. Isabis? What do you think?"

"I don't see a thing!" she says.

"Good," Sabeena says. "Now come on. Based on our preliminary observations, the people staying here will be back soon."

Until Mim informed me of the meet-up she's planned for midnight, setting up the camera was my only task for the evening. Still, our surveillance gear is in place by six, leaving me hours to work on assignments and play cards with my sector mates before twelve o'clock approaches.

The night is clear and, when the allotted time comes, the moon is so bright we don't need flashlights as we venture to the dock.

"I don't know why the girls didn't meet us here," Dylan says, trudging onto the sand in a white shirt and swimming trunks decorated with cartoon dogs.

"You don't know anything about what Mim wants from us?" I ask for the third time.

"Nope," Dylan says, sounding a touch annoyed. "I didn't even know she'd invited half the sector. I thought it was going to be the two of us."

Meander smirks, and I try to keep the smile out of my voice when I reply, "Sorry we're imposing."

"It's fine," he grumbles, rubbing his hair in an agitated manner. "We haven't seen much of each other lately, but… Whatever, it's not your fault." He steps faster, getting ahead of us as he makes the short trek to the taxi dock.

"*Trouble in paradise*. Isn't that what people say?" Meander asks.

"Looks like it's literal for him." I smile. "But to be fair, I don't think he's done himself any favors."

Meander hums in agreement as we approach Dylan's position at the foot of the dock. He stares past us and, when I glance back, I see the girls are not far behind. They hurry to meet us, and we reach the dock at the same time.

"Good, you're all here," Mim says, standing with one hand on her hip. Her bikini is only partially covered by a crocheted lace dress, while her hair has been parted into pigtails, the look reminiscent of the style she wore most of last summer. Dylan can't take his eyes off her. By the satisfied expression she wears, I'm guessing that's the reaction she was hoping for.

"Like it?" she asks, motioning to her dress. "I made it myself."

"It looks great." Dylan grins.

Mim steps up to him, smiling when he wraps his arms around her waist. Kornelía slinks around them, her sporty blue swimsuit and beige towel far less conspicuous.

"So, uh… Why are we here?" I ask before Mim and Dylan forget they're not the only ones present.

Mim twists so her back is pressed to Dylan's front, his chin on her shoulder. "Later," she says. She looks more like herself than she has since camp started more than five weeks ago. "Right now, we're going for a swim."

She grabs Dylan's hand and spins him, then drags him to where Kornelía waits further down the wooden planks.

"Those waters are awfully black," Dylan says, peering over the dock's edge. "Are we sure we're not going to be attacked by, like, sharks or something?"

Mim laughs. "No one's going to be attacked by a shark," she says, peeling off her dress. "Not tonight. We're here for a purpose. We'll be fine."

Meander looks at me, his expression doubtful. I nudge his shoulder and kick off my sandals. I'm not as convinced about our safety as Mim, but I'm willing to push aside my concerns to enjoy the experience of splashing in the Pacific under the glow of the midnight moon.

Mim allows Dylan to ogle her bikini for a few seconds before she dives off the back edge of the dock. Once she's underwater, he throws off his shirt and jumps in, while Kornelía lowers herself over the edge before wading into the water.

I throw my shirt with the others before I notice Meander standing still, his t-shirt and sandals still on.

"Coming for a swim?" I ask. My voice is strangled as I struggle to pick the correct tone—too indecisive whether to be suggestive or to keep the offer as platonic as possible.

Meander slides his hands into the pockets of his swimming trunks, an uncertain expression on his face. I survey his outfit again, remembering what he said on our first night when we contemplated escape routes before initiation began.

"Is it because you can't swim?" I ask in a quieter voice.

He looks confused for a moment. Then he laughs, pulling his hands from his pockets and shaking his head. "You're such an idiot." He smiles and pushes me off the dock.

Blackness rushes around my head as I sink into the water, until I kick up with enough momentum to break the surface. Pushing back my hair, I look up to see Meander smirking. He watches me for a moment, then dives in.

When he reappears close beside me, his curls have straightened at their roots, though tendrils still twist and loop against his neck.

"You know how to swim, then," I say, splashing water in his face and back paddling away from him as he tries to retaliate.

He's still wearing his shirt, which is weird because I never expected he'd be shy about his body. But when he catches up to me, his hand grazing the bare skin of my stomach and his legs tangling with mine under the water, I'm relieved I don't have to handle his lack of clothing on top of everything else.

"I live near the coast," he says, shaking hair out of his eyes. "I'd be a sad sod if I didn't at least know how to keep myself afloat." He glances up at the moon, then down at its shining reflection on the water. "Can't say I've ever been out this late, though. The water's different like this, isn't it?"

"Yeah, it is," I say, like I'm invested in the ocean's appearance and not watching him instead.

"I used to think it'd be nice to swim this late," he says, his voice easy. "With no people around to spoil the peace." His arm brushes against mine as he turns and faces the invisible horizon. "I'm going to swim out a bit, see if it's as nice as I dreamed."

He pushes forward, stroking his way out. As soon as he's a few feet away, Dylan's shark comments swim back into my head, this time sounding far more plausible.

"Don't go out too far!" I call.

I watch him retreat a little farther before I sigh and dip underwater. Being submerged is like floating in a sensory deprivation tank, everything weightless and dark. I sink, enjoying the surreal sensation of bobbing in space until the logical portion of my brain reminds me this is an ocean with predators and undercurrents—and the illogical part wonders if anybody has been murdered in these inky depths.

With a jolt of alarm, I swim upwards, relieved to resurface after only a few panicked kicks. With hair dripping into my eyes and salt water coating my lips, I take a shaky breath under the night sky.

I'm still dizzy with unfounded anxiety when Kornelía floats into view before me. "One thing I missed last summer was the water," she muses. Her voice is serene, the words pouring forth as if we've been talking this entire time. "I'm not big on swimming—but *soaking* is an altogether unique form of meditation."

She glides on her back, her long hair splayed and her eyes closed. After my brief anxiety attack, I marvel at how calm she is floating around blind. But then I remember who I'm staring at, and marvel instead at what it must be like for her to have such a strong sense of her surroundings.

"You do that a lot at home?" I ask, only half paying attention. "Soak?"

Kornelía smiles."There's nothing like Icelandic water, you know. Near our farm, there's a hot stream I soak in all the time." She opens her eyes and flicks water at me. "You should swim," she says, perhaps sensing how tense and coiled I've become.

I give her arm a push, sending her in a slow cartwheel through the water. She laughs, and I dip once more, keeping just below the surface for a long moment before I press back up into the open air. The water is nice, the temperature far warmer than the beaches in Ontario. I'm accustomed to toe-numbing cold you can't get used to unless you jump straight in and spend all of your time in motion. Being able to bob in the water without fear of a cool breeze setting my teeth to chatter is a pleasant treat.

On the far side of the dock, Dylan says something to Mim before he climbs onto the wood boards. He pretends he's going to bellyflop forward, but then he turns and backflips off the edge.

"You're a good swimmer," Mim says, holding her arms out as he swims into her embrace. "And I thought you could only… What do you say… puppy-paddle?"

"*Puppy*-paddle?" Dylan laughs. "Hey, I'm no pup." He slides his arms up to her shoulders and dunks her. Then he takes off, forcing her to swim after him once she's back above the surface.

"You are done for!" Mim yells. She shakes her bangs from her face as she closes in on him.

Dylan lets her get close, then swims further away. "How's my paddling?" he calls over his shoulder.

I watch them until Mim catches up and they lean

together for a kiss. Then I sink back under the water and swim in the opposite direction. Keeping close to the dock, I allow myself a bit of space to work in a few strong kicks. Even once Meander returns, I keep my distance, swimming by myself for a few quiet moments before heading back.

By the time I start my return, Meander is seated on the dock, his legs dangling in the water. He watches as I approach, his expression thoughtful.

"Nice swim?" he asks as I glide next to the dock.

I fold my arms on the water-logged boards and glance up at him."Water's warm," I mumble. "It's wonderful. You've had enough?"

He smirks. "One lap's good. I don't mind the water, but I've always preferred observation to participation."

"You've always preferred being left alone with a book," I tease.

"Not *always*," he corrects. "I didn't pick up a book until I was in school. Couldn't properly read until I was seven."

I tilt my head further back to see him better. "Really?" I ask, surprised.

Seven isn't late for a kid to read. Rose didn't start understanding her books until she was six and a half. Even at eight, she still struggles from time to time. But the revelation doesn't fit him. I've never given much thought to what Meander was like as a little kid, but the idea summons an image of a curly-haired toddler with a picture book in his lap.

I guess I'm shocked less by the discovery that he couldn't read than by the realization he never held a book until he was in school. I couldn't always play the violin, but there are photos of me at the age of two sitting on my grandfather's knee, holding the instrument that would one day become mine.

Meander shrugs, his feet tracing lazy circles in the water. "Mum doesn't read," he says, his voice tinged with distaste. "I'm not sure she even knows how, aside from the basics. She used to have Liam read her mail and the like. We didn't have books around the house when I was little."

The topic of Meander's upbringing fills me with sad frustration, but I swallow the discomfort, knowing he wouldn't want me to comment on it. Those are conversations reserved for home, when we're alone in our respective rooms and feeling safe enough to discuss more sensitive matters. I file this new fact away, so I can pull it out on a rainy autumn day when we are both in need of a serious chat. Then I smile, shifting the conversation as subtly as I can.

"We're all at the mercy of our parents' interests for a while," I say. "I've loved classical music for as long as I can remember because of my grandfather. But we never listened to it at home. My mother had grown up with nothing but symphonies and concertos when she was younger, which meant all we ever listened to was Top 40 crap."

I don't mean to make a face, but I must because Meander laughs.

"Parents suck, don't they?" he says. He tugs at the bottom of the wet shirt clinging to his chest, his finger twisted in the hem of the dark fabric. I push myself up to sit beside him, and when I face the water, I see that Mim and Dylan have swum close. They have also overheard at least part of our conversation.

"We never listen to music at home," Mim sighs,

swimming up to the dock. "Mama doesn't like it. She used to, but… It's been a long time."

Dylan scoffs. "Not us," he laments. "My dad thinks an appreciation of good music helps make a well-rounded life. He's big on jazz, and some of the classical stuff Cal's always listening to. And disco. He's got a thing for awful seventies shit like the Bee Gees."

"I love the Bee Gees," Meander says, and I look at him, the laugh starting before I even have time to gape.

"*You* love the Bee Gees?" I ask.

The innocent smile playing about his lips sets my heart pounding so hard I'm sure everyone would be able to hear it if it weren't for the gentle rush of the waves around us.

"Who doesn't love the Bee Gees?" he asks, his eyes bright even in the dark of the night.

I'm glad the others are here. If they weren't, I think this pointless tidbit of unexpected information might be the thing that pushes me over the edge.

"What are Bee Gees?" Mim asks, her voice a firm reminder Meander and I are not alone.

Dylan smirks, kissing the back of her neck. "Not up on popular music of the 1970s?" he murmurs.

"I told you, we don't listen to music," Mim repeats. She leans her head against his shoulder so they can share a lingering gaze. When she lowers her face again, her smile has flattened. "Anyway, we didn't come here to talk about our parents. Where's Korni? We've got important business to attend to."

"I'm right here," Kornelía says, sidling up to the dock.

I wonder if she was nearby this whole time, listening to our conversation but choosing not to be a part of it.

If she was, I'm curious to know why.

"Good," Mim says. She breaks away from Dylan and hauls herself onto the dock. "Let's talk. I've got something to say."

wood as Mim wrings out her pigtails and begins to speak.

"I've been doing a lot of research," she says, looking between us. "And I've decided to complete an incredible project before we leave camp."

"Are you talking about ghosts?" Dylan asks.

"Obviously," Mim says, shooting him an impatient glance. "I don't know about the rest of you but, after I returned home last year, I felt useless. We ended the summer by releasing a ghost, which was wondrous. Then we went home and—" she makes a 'poof!' gesture with her hands, raising her eyes to the sky as if watching the skills she learned dissipate into the air.

"So, you want to learn a tactic you can use once you're away from here," Kornelía says, nodding.

"Sort of." Mim smiles. "I couldn't handle sitting around like a pathetic lump, waiting for camp to arrive again. So, when the new year began, I started… practicing."

"Practicing at home? On real spirits?" I ask. Her suggestion sounds dangerous. I have to remind myself that this is what the Oracle wants for us. For most of us, anyway.

Mim leans back on her hands, looking proud. "I released two ghosts," she says in a quiet, confident voice.

"By yourself?" Kornelía asks.

Mim nods. "Yes. I started travelling around, anywhere I could get to and from in a day," she explains. "I investigated twelve stories of hauntings, and found three ghosts I could see. I managed to release two of them."

"How come you never told me this?" Dylan asks. Just as when Kornelía failed to mention her new glasses, Dylan looks wounded to discover Mim has been withholding information.

Mim considers him, but no apology rolls off her tongue. "Our lives at home are separate from life here," she says, her tone indifferent.

Dylan opens his mouth to respond, but then he shuts it tight, rubbing his hair and staring at the water.

"Does the Oracle know what you've been doing?" Kornelía asks, sounding far less bothered than Dylan.

"Yes," Mim says again. "I didn't tell them, but they must have eyes everywhere. They found out, and they're proud of me. I'm making their investment worthwhile."

"What are you talking about?" Dylan asks, looking back at her. "What investment?"

Mim sighs. "You think this is cheap?" she asks,

motioning around us. "That all of this is for fun? It's not. They gamble on us when they let us come here. We owe them."

"We don't owe them anything," Dylan snaps. "We never signed a contract when we agreed to come to Wanagi. It's our choice what we do with our abilities."

"You're both right," Kornelía says, trying to keep the peace. "What we do with our talents is up to us. But we do owe the Oracle gratitude for giving us the chance to be here."

Mim and Dylan continue to glare at each other, so I help Kornelía by pushing the conversation forward. "What is your plan, Mim?" I ask.

Mim takes a deep breath, composing herself after her exchange with Dylan. "I know how to release ghosts," she says. "Now, I want to attempt a more complex feat. I want to release a *resistive* spirit."

"Resistive, as in, doesn't *want* to be released?" Dylan balks.

"Maybe," Mim says. "Spirits can be resistive for a number of reasons. Not wanting to leave is only one of them."

"Mim, that's advanced work. It could be dangerous," Kornelía cautions.

"I know," Mim says, sounding unperturbed. "Which is why I'm telling you." She looks at all of us as she straightens her spine and crosses her legs. "Last year, I made a mistake. I tried to tackle a ghost on my own. I needed help, but I was too stubborn to ask for it. So, I'm asking now. I have a spirit in mind, one on this very island. I want to release it."

"But if it's resistive..." Kornelía begins, looking worried.

Mim meets her gaze, not shying away from the topic. "I want to perform an exorcism," she declares.

Until last week, I had no idea *exorcism* was even a concept discussed at Camp Wanagi. The idea of Mim tackling something so huge makes my head spin, even if the news is not a total surprise. Mim told us there was an exorcism candidate on this island when she asked Meander if he knew any Latin. I guessed she was either intrigued by a course project or was trying to avoid whatever drama is going on between her, Dylan, and Kornelía. That she was, in truth, working out the details of performing an exorcism herself never occurred to me. Still, if anyone was going to spring an announcement like this, I'm not shocked to hear it from Mim.

"Whoa," Dylan says, shaking his head. "You can't perform a freaking exorcism. For starters, don't you need, like, an old priest and a young priest or something?"

"Dylan, not everything you see in the movies is real," I remind him.

"No, I think this time he's right," Meander says from beside me. "She needs someone from the church, anyway."

"I would," Mim says, "if I wasn't a Sender. The rules are different for us."

"Okay, even if that's true," Dylan continues, "there's got to be a middle ground between releasing a few ghosts and performing an *exorcism*."

"Of course there is," Mim says. "But I don't have time for all of that. So, I'm skipping some steps." She meets Dylan's frustrated expression with a determined gleam in her eye. "And nothing you can say will make me change my mind."

"What do you need from us?" Kornelía asks before Dylan has time to respond.

"I want you to come with me," Mim says, glancing between us again. "Last year, I thought I could do everything myself. This year, I'm being careful. Exorcism is dangerous. I'm prepared, and I know what to expect. But I also know things don't always go according to plan. So, I'd like you to be with me. For support."

"What, all of us?" Meander asks, sounding confused.

Mim nods, looking him up and down. "It was the five of us last year." She shrugs. "I want it to be the five of us this year, too."

"What if we refuse?" Dylan mumbles.

"I'll do it by myself if I have to," Mim says. "But I'd feel better with your help." She places her hand on Dylan's knee. He looks like he wants to shove it off.

"Mim, this is asking a lot," Kornelía sighs. She slumps forward, her elbows pressed into her knees and her chin cupped in her hands. "Do any of the instructors know what you're planning?"

"No." Mim shakes her head, her fingers squeezing Dylan's leg. "And you can't tell them. They're happy to let me work with ghosts at home but, while I'm here, they want to keep a closer watch."

"For good reason," I say. I wasn't planning to chime in with any further remarks, but I can't let her go into this without at least trying to make her see sense. "Mim, you have to let *someone* know. What if things go wrong?"

"That's why I want you there with me," Mim says.

"But what if something goes wrong for all of us?"

Meander asks.

Mim pauses, considering his words before she sighs. "I've already thought of that," she mumbles, her voice low and almost hesitant. "One of us will stay behind. If we don't come back at a reasonable time, he can let the instructors know."

"Back from where, Mim?" Kornelía asks. "Where is this spirit?"

"Swallow's Cave," Mim says.

I start, looking at Meander. "We've been there," I say, my eyes still on him. "We heard it was supposed to be haunted, but we didn't feel anything."

I glance back at Mim to see her frowning in mild disappointment.

"Oh, well… maybe you can't see it," she says, perking up again as she talks. "The stories are that it was a jilted lover who threw himself over the cliff above the cave. He landed in the water, hit his head on a rock, and drowned. I haven't seen the spirit yet myself, so maybe you all have nothing to worry about. But there *is* a spirit there, one not keen to move on. That much I know from Oracle-approved sources."

"If you haven't even seen the spirit yet, when do you plan to exorcise it?" Kornelía asks.

"In a few weeks," Mim says. "I still need to confirm contact, get some supplies, and practice what I'm going to do. But I wanted to get you up to speed first."

"And who is going to stay behind?" Kornelía continues. It's as if she's working through a mental checklist, ticking off the boxes one by one.

"I—" Meander starts to volunteer, but he's interrupted by Dylan.

"Should be me, shouldn't it?" he says, his voice

dark. "I'm the useless one."

"You're not useless," Kornelía says, but it's not Kornelía who should be saying it.

Mim's still got her hand on Dylan's knee, but she doesn't look at him when she replies. "I think that makes sense," she says, her voice suggesting he was always the one she intended to act as watch.

"Right, sure."

Dylan's quiet for a moment, before he stands and storms down the dock towards the beach. Mim looks like she wants to stay and discuss her plans further but she gets up with a sigh. She pulls Kornelía up, too, dragging the reluctant girl with her as she goes to try and make peace.

Meander and I watch their retreat. When they've all reached the beach, I turn to him. "What do you think?" I ask as his eyes shift from the fading figures in the distance to me.

"I think it's a stupid idea," he says. He sounds uncomfortable, and it's not hard to guess why.

"She might not have anything to work with, anyway," I say, shrugging. "We went to that cave. I didn't notice anything."

"Neither did I," he admits. "But we weren't exactly on the lookout, were we? Who knows what we could have missed."

"Maybe I can't see the spirit, but I find it hard to believe you couldn't. If it needs an exorcism, there's got to be some anger there."

"Yeah, but we didn't get out of the boat," he says, drawing his legs into his chest. "Besides, I was distracted."

The sentence drops into silence, like maybe he was

going to say something else but decided against it. My cheeks are warm, but I don't dwell on what he might or might not have meant by being 'distracted'.

"Maybe her plan will fizzle out," I say, doubtful. Mim's not one to give up on ideas. If she's been hunting for spirits on her own time, I can't imagine she'd lose interest in her grand scheme now.

"Yeah, maybe," Meander says, sounding equally dubious. He lets out a long breath and lowers his legs to the dock. "You ready to head back?"

"Yeah, I guess so," I say.

My gaze settles on his face. I study the line of his scar, the curve of his lips, and the small spray of lashes around eyes that notice my staring.

"What?" he asks, a smile in his voice.

I shake my head, releasing what I hope is an unburdened breath as I scramble for something pointless to say. "I still can't believe you like the Bee Gees," I manage at last.

Meander laughs."We all have our little secrets." He stands and gives me a look full of joyful snark as he helps me up. "Like how someone I know still has a cartoon moon lamp beside his bed."

My face floods with mortified heat, and I jolt back, dropping my hand as soon as I'm on my feet.

"I just... I haven't gotten around to redecorating," I stammer.

I make a mental note to throw away the lamp, an illuminated moon I've kept because, on long ago nights when I was afraid of spirits sneaking into my room, its soft glow made me feel better. Obviously, I need to throw it away, or at least hide it in a closet. At a minimum, I'll remember to shove it under my bed while I'm talking to him over video from now on.

"I like it," he promises.

I groan, running my hands over my face in total embarrassment. "Let's go," I mutter, starting forward.

My sandals flop against the wooden dock for two or three steps before I hear Meander's voice. The noise is so soft it's almost inaudible but, when I decipher the notes, I realize he's singing in a quiet falsetto. I'm positive the tune is by the Bee Gees. I stop and turn as he finishes a word that sounds remarkably like 'lamplight'. He smirks, and I'm lost for words, stuck between lingering embarrassment and a swell of longing that topples all the other itches of interest I've experienced over the last couple weeks.

The words won't come, even if I want them to. So, I don't try to speak. I simply snatch the sandals he's carrying and pull the towel from around his neck, dropping them both on the dock before I shove him back into the water.

I'M NOT SURE WHAT HAPPENED WHILE MEANDER AND I WERE STILL AT THE dock. By the time we returned to our fale, both of us tired from a second swim, the girls were gone and Dylan was in bed.

In the morning, it quickly becomes obvious Mim and Dylan aren't speaking to one another. Poor Kornelía is forced to play intermediary between them, which means she spends as much time avoiding them as she can. By Tuesday, almost a week after Mim's announcement, Kornelía's spending most of her days hanging out with Isabis and some of the other Entity campers. The only time I see her outside of our courses is when she stops by to check the daily tapes from the treehouse.

"Anything interesting yet?" she says that afternoon.

We've taken turns watching the footage. Today I'm in charge of the tapes, but Kornelía stares over my shoulder, her chin resting on the back of the couch.

She must be uncomfortable, crouching awkwardly to see the screen of the tablet we borrowed along with the camera. She refuses to sit on the sofa in case Mim or Dylan arrive to pester her—even though she knows Mim's tutoring Reed and Dylan's in the middle of a course.

"Nope. Those people are still there. They must be staying for a while," I inform her.

The same couple has been in the treehouse for as long as we've been spying. The footage we've collected is a nearly identical parade of watching them come and go, a few outfit changes the only thing to differentiate the date.

I peel off a slice of orange and pop it into my mouth while fast forwarding through empty footage, hours when the people were inside or out back on the private stretch of beach. When the couple appears again near the end of the day's footage, I slow the tape to normal speed.

"I can't hear anything," Kornelía says, leaning closer to the tablet.

"I've got the sound off," I say. "Watching them is creepy enough, Kornelía. I can't abide listening to their conversations, too."

"Yes, but look!" She points at the screen, and I pause the video to see what she's noticed. "The woman's eyeing her watch while she speaks. She might be talking about time."

"What does it matter if she is?" I look sideways at Kornelía. "They don't have any luggage with them. They're coming back to the house."

"Just watch it again," she says. "*With sound.*" I give her an annoyed glance, and she smiles, pushing her hair back behind her ears and adjusting her glasses. "Please," she adds, leaning her head against mine.

"Only because you said the magic word," I sigh, eating another orange slice and un-muting the footage. I reverse the clip to just before the woman on the screen looked at her watch, and then press play so we can listen to what she said.

"*Come on, Chris. We're going to be late.*"

"*We've got plenty of time. The restaurant's, like, five minutes from here.*"

"*But we need to finish dinner and get to the yacht afterwards.*"

"When did you pick up these tapes?" Kornelía asks. Her eyes dart around the screen, like she's trying to ensure she doesn't miss the slightest detail.

"I don't know, half an hour ago? Maybe forty-five minutes?" I pause the video as the couple gets into their rental car. "Why?"

"They're gone," Kornelía explains.

"Yeah, for dinner." I glance back at her, eyebrows raised. "Which they've probably finished by now."

"But they'll still be out afterwards," Kornelía says, standing up. "On the yacht."

"So? We don't know what that means."

"No, but we can guess." She digs in her pocket and pulls out a hairband. "She was worried about getting through dinner, which means they've likely *reserved* a time for something afterwards. And if they're going to a yacht, they're probably going for a sail. Maybe a sunset cruise."

"So?" I say again. "Sunset's in about an hour. Even if they are going out for a sail—which we don't know for sure—they could still be back in a short amount of time. We need a full night, at least. We can't go there when people are in the house."

"Not to release the spirit," Kornelía agrees. "But…" she pauses, pulling her ponytail tight. "If we wanted to get a closer look and a better sense… I mean, we could stop in for just a minute."

"Kornelía!" I drop the tablet onto the sofa and twist around to face her.

"I know, it's wrong and something we definitely shouldn't even be thinking about." She comes around and sits on the second couch, pulling one leg under her. "But I haven't found anything about the spirit. No stories or death records I can trace to that location. If we get a night in the house, we need to be prepared. But we can't be prepared if we know nothing about what we're going to face."

I lean back, closing my eyes and rubbing my temples. "Between you and Mim, this summer's turning into an audition for juvie hall."

"Sorry, Cal."

She reaches over to give my knee a pat but, when I open my eyes, she has snatched the tablet and is studying the frozen video footage. "Mim wants me to go with her to the cave this weekend," she says after a moment, her voice more subdued.

"This exorcism plan is bad, Kornelía," I say.

She nods."I know," she agrees, but then she smiles. "Or, I don't. Mim's the only one of us who has released spirits on her own time, so maybe she knows what's she talking about. And she's right, about keeping it secret. If we tell anyone, they'll stop it."

"Yeah, but maybe it *should* be stopped," I say.

Kornelía stares at the tablet, pushing her glasses to

the top of her head. "Unless she's doing what she's supposed to. You think other kids here are so well behaved?" She grins as she glances at me. "Do you think Robbie played by the rules when he was a camper?"

"I've never thought about it." I shrug. "But it's not hard to imagine him getting into trouble. Still, that doesn't mean he sought it. Besides, it's only our second summer here."

"Which means in four weeks time, when this summer is finished, we'll be halfway through Camp Wanagi."

The statement is jarring, although I know she's right. Camp Wanagi only spans four summers. And after our short time with the Oracle is over, we're supposed to decide whether we want to devote our lives to releasing spirits, or spend the rest of our days trying to ignore them.

Like we have a choice. Working for the Oracle doesn't sound too appealing for me. But spirits won't leave me alone, even if I choose a non-Sender path.

"It's not enough time," I say, eating the last slice of my orange.

"It's not, and it is," Kornelía muses. "We're given a lot. The Oracle provides us with courses and lets us test our abilities in a monitored environment. Mim's right that we owe them our assistance, even if they don't expect it of us."

"You're going to help her, then?" I ask.

"Aren't you?" she replies with a pointed stare. "I'm at least going to the cave to see if a spirit is there. If Mim's determined to do this, there's not much we can do to stop her. But if we're there for support, she's more likely to be successful."

"I suppose," I grumble, resigned to my fate.

I won't tattle on Mim, or refuse to go with her if this all plays out like she's expecting. But that doesn't mean I have to be happy about it. Not knowing what a Sender-related exorcism might involve is not a blessing. I shouldn't have wimped out of taking Resistive Release. The course would have at least given me an inkling of what Mim is planning.

Kornelía rewinds the video clip and presses play again, listening to the short segment of conversation. "This is our chance," she mutters, fast forwarding the video through the rest of the footage to ensure they haven't returned.

"Even if they were still out when I picked up the tapes, they could be back by now," I remind her.

A spare battery and a spare memory card means that while we're reviewing the day's events, the camera is still at the treehouse, recording the front drive. Without the most recent seconds of footage with us, however, there's a valid possibility the couple's evening excursion has come to an early end.

"Or, they could be out," Kornelía argues. "Long enough for us to get inside. We need to see the spirit close up, Cal. We need to get a better sense of who it is."

"We know who it is!" I snap, annoyed that reason seems to have escaped Kornelía as well as Mim this year. "It's a child. A girl. One who was murdered."

"Yes, except I've been poring over death records and newspaper clippings—as have Sabeena and Isabis—and do you know what we've found? Nothing. No reports of a murder. No records to show that someone fitting our vague description was killed."

"So, maybe the death wasn't reported as a murder," I say, weary of the conversation. I expected to review the footage and then spend the next hour out on the beach with my earbuds for company. I'm not pleased Kornelía is once again modifying my plans. "Maybe it was recorded as an accident."

"Okay, fine, maybe it was," Kornelía agrees. "And maybe that's why the spirit is still around. She might want people to know she was murdered. Just like Isabelle Levasseur."

I suppose she's right, although the spirit we freed last summer is not the one floating through my mind just now. I'm thinking of Maggie, another murdered little girl, and the first spirit to guide my will in order to help people figure out who killed her—years before I had any idea the Oracle of Senders existed.

"I understand you want to help," I say, watching as Kornelía studies the speeding picture on the camera. "But you're suggesting we go there tonight. When people are staying at the house and will be back after a few hours."

"We can make it," she assures me, deleting the footage so no one will stumble upon it and discover what we've been doing. "If we hurry, we can sneak in just long enough to see if the spirit has anything useful to say."

"*Even if* we can make it there and back before the couple returns, we're only two members of a group of five," I continue. "We don't know where anyone else is."

The excuse is weak—not to mention untrue—since I know Meander's in the library, doing research for his history course. But keeping the location of all remaining group members hidden is my best chance of getting out of this ludicrous plan.

"It doesn't matter," Kornelía argues. "We're not going to release the spirit. We're just going to spend a little time with it."

"You're suggesting we go alone?"

I stare at her wide-eyed as she nods, her smile bright, as if she's suggested we go get an ice cream cone.

"Yes. And now," she pleads. "It won't take long, Cal. But we need to leave."

She stands up and offers me her hand, which I study with trepidation.

"I never said I agreed to this," I say.

She huffs, grabbing my arm and hauling me up with the strength I've forgotten she possesses.

"Come on," she says. She pauses for a moment before offering me a grin. "Do this, and tomorrow I'll buy you an ice cream."

I'm too startled by her plucking a random thought from my head to resist as she takes the tablet and drags me from the room.

Outside, the sky is scattered with clouds and the sun hangs low over the horizon. I slide my free hand into my pocket and clutch my phone, wondering if I should text Meander. But he's working on a paper and, while I doubt he cares if the paper gets finished, I don't want him slacking off on my account. Not when I know he won't enjoy what we're about to do.

We stop outside the girls' fale, and Kornelía makes a quick sweep for Mim before she ducks inside to hide the tablet. When she returns, her large ears sticking out from beneath her ponytail and her oversized glasses taking up half of her face, she looks goofy and sweet, not like someone eager to break into a stranger's home.

"Ready to go?" she asks.

With a reluctant nod, I fish out my phone and unravel my earbuds, blasting Mozart's "Violin Concerto No. 5" as we head in the direction of the treehouse.

# 23

I FIGURE WE'LL BE APPROACHING THE PROPERTY FROM THE BEACH, surveying the back windows before sneaking around to the front. But when we arrive at the treehouse near dusk, Kornelía goes straight for the wraparound staircase.

"What are you doing?" I ask in a panicked whisper as she drags me along behind her.

She climbs the steps and nears the front door, glancing back at me with a puzzled expression. "Entering the house," she says. "Like we discussed?"

"Going to ring the doorbell, are you?" I ask, my fingers gripping the phone I stowed in my pocket when we reached the dirt path.

She ignores my comment and drops to her knees in front of the door's handle. "I brought these," she says, holding up a couple bobby pins.

My mouth gapes for a moment, then I rub my hands over my face, exhausted from trying to figure out what my friends are capable of doing. "You know how to pick a lock?" I say, my voice weak.

Kornelía shakes her head. "Nope. But I watched a video about it, and I mean… It can't be that difficult, right?"

I lean next to the door, watching in stunned amusement as Kornelía attempts to pick the lock. I'd laugh, if I weren't so stressed about the likelihood of getting arrested for breaking and entering at some point tonight.

"What if there's an alarm system?" I ask after a few minutes.

"There's not," Kornelía says, her voice tight as she works to jiggle half of one bobby pin inside the lock.

I sigh, listening for sounds of life inside the house or a car approaching from the dirt path. When no worrisome noises meet my ears, my gaze shifts upwards.

"The sun is setting," I point out.

"Not helpful, Cal," Kornelía grunts. "Complaining is not going to speed up this process."

Complaining was not my objective so much as trying to convince her to give up this insane idea. The wrongness of the situation is overwhelming. I've never intentionally broken into someone's house before. The closest thing I can compare this with was last summer in Paris, when Meander and I went to his aunt's apartment. He had a key—he knew the owner— and, even then, we left the apartment in disarray. If anything gets out of place here, or if Kornelía does something stupid like breaking a pin in the lock, we're in serious trouble.

"Well, what *will* help?" I ask, forcing away my fears

about a near-future disaster.

"I need more light," she says, turning to me. "Can you hold out your phone?"

I push off the wall, then pull out my phone and switch on the flashlight. Kornelía positions my hand at an angle above the keyhole, mumbling her thanks as she returns to her task.

Even with the light, it takes Kornelía way longer than it should to get the lock unlatched. The sky is nearly dark by the time she squeaks in excitement as the door clicks open.

"Good, we've established you're able to pick a lock," I say, staring over the rail at the drive, poised to react should headlights shine through the darkness. "Valuable information for next time. Now, we need to get back to camp."

"Are you kidding me?" Kornelía stands up, wincing as she rubs her knees. "We can't leave now. We just got the blasted door open."

"They're going to come back," I half-whine.

"They won't come back," Kornelía insists. "And we'll be quick. In and out, I promise. But first I need to get a better sense of what's waiting for us."

She pushes open the door and steps inside. I stand on the threshold, mired in indecision, until I hear her on the stairs. Stupid plan or no, I can't let her go into the house alone—not after the chilling experience of her last spiritual encounter. Muttering a few curses under my breath, I walk in behind her, closing the door and twisting the lock to make sure she hasn't busted it.

When the lock clicks closed, I survey the dark room. The layout is strangely familiar after browsing the photos from the vacation rental website. The only difference is that everything is now cast in long shadows. The wide windows are open, but the beach beyond the panes is as dark as the cloud-filled sky.

Shining my phone's light ahead of me so I don't trip, I make my way across the tiled entryway to the spiral staircase. Kornelía is at the top of the stairs by the time I reach the bottom step. She leans over the upper balcony, beckoning me to hurry.

"Hold on!" I whisper, treading carefully up the steps.

"You don't have to whisper," she reminds me in a normal volume.

The night is warm but, by the time I've reached the second storey, the air is cold. I put away my phone and shiver as we cross the hallway to the closed door of the room we both know the spirit inhabits.

"Are you ready?" Kornelía asks.

The first waft of putrid vanilla furls around my head, and I hold a hand over my nose, breathing the remnant scent of citrus from my orange. "No, but let's go in, anyway," I say with a hard swallow.

She nods, twisting the knob and pushing the door open. The room inside is dark and, at first, I don't notice any activity or feel anything more than a slight chill. The smell doesn't grow stronger, either. Not until we step through the door.

Kornelía enters first and seems fine, which I idiotically take as a sign that I will be okay as well. But as soon as I cross the threshold, I stumble back against the open door. The vanilla ripens, rots, and swims under my nose like someone's holding a tub of fermented imitation extract in front of my face. I cough and shiver as the temperature plummets, the warmth of the Tongan air cut by striking bursts of frozen breeze.

"Damn it!"

I hold my head as the static switches on for the first time in weeks, crackling so loud pain starts behind my eardrums with immediate and drastic force. I've never experienced spiritual activity so contained before. Outside this room, there was only a trace of smell and no sign of movement or noise. But now, an inch inside the doorway, the spirit emanates scent, chill, and pain with full strength.

Struggling to keep upright, I look at the dead girl who stands across the room from us. Her extremities are more focused than anything else— her wispy blue-white feet so well formed I can make out all ten bloodless and transparent fingers and toes. One hand is clenched in a fist, and she pounds it against the wall, rattling the framed picture above her head.

"Are you okay?" Kornelía asks, bending to meet my gaze.

The pounding noise is excessive. The girl continues her deliberate attack on the wall, even while her face is turned towards us. She's unsettling. Her long hair flows down to her waist, and her eyes are nothing but hollow sockets of mist. Aside from the movement of her fist, she's as still as a wispy mass can be. No wonder it was difficult to tell if she was watching us from outside.

"Can you… see her?" I manage in response to Kornelía's question.

She frowns, standing up and closing her eyes, hands on her hips as she turns her head from side to side.

"Yes," she says, her voice troubled. "But there's still something else. Something muddling her energy."

"I don't know about her energy," I say, squinting through the pain in my head as I attempt to study the girl more closely. She's wearing a dress, but I can't make out its style or get any indication of what time period she may have lived in. "We're here to ask a few questions and investigate what's available to us, remember? We don't have time for anything else."

"You're right." Kornelía nods, stepping nearer to the girl by the wall. "Don't be afraid," she says, her chin tilted in the spirit's direction. "We're here to help you."

The girl ignores her. Her eyes—her lack of eyes—are fixed on me, and she continues to beat the wall in a slow, rhythmic fashion.

"I don't think she heard you," I mumble.

Kornelía lets out a frustrated breath. "I can't communicate with spirits," she says, a confirmation that this aspect of her ability hasn't changed. "You'll have to do the talking."

I groan in disapproval, but take a few steps into the room. The spirit continues to watch me, and I do my best to interpret what I see. I can't get a clear indication of what killed her, though. No noticeable slashes or spots mark her, which is unusual. Her mouth looks a little puffy, but she may have had thick lips, or it may just be the accumulation of mist comprising her face. Even if it's not, a puffy mouth doesn't narrow the possibilities enough for my liking. She could have choked, suffocated, been poisoned, drowned—for all I know, she could have had a fatal cut somewhere around her lips.

I can deduce she was sick, based on the fact Sabeena saw her the first night we were here. But the spirit could have been poisoned over a long period of time, or she could have been choked while illness weakened her.

I understand why Kornelía's frustrated. I may not feel something unusual in her energy, but I can't get a decent sense of how this girl died, or what the vanilla smell might mean in connection to her lingering presence.

"Don't… don't be afraid," I say, repeating Kornelía's greeting. "We're here to help you."

She doesn't respond. With her eyeless face still trained on me, she continues to beat the wall. The static in my head is loud, but no words burble through it, nothing to help us figure out why she's still here.

"How can we help you?" I try. "What do you need?"

The girl's stance remains unchanged. She must be capable of moving, since she first watched us through the window across the room from where she's standing now. But if I didn't already know that, I might think her endless pounding was the only movement she can manifest.

"Is she saying anything?" Kornelía asks without hope.

"Nothing," I reply. I take several deep breaths and allow myself to stagger back to the door. "I don't think we're going to find anything. Maybe with help… Sabeena might know something. Meander might… Meander's great at getting spirits screaming."

"I know, but—"

Kornelía steps over to me, while something elsewhere in the house rattles. I grab her arm to stop her as the sound of a door swinging open bellows below us.

"Let's just watch a movie and call it a night," a man's voice says.

"I can't believe that guy," a woman replies. "Cancels the ride because of a little rain? Ridiculous."

"He said there was a storm coming."

"It's barely spitting out there. He just forgot and didn't want to work. I'm so fed up with this place. I can't wait to go home."

"*Kornelía*," I hiss, my fingers tight on her arm.

The spirit continues to hit the wall, but still she watches us, waiting to see what we're about to do. I'm curious myself. For the moment, I'm frozen near the open door. Despite my conviction it would happen, it turns out I wasn't *actually* prepared to deal with getting caught.

"Okay, okay," Kornelía whispers, prying her arm away from me. She makes a quick sweep of the room, then nudges me out of the way so she can close the door behind us.

"We need to get out of here," I say, watching as she inches the door shut until it clicks. "We're not supposed to trap ourselves inside!"

"They're downstairs," Kornelía reasons. "So, we'll have to stay up here until they leave again. Or go to bed."

"But isn't this the bedroom?" I ask, pointing to the double bed against the far wall.

"It's a big house," Kornelía says. "Do you see any suitcases or personal items? The people who were staying here the first night we came by used this room. But it doesn't look like this couple is. They must be staying in another room, which means they won't come in here."

"That seems like pretty flimsy assurance," I sigh, holding my stomach. "What if they come in here, anyway?"

Kornelía is about to say they won't, but a sharp look from me makes her cross her arms over her chest and turn to the closet. "Let's go in there, then," she suggests. "Very little chance they'd come into the room *and* look in the closet."

"Unless they notice *her*," I say, motioning to the ghost incessantly pounding the wall.

Kornelía considers the shaking picture frame above where the girl hovers. "No one has come to investigate so far," she says, her tone shifting from indecisive to resolute. "We'll have to assume they can't hear her. It's our best shot."

She heads for the closet and I trudge behind her, one eye on the spirit watching us from beside the closet door. We slink inside and slide the door shut, and I'm grateful there's enough room I can slump into a ball and grip my aching head.

"How are we going to know when we can leave?" I ask.

"The television's on downstairs," Kornelía says, ignoring my question.

"Is it?" I mutter. The static is too loud for me to hear Kornelía well, let alone the TV on another floor.

"They must be settling in for a movie," she continues.

She looks at me, then past me, her brows furrowing. I turn, jumping when I realize the spirit is in the closet with us, wedged between me and the wall.

*What is it with this spirit?* She makes no vocal sound,

and I didn't even notice the shift as she got closer. She's nearly touching me, but the pressure in my gut and the shiver of my spine is the same as when I first stepped into the room.

"With our luck it'll be a double-feature," I moan, glancing away from the spirit, unsettled to know she is still watching me.

Kornelía offers a sympathetic smile. "Gives us more time to try and figure out what the ghost needs, at least," she says.

We end up having lots of time to hang out in the closet. Kornelía sits and stands in turns, while I stay hunched low, wondering how it's possible I've already found myself in a worse situation than being stuck on a haunted airplane. The spirit won't talk. I make a few more attempts to ask her questions or lead her into conversation. But she only stares at me, occasionally swinging her fist back against the wall behind her and sometimes disappearing from sight for a minute or two.

After a while I give up trying to converse. I try taking out my phone so I can text Meander and tell him what's happened. When I pull it from my pocket the battery is dead, drained from the girl hovering to my right.

When a word comes through the static, at least an hour in to our hiding, it takes a full minute before I realize I've heard anything. When I do, my head snaps up, my limited vision swimming with the sudden movement and its accompanying shock of pain. I turn to the spirit, but nothing has changed. She's still there, staring at me, her fist clenched but hanging at her side. I watch her until, at last, the word scrapes through once more.

*"Bean."*

Her mouth hasn't moved. Then again, the word's in my head, not in my ears, so maybe she doesn't need to form the word with her misty lips.

"Kornelía," I whisper, my voice broken from the effort of keeping sickness at bay. "She said something."

"What?" Kornelía slides down to crouch beside me, her long legs bent at an awkward angle against the closet door. "What did she say?"

"Bean, I think," I say, scrunching my nose as I try to translate what I heard into something that makes more sense. But saying it out loud has made the spirit echo it in my head, the word clearer now I know what to expect.

*"Bean."*

"Bean," Kornelía repeats, thinking. "Why'd she say something now? We've been here for ages."

"Maybe she thinks we've moved in," I say. Kornelía jabs me with her elbow, and I bury my head in my hands again. "I don't know why. She's—" I glance up to see that the spirit has disappeared again. "She's gone, at any rate."

"No she's not," Kornelía says.

She squints at the space to my right where the spirit was. Then she closes her eyes. Even with her eyelids closed and the glow from the spirit dampened by her disappearance, I'm able to make out surprise spreading across my friend's face.

"Of course," she says, her low mumble giving the words an Icelandic accent I rarely hear in her speech. She opens her eyes and smiles at me as a creak below us makes us both tense. We listen as the couple heads up the stairs. The squeak of a second-storey floorboard is audible even through the static.

I feel bad for these people, oblivious to the two strangers hiding in their guest room closet. Not as bad as I feel for myself, but still.

The room next to ours must be the bathroom. Shortly after the floor squeak, a sound of running water issues close by our backs. A few minutes later, I hear the blessed noise of a door closing farther down the hall.

"Let's go," I say the instant the sound has stopped.

Kornelía nods, grabbing the doorknob and opening the closet door. She falls out but manages to catch herself before she crashes to the floor. The spirit has returned, and she gives a final slam against the closet wall as I crawl out.

"Should we leave quietly, or make a run for it?" Kornelía asks, helping me to my feet.

"If I try to run right now, I'll fall face-first down those stairs."

I lurch forward and rest against the wall next to the door, annoyed there's no relief now that I'm further away from the spirit. This entire room is buzzing from her energy, or whatever is causing the static in my head.

"Okay, we'll go slow," Kornelía says.

She opens the door and peers into the hallway. A light shines underneath a door further down, and she gives me another nod before we tiptoe out. Two steps into the movement I realize we should have taken off our shoes, but mentioning this detail out loud would be more troublesome than dealing with the soft tap of our sandals.

When we're out of the room, I take gulping breaths, pressing my forehead to the wall while Kornelía closes the door. She pats my back, then signals for me to follow her. My head is clear, my stomach settled, and most of the warmth back under my skin by the time I'm halfway down the hall. The vanilla scent lingers but, after what we've been through, I can handle a bit of a bad smell sticking in my mouth and nose.

We creep down the stairs, peering over the banister to make sure no one is still on the first floor. What we can see over the railing is an empty room, which is a relief. But when we're three quarters of the way down the steps, the door upstairs clicks open.

With a wild look of panic, Kornelía mouths *run*, and we sprint down the remaining steps with no thought to caution.

"What was that?" the woman says, as Kornelía fumbles with the lock on the front door.

"I don't know. Sounds like…"

"Go, Kornelía!" I whisper.

She gets the door open, pulling it back so we can rush outside. I slam it behind us, grabbing Kornelía's arm as we hurry across the raised porch and down the stairs. The lights on the first floor of the house switch on, and we duck through the brush, running between branches and leaves until we hit the main road.

WE DON'T STOP RUNNING UNTIL WE BURST THROUGH THE DOOR OF THE boys' fale. My fitness has improved after weeks of working out with Althea, but my lungs are still on fire when we knock open the door and slide into the room.

"Looks like someone had an eventful evening," Sefa says, glancing up from a game of solitaire.

"What's wrong?" Meander asks at the same moment, his concerned words drowning Sefa's amused ones. He closes his book and grabs his phone off the sofa's armrest before he stands.

"We were at the treehouse," Kornelía says between breaths.

Dylan brings us each a bottle of water, and I gulp mine down in one go. I don't know how long we were stuck in that room, but we've missed dinner and, now that I'm not sick, I feel like I haven't had food or water in days.

"You were *where*?" Meander asks, fixing his gaze on

me.

He expects me to respond. But, while I'm busy wiping my mouth with the back of my hand, Kornelía answers in my place.

"We went to check on the spirit," she says. She offers a brief explanation of what happened, of how we saw an opportunity to make initial contact, but then got stuck inside the house. Dylan laughs, but every word makes Meander's features settle further into a stony mask.

"You are amazing," Dylan says when Kornelía is finished relaying the tale.

She smiles, looking relieved to have an excuse to be near him without it turning into a discussion over how annoyed he is with Mim.

"You're crazy," Sefa chimes in, his tone not so joyous. He considers her, then offers a small bark of laughter. "But you're dedicated, I'll give you that."

"I can't believe you went there," Meander says in a low voice, his statement again directed at me.

I put the empty water bottle on the nearest end table and shake my head. "We didn't mean to," I say.

His eyes widen with incredulity. "You didn't *mean* to?" His voice is sharp, the volume rising with each word. But then he stops, staring around the room like he's only just realized we're not alone. His jaw tight, he gives me an unmistakably pointed stare before storming outside.

"What the hell's wrong with him?" Dylan asks.

"No idea," I mumble, although an abundance of ideas filter through my head as I process his reaction. I didn't expect him to be so upset about the events of our night but, still, I can imagine a dozen different reasons why he stormed out. I turn around, ready to follow him and find out first hand which inkling is correct.

"Cal," Kornelía says, touching my arm as I step towards the door.

"Tomorrow, Kornelía, okay?" I say, stepping away from her. "I promise. Tomorrow."

I know she wants to talk about what we experienced and what it all means for trying to release the girl in the treehouse. But right now, I'm far more concerned with the boy who just left the room.

She looks like she wants to argue, but she holds back, instead giving me a small nod. "All right, tomorrow," she says, waving me off.

I jog outside, searching through the darkness to see where Meander went. The lady staying at the treehouse doesn't seem like an overly pleasant person, but she may have been right about why the yacht captain cancelled their trip. Any rain had stopped by the time Kornelía and I made our escape. Now, the clouds are starting to break apart, a few stars visible in glimpses of the bright sky stuck beyond the gray.

Meander's not difficult to locate. He's near the shore, still visible from our front door. When I reach him, he stands with his back to me, his arms crossed over his chest.

"Hey," I begin, unsure of what to say.

"I can't believe you went there," he repeats, continuing the complaint he started indoors.

If I'd known our outing would bother him so much, I would have texted him earlier. I thought I was doing him a favor, but now my limbs are heavy with disappointment that I misinterpreted his reaction.

"It was Kornelía's idea," I sigh, tired and despondent.

"That doesn't mean you had to go along with it!" He turns around, glowering. "That was bloody stupid of you."

"I'm not going to disagree," I say, the first tinge of annoyance sparking under my skin. After what I've been through tonight, I don't need to be yelled at. Especially not by him. I thought he'd be worried about my absence, or tease me about getting trapped. This is not the greeting I anticipated, and I'm not equipped to handle his displeasure.

"I couldn't stop her from going in," I continue, trying to make him understand my motives. "I thought it'd be better to go with her than have her sneak in alone."

"And it never occurred to you to let someone else know what you were doing?"

*Someone* means *him*. I curse myself again for not texting him before we left.

"I didn't want to interrupt your work," I mumble, the words lame even to my ears. "And I tried to send you a message when we were inside, but my phone was dead."

He shakes his head, not believing me or maybe just not caring. "You are such an idiot," he mutters.

This time I don't stop the anger when it flares. "What is your problem?" I ask, my legs starting to shake from exhaustion and the sick sensation of fighting with him. "I didn't think you even wanted to deal with this spirit. Are you really that upset you didn't get to come with us?"

His eyes widen for a fraction of a second before he gives a derisive laugh. "I don't care about the damned spirit," he mutters.

I nod. It's the response I expected, even though the answer leaves another question in its wake. "Why are you so bothered, then?"

Meander puts a hand to his forehead, like he can't believe I'm this ignorant. "Because you could have been hurt," he says, the words tight and short, staccato notes that strike against my chest.

I flounder, trying not to give myself a good slap because *of course* he was worried and I'm not sure why I ever entertained the idea he might not be. "Well, then why aren't you berating Kornelía, too? She's the one who came up with the plan."

"Because she's not the one liable to do a spirit's bidding," he says.

I've shared my fears with Meander many times. He knows how worried I am about being manipulated by a spirit's will, but discovering *he's* concerned about the possibility as well grates against my skin. I always figured he was humoring me when he listened to my ramblings. I didn't realize he agreed that I'm unfit to face ghosts alone.

"You think she can handle herself, and I can't?" I ask, failing to keep my voice from cracking with frustration.

He takes a deep breath as his arms drop to his side. "Of course not," he says, his tone scolding but not nearly so vehement anymore. "But I've seen what spirits can do to you, Cal. You can't put yourself into a vulnerable position like that without being prepared for the risks—without having a way to escape."

He's right again, but this time I'm not so ready to express my agreement. "I don't need to be supervised," I snap. I'm not sure when the topic changed from me being at the treehouse to me being incapable of dealing with spirits altogether, but I resent the notion I need to be aided like a weak child. "It's not like I can rely on a team of helpers to bail me out of danger for the rest of my life. For all I know, this is how my ability is developing. Maybe by next year, spirits will guide my will every time they're nearby. I can't *prepare* for those kinds of risks."

"You don't know what will happen next year," Meander says with a shake of his head. "I know you can't control what spirits find you at home. But you're not at home, Cal. You are *here*, with people who can help." He takes a shaky breath, his voice stuck between aggravation and a strangled timidity. "People who care a hell of a lot about you being safe."

The statement makes me start, the topic shifting again without me knowing where one thread ended and another began. My heart pounds, not so much from his words, but from the way he's now looking at me—the way I *think* he's watching for my reaction. His expression is unsure and, in my confounded state, I only manage to cling to one hope for why he's nervous about admitting there's someone here who cares.

For the first time in a long while, I don't let myself overthink the moment. With a deep breath, I venture forward until we're only a foot apart.

"People like… *you*?" I ask, trying to keep my face serious and my expectations low.

Meander's eyes gleam with something I've been desperate to see for weeks, a confident uncertainty I wasn't sure would ever be waiting for me. I have to bite the inside of my cheek to force down a smile when he speaks again.

"Yeah, like me," he admits, the words hesitant and inviting all at once. He pauses, then nods like he's convinced himself to say something more. "I don't think I've ever mentioned it, but… you are my favorite person, Callum." He falters, looking at his feet, then glancing up with a smile. "Which isn't quite explaining it right. I don't like people, generally speaking. But even if I *did*, you'd still be top of my list."

For a minute, our eyes lock. My head swims and my stomach churns. It's like the opposite of seeing a spirit. Instead of getting away, all I want to do is move closer.

But then Meander looks down again, and everything in his manner shifts. "Which is why I don't think I should be a part of Mim's exorcism," he tells me.

His unexpected words leave me muddled."Mim's exorcism?" I ask, disappointed and confused. "What does that have to do with anything?"

"It has to do with you," he says, not stepping away but still putting up his guard again. "I'm dangerous, Cal. And I don't want you to get hurt. I don't want that *ever*, but absolutely not because of me."

"I won't—" I begin, but he cuts me off with a look.

"You already did," he says, his fingers reaching out to brush the spot on my forehead where a rock struck me last summer. "I haven't been working on a history assignment, you know. I've been in the library reading up on exorcisms. They're notoriously savage, even for people without a talent like mine. I know Mim won't change her opinion, and I suspect I'll have no luck telling you to stay behind. But I *can* stay back. I can be the one waiting for you to return."

"We need you with us," I say, frazzled by yet another

new aspect of this conversation.

Meander scoffs. "No, you don't. And I don't want to put anyone at risk."

"But we're aware of the danger, Meander," I say, pressing a hand to my forehead. "No one thinks this is going to be a breeze." I feel lightheaded, whether from hunger or this discussion I'm not sure. Regardless, I push it back, touching his arm to keep him close and myself upright.

He stares at my fingers for a moment before he shakes his head."Everyone else can do whatever they want," he says. He touches my fingers with his. "But I can't be responsible for *you* getting hurt again. I just… I can't."

"I know the risks, too," I say as he drops his hand and I carefully lower mine. "And I, uh, won't lie… I really, *really* like that you want to keep me safe." I smile at him, then set my gaze into a stern mask. "But you can't hide away because of an occupational hazard."

He smirks at my terminology, but I don't give him any time to respond. "You want to keep yourself tucked away from spirits, but we both know that doesn't work," I continue in my best tone of caring reprimand. "It makes more sense for you to learn how to use your ability than for you to try and pretend you don't have it. You are *so* useful, Meander. I know you don't think so, but you are. And that's why Mim wants you to come. She didn't invite you simply because you were present last year. You played an important part in releasing the spirit of Isabelle Levasseur, and she knows it. We all do."

"I'd rather be safe than useful," he says.

"I'd rather not be hounded by murder victims, but

unfortunately we don't get to choose what abilities we have," I sigh. My eyes drift to his forearm, and I imagine the scar on its underside. "I understand why you hate your ability. But we have to deal. *You* have to deal. Because if you don't, you're going to end up a half-insane hermit living off tea and Hobnobs while trying to pretend you don't exist."

He smirks again, and I smile, kicking his shoe.

"And the thing is, I want you to exist," I confess, finding his eyes and not letting them go. "*Very much*, I want you to exist." I swallow, and let out a trembling laugh. "And, if I'm being greedy, I also want you to be close to me. Like, all the time."

He opens his mouth to respond, but then closes it with a nod. The smirk softens into a quiet smile, and for a while we stare at each other, a feat simultaneously awkward and amazing.

The anger of our brief fight has twisted, flipped, and catapulted us towards something infinitely better. I would be happy to stand like this for hours, except my stomach is clenching with hunger and I don't want my growling gut to be the thing that ruins the mood.

"I was thinking…" I start, breaking the silence before I've figured out what my excuse will be. "After I eat something, I was… going to play my violin."

After being trapped in that closet with the spirit's hollow sockets of foggy mist watching me, followed by the revelation of Meander's confession, I need to process my thoughts with a bow in my hand. But I'm not going to let this night slip into the past as if it were only a dream. My smile turns shy, and I press my lips tight before I make myself say the words.

"You could come with me, if you want."

"Really?" His voice is surprised, but his expression is pleased. The look alone is worth my unease.

"Yeah." I nod and, when the beginnings of a rumble prepare to remind me of the dinner I haven't enjoyed, I add, "but I need to eat something first. You're welcome to join me in the dining hall, too. Shoving food in my face with company is somehow far less intimidating than playing a few bars of music."

He laughs, falling into stride beside me as we head back up the beach. As we walk, our arms dangle close together, his fingers grazing mine with the sway of our steps.

# 25

 broken into a private property tonight means I have no qualms climbing through the unlocked window to sneak food from the camp's supplies. As I make sandwiches and eat more than my fill, I relate further details to Meander about what happened at the treehouse. When I'm satiated, and he has asked all his questions, I retrieve my violin.

I'm glad the library has become my go-to place for playing the violin this summer. I can't think of anywhere better for my first performance in front of Meander.

My fingers shake as I take out my instrument and unfold the music. Plucking absently at the violin's strings, I will the tremor to stop and my breathing to even. When my hand finally rests still against the fingerboard, I pick up my bow and tuck the violin under my chin.

My first notes are soft but steady, the familiar sound of my strings breaking through the surreal nervousness of having Meander nearby. He laughs when I start with Brahms Lullaby, assuring me it's the best lullaby rendition he's ever heard. His happiness furthers my comfort, and I relax into the music as if I'd never been frightened to play.

When I switch to a concerto by Hans Werner Henze, Meander grows quiet, leaning back in a chair and becoming absorbed in my performance. I'm not used to such a captive audience. Mom and Dad work on their own projects when I practice at home, and Rose interrupts me all the time to insist I play her favorite pieces. Meander doesn't demand specific movements, nor does he tell me to lower the volume so he can concentrate on something else. Three pieces in, he starts to wander around the library, touring the stacks and flipping through random books. All the while, I know he's still listening. Each time I complete a piece, he reappears to offer a quiet round of applause while asking me to continue with something else.

Brahms and Henze make up the majority of my concert, but I include a handful of short selections from works by Mozart, Paganini, and Chopin as well. I didn't plan to play so much, but I'm more comfortable than I thought I'd be. The small smile that never leaves Meander's lips draws a blush to my cheeks. But unlike the flush of embarrassment I'm used to, this heat is wonderful—especially when I notice the pleased reaction in Meander's eyes.

The glances we exchange and the music we share makes the evening rocket forward, a complete change from the dragging hours I spent in the treehouse. By the time my arm aches and a crick stiffens the muscles in my neck, Meander's presence is so familiar and enthralling, it's like he's always been around for my practice sessions.

We get back to the fale around midnight, where we watch a movie with the other guys, one of the few times all five of us have hung out together this summer. Despite sleeping in the same room, I haven't seen much of Sefa, and even less of Naasir and Reed. Hell, I haven't even seen much of Dylan. Last year the whole sector was close. We had our own floor in the château, and we kept near the only people who shared the uncertainties of being new. But this year the girls are in another building, and we've got a tropical beach to utilize.

Still, it's nice to spend time with them. Dylan and Reed root for the killer in the horror movie, while Naasir questions why every scene needs to be gory— and Meander mutters sarcastic comments about the characters' foolish decisions. Once the final girl has claimed victory against the slasher, we laugh about the film's cheesy effects and questionable acting while we prepare for bed, the discussion lingering long enough none of us get to our bunks before two o'clock.

Which would be fine, if it weren't for Kornelía's six a.m. wake-up call.

She beats on the front door, calling our names and eventually resorting to hitting the small bedroom window with a rock until Naasir stumbles out of bed to let her in. Once she's gained entry to the main part of the fale, she barges into the bedroom, rousing all of us and sending Sefa into a tired tirade.

"You can't come in here," he says, his face half-buried under a pillow. "It's not decent."

Kornelía rolls her eyes, crossing the room to sit at the foot of my bed."It's not like you're naked," she says, her voice suggesting she wouldn't care even if he was. Kornelía lives in a farmhouse full of siblings. I have the feeling she's not embarrassed by much when it comes to issues of privacy.

"If I said that while standing in your bedroom, I'd get pummeled," Dylan says. He lays on his stomach, his dark hair a wild mess.

"By me or Mim?" Kornelía replies.

He laughs. "Lu, most likely."

I give Kornelía a small kick before she has time to respond. "What do you want?" I ask through a yawn.

"You said we'd talk," she says. She twists so she can see my face. "You promised."

"You didn't say our talk would be so early," I groan, propping myself onto my elbows.

"You didn't stick around long enough to negotiate the time," she retorts. "We've got a lot of work to do."

She stands up and walks over to Meander's bunk. He's nowhere to be seen, his bed nothing but a massive pile of blankets. Throughout the summer he's collected them, snatching them up whenever someone kicks off their cover claiming it's too hot. I don't know how he doesn't melt, but I'd be lying if I said I didn't find the quirk adorable.

"You should come, too," she says to the mound, crossing her arms on the bed frame.

His sheets rustle and his face appears, eyes narrowed in annoyance. "Too sodding early," he grumbles.

Kornelía only smiles before turning away."I'll be in the library," she says, looking back at me as she walks towards the door. "Sabeena's waiting until Isabis is up. Then she's going to join us as well. *So, hurry up.*"

When she's gone, the main door of the fale falling shut behind her, Sefa huffs. "She *is* crazy," he complains.

Dylan smirks before turning his head towards the wall and falling back to sleep. I swing myself out of bed, glancing up at Meander.

"You coming?" I ask, keeping my voice quiet so I don't disturb the others anymore than Kornelía already has.

"I guess I better," Meander sighs.

He runs a hand through his hair, his fingers sticking in the tangle of his uncombed curls. With a grimace, he tugs his fingers loose and looks at me with a resigned pout. I laugh, and he smiles, his eyes watching my lips in a way I've never noticed before. My gaze slides down to his lips, too, and then I look away, focusing on getting up before the memory of last night's conversation sends me into a happy daze.

True to her word, Kornelía is in the library when we arrive, books stacked around her and a tablet under her nose. She doesn't look up when we approach, only pointing to the chairs across from her as she tells us to sit. I exchange a tired glance with Meander, but we follow her instructions to avoid a scolding.

"I know why the girl is still around," Kornelía says, one long finger scrolling through whatever she's studying on the tablet. "I mean, I'm pretty sure I do."

I lean back and run my hand across my forehead, pushing at the fringe of hair dangling too far down. This morning, I could list a thousand reasons I'm not looking forward to going home in only three weeks time. But, if there's one positive to our upcoming departure from this glorious place, it's the appointment I've booked for a quality haircut when I get back.

"How could you know about the girl?" I ask. "Did you find something online? A news article?"

Kornelía shakes her head. "Haven't found a thing," she says, eyes fixed on the screen.

I wait a beat, hoping she'll continue. When she doesn't, I sigh. "Kornelía, look up and explain what the hell you're talking about, please," I say.

Meander grabs a book from the stack and peruses it as Kornelía raises her head, looking as confused as I am by the lack of understanding between us. After a pause, she seems to realize the problem.

"I'm sorry," she says, shaking her head and slipping off her glasses. She pinches the bridge of her nose in discomfort, giving the frames a hateful glance. "I got ahead of myself. You said last night that the girl disappeared from the closet."

"Yeah, she—"

"She didn't disappear," Kornelía says, cutting me off. "I told you her energy was muddled. I couldn't get a clear sense of the place, and I think I know why. There's something behind that wall. Something the girl wants us to see."

"But..." I struggle to make sense of what she's saying.

"A hidden space?" Meander asks. He puts down the book and folds his arms on top of its cover. Under the table, his leg rests against mine.

"But," I start again, more coherently, "there's another room on the other side of that wall. The bathroom, remember?"

"Yes, that's what I thought, too," Kornelía agrees. "But I couldn't stop thinking about it. What was the one thing the ghost did while we were in there with her?"

"She banged on the wall," I say, working to catch up with her. My brain is too languid, like a symphony unable to work at anything more than a walking pace.

"Right," Kornelía nods. "The wall across from the window. And then, when we were inside the closet—"

"The wall behind her," I say, the pieces slowly swirling together. "Which was the wall adjacent to the one she'd been banging before."

Kornelía places the tablet on the table and gives us both an excited smile. "I've been studying pictures of the house from that rental website," she says with a nod. "The closet we were in was small, and the bathroom beside it looks small, too. I think a whole area of space is being wasted."

"Wasted, or used for something else," Meander concludes.

"You mean like a... secret room?" I ask, looking between them.

"Maybe," Kornelía nods. "It'd be small. But there's something else there, I'm sure of it."

"And you think it's worth checking out?" Meander asks.

"Depends on what it is," Kornelía sighs. "Maybe. A corner between the closet and bedroom... The space could have been a clubhouse, somewhere she played. Or, an object could have been walled up back there. A doll, maybe. Cal, you said she muttered the word 'bean'. Maybe that's the name of her teddy bear, or something that reminds her of her family. It'd be helpful to know who she left behind. A living relative might have insight into a toy she lost before her death. But I still haven't found any death record to match hers, which means we don't know who her family is."

Meander looks at me, a disconcerted expression in his eyes. "What if there isn't any record?" he suggests in a quiet voice.

A sick feeling swells low in my stomach, spreading out from the place in my core that's always given me an intuitive edge when dealing with spirits. My brain may be slow to process new information, but my talent is not.

I widen my eyes in silent question, and he answers with a grave nod.

"You think the record doesn't exist?" Kornelía asks, confused. "That doesn't make—"

"There'd be no record if there was no body," Meander interjects.

Kornelía's face brightens until she realizes what he's suggesting. I hold a hand to my forehead, thinking about the possibility that all the time I was stuck crouched in that closet, a corpse may have been slumped on the other side of the wall. An involuntary groan escapes my throat, and Meander begins rubbing my back. I lean into the press of his hand as I look up at Kornelía.

"She *was* trying to communicate," I say, my voice thick.

Kornelía nods. "She was. And we've got to get back in there to help her."

"You can't be serious," Meander says. "If we suspect someone murdered a girl and walled up her body, we've got to go to the police."

"And claim a ghost told us about the crime?" Kornelía asks, one eyebrow arched.

"Then we tell the Oracle," I say. "There's no reason for us to return to the house."

"Even if the Oracle believes us, the owners of the house won't," she says. "There's no way we'd get permission to knock down a wall based solely on a supernatural hunch."

"What if the owners were the ones who committed the crime?" I ask, the thought occurring quick and sharp, like a crack of glass behind my lungs. I'm not sure whether it's intuition, or simply a morbid guess. "They refused to let us investigate. And *someone* who lived in the house killed the girl. If the body was walled up, it couldn't have been a vacationer."

Kornelía taps a finger against her lips in thought. "You're right," she says. "The owners had to have done it. But I don't want to assume it's the people who own the house right now. I mean, they wouldn't rent it out if they knew there was a body inside the walls, right?"

"Depends," Meander says with a soft, scoffing breath. "If they're confident enough—or *mad* enough—they might."

"Okay, so first we need to figure out when the murder took place," I say. "And we need to find out how many people have owned the house. I couldn't make out much of the girl's clothing when I saw her. Did you Kornelía? I know she was wearing a dress, but I'm not sure what style. That could give us a clue as to when she died."

Kornelía shakes her head. "She's not wearing a dress," she corrects. "She's wearing a nightgown.

Which doesn't give us enough to go on. It's too plain."

"Well, we can start by figuring out how old the house is," Meander says, his hand still on my back. "That would provide a probable time frame for the murder. If nothing else, it would eliminate any dates before the house was constructed."

"You're right," Kornelía says. "We should start looking through records of missing children, too. See if we can find her. If we locate any concrete evidence— find out who the girl is and make a reasonable guess for when she was killed—we'll go to the Oracle. But if our search turns up nothing… We're going to have to figure it out ourselves. We can't risk the owners getting suspicious and keeping us out of the way, whether they're guilty or not."

We agree to her plan, and waste no time getting our searches underway. Kornelía surrenders the tablet to me while she goes to one of the computer stations. Meander sifts through the pile of books Kornelía amassed before we arrived and, when he finds nothing useful amongst their pages, he ventures over to the collection of archive records the Oracle has scrounged up from the surrounding islands.

We work in silence, each of us on the hunt for a slice of the girl's story. Thinking about a body enclosed in a place people now relax in is eerie but, once our search gets underway, I realize I'm bothered less by the thought of a corpse than I am by the possibility of once again trying to release a trapped spirit. With each real estate search that turns up nothing to help us, the despair of winding up back in the treehouse engulfs me with fresh waves of nausea.

Our searches take us through databases, books, and

old website pages until nine, when Sabeena and Isabis arrive to aid our efforts. Sabeena enters the library carrying some kind of dessert. When she sets it down in the middle of our table, I realize part of my sickness might be because I haven't eaten anything today.

"Did you make this?" Kornelía asks, stretching her arms over her head while she walks back from the computer station. She doesn't have to worry about keeping her voice low, as we're the only ones in the library—nine o'clock is early for most Senders-in-training.

Sabeena snorts. "If you ever see me baking, do yourself a favor and run away." She pulls napkins and forks from the messenger bag slung over her shoulder. "Isabis made this."

"You helped," Isabis says from beside her. She considers the dessert for a moment before she smiles. "It's a milk tart. My mamma makes them. Thought it might be nice, since Kornelía said we'd be busy researching all day."

"Most of the day," Sabeena says, looking around the table. "Four of us have Sender Mythos at noon."

"Which gives us plenty of time to eat and catch you two up," Kornelía says.

Sabeena nods, pulling a plastic knife from her bag and cutting into the tart.

"I'm going over to the dining hall to get some tea," Meander says in a low voice close to my ear. "Want anything?"

"Juice would be nice," I say, my skin tingling beneath his breath.

"Orange?" he asks, knowing it's my preference.

I nod. He walks away, and I smile when he reaches

the door before it must occur to him he should make a similar offer to the others. Kornelía asks for water, and Meander looks relieved when the others decline.

I watch him leave, then I take a slice of tart as Kornelía tells Sabeena and Isabis what we've discovered.

## 26

SABEENA WANTS TO RETURN TO THE TREEHOUSE.

"I didn't get a chance to speak with her," she argues between bites of tart. "I might have better luck getting her to communicate."

Kornelía is on board with the idea, and her enthusiasm for the plan only grows as the morning hours dwindle without us finding anything helpful. When the four of us have to leave for Sender Mythos, Isabis stays behind in the library, working through lists of missing children even though we're doubtful her efforts will yield any positive results. She has a course starting at four, but she agrees to stay in the library until then, and email Sabeena a summary of her findings so we can pick up the search after she's done.

Sender Mythos drags by, despite its interesting lesson plan. Mrs. Buxley leads us through an overview of ludicrous theories various Senders have put forth over the years. One woman's suggestion is that Senders are people who have regained life after an unnoticed scrape with death. Another man holds a bizarre, depressing belief that Senders imagine all the spirits they see—and that any physical harm we experience is subconsciously inflicted on ourselves to atone for some hidden source of guilt.

Listening to my sector mates and the Revenant kids bantering about the ideas should be fun, especially once they start making up their own ridiculous theories to match the ones we've heard. But my knee bounces anxiously, and my thoughts refuse to stay focused on the conversation at hand. I can't appreciate the joys of the peculiar. I'm too preoccupied thinking about the solemn spirits waiting beyond the safety of this class.

Before our course began today, Mim exchanged hushed words with Kornelía, telling her that tomorrow is the day they'll investigate Swallow's Cave. Between the two of them, this summer is spiraling out of control. Mim's looking more drawn out than ever, the shadows under her dark eyes rivaling Dylan's ever-present bags. And while Kornelía agreed to the trip, it's obvious her attention is on her own task, an immensely different assignment every bit equal in its insanity.

In France, our projects were controlled, selected by instructors and monitored until they were complete. Here, we're working in secret, and the catastrophes looming behind walls and in the recesses of a dark cave are too close for comfort.

"You doing all right?"

The whispered words are like a quiet tide washing

back the panic. I smile, glancing to where Meander watches me, no book in his hands and nothing distracting his attention.

Our relationship is also spiraling out of control, but in a decidedly better fashion. A day ago, I was keeping my space, trying in vain to work out the meaning of each flitting look and casual touch. Now, Meander's foot touches mine, and I know it's not unintentional. He stares into my eyes, and I know there's something purposeful in his searching gaze.

"Yeah, I'm fine," I tell him and, for at least a few blissful seconds, the statement is true.

"You don't have to go back," he says, leaning close. "I know the others want to, but that doesn't mean we have to."

I make sure Mrs. Buxley hasn't noticed we're not listening to the current debate over the validity of a theory involving magnetic sensitivities before I answer. "I spent a good amount of time with that girl," I whisper when I deem it safe. "I've got to help her, if I can. And you're coming, too. Unless you're worried about, you know, the *body*."

Meander shrugs, leaning back as Mrs. Buxley gives us a sharp glance. "Can't say I'm looking forward to it," he says once she's turned away. "But a dead body doesn't pose any threat. Spirits are much more troublesome."

"So, you'll come?" I ask.

With a sigh, Meander nods. "I'll come," he mutters, kicking my foot. "But only for you."

When Mrs. Buxley at last dismisses us, I pretend not to notice her stare as I hurry from the room. I don't want her pulling me aside to ask about the camera I borrowed. With my eyes downcast, I rush past her desk, step through the doorway and almost smack into Isabis.

"Good, you're finished," she says, waving away my apology. She sounds aggravated. The tremor in her voice is worse than usual. "I've been waiting."

"Are you okay?" I ask, stepping to the side to let my other classmates pass.

"There's nothing wrong with me," she says, her eyes fixed on the doorway while she waits for Sabeena and Kornelía to join us outside. When the girls appear a few seconds later, Kornelía makes us move away from the fale so we won't attract Mrs. Buxley's notice.

"You should be in class," Sabeena scolds once we're down the road.

"Yes," Isabis sighs. "But I thought this was more important."

"Did you find something?" Kornelía asks.

Isabis digs one of her crutches into the sand, her lips tight with annoyance. Kornelía takes a step back, putting a fist to her mouth to keep herself from interrupting again.

"I couldn't find anything," Isabis explains after a moment of quiet has passed. "And I got bored. So, I went to the house to look at last night's footage."

She pauses, inhaling deeply.

"Cal and I were there last night," Kornelía reminds her, too eager to stay silent as Isabis catches her breath. "Did you find anything else on the recording?"

"I never watched the recording," Isabis says once she's got her breath back. "There wasn't any need. When I got to the house, the people who have been staying there were headed out to their car. They had suitcases."

"They've left?" Kornelía asks.

She turns to me like I might have some kind of insight into the couple's sudden departure. I wonder if they were always planning to leave today, or if last night's intruders made them decide to shorten their stay.

"Guess you picked the wrong night to investigate," Meander says.

"That's my point," Isabis sighs. "They're gone. So, if we want to go to the house, we need to do it tonight."

"Tonight? That's too soon," Sabeena says in a panic. "We're not prepared. Especially not after what you told us this morning, Korni."

"We don't have a choice," Isabis says.

"She's right," Kornelía agrees. "We leave in three weeks."

"So?" I glance at Kornelía, still somehow surprised by her fierce determination. "What are the chances the next vacationers will be staying for three weeks? We'll have another shot."

"Maybe not," Sabeena argues. She crosses her arms over her chest and thinks. "We can't go into this with only a couple days to spare. We'll need time to recover, if we plan on being successful. Which means we've got to tackle the ghost as soon as possible."

"We could even end up needing more time with her," Kornelía adds. "We can't waste the opportunity to get as far as we can."

I hate every aspect of the plan now hatching among the girls, but I don't have any more arguments to make. We're in a curious position, knowing what we do. Even if we find enough evidence to safely tell the Oracle and ensure a proper investigation gets underway, there's no guarantee the spirit will be freed from the house. If our hunch is correct and her body is behind that wall, her unfinished business may well be connected to the fact she's never been found.

But if we're wrong? An investigation would tie up the house for ages. Who knows when anyone from the Oracle would be able to get back inside.

I glance at Meander. He gives me a sympathetic smile, and I smile back, trying not to sulk. He doesn't want to do this anymore than I do—probably wants it less, since it was my idea to get involved in the first place. If anyone should be complaining about the turn of events, it's him. But he remains silent, listening to the others discuss what equipment we'll need and what time we should meet to head over. So, I stay quiet, too, making a mental list of what supplies I want to bring along—like a sweater and some sort of hammer to help knock down a wall.

Once the plan is settled, Kornelía returns to the library while Sabeena goes with Isabis to tell her instructor why she'll be missing her course. When only two of us remain, Meander finally speaks.

"This is a terrible plan," he says, his tone almost conversational.

Our job is to track down Robbie and tell another lie to convince him we got a last minute room booking for tonight. I never thought I'd be looking forward to telling the truth as much as I am when this summer is over.

"We seem to be full of terrible plans this summer," I say as we start towards the leads' fale. I give Meander a sideways glance as we turn down the main road. "Am I weird for believing this summer is way worse—and way better—than last year?"

"Yes." He steps closer until our arms brush as we walk. "But I'm of the same mind. So, I guess we'll have to be weird together."

I let out a small laugh, the tide rushing in to once more push away my nervous thoughts. "I don't so much mind being weird when it's with you," I admit with a smile.

"Funny that," Meander replies, his words soft as the distant rush of waves on the shore. "I was just thinking the same thing."

"Y'ALL ARE GOING TO DO GREAT," ROBBIE SAYS WITH A GRIN. HE LOOKS between me, Meander, and Kornelía, appraising his troops before he sends us out on our mission. "That spirit doesn't stand a chance."

"They're not trying to *kill* it," Mim says from across the room.

"You know what I mean." Robbie twists one of the piercings in his left ear, his sights focusing on Kornelía. "Looking good," he says, eyeing her ensemble. If we were at a normal summer camp, his comment might be considered inappropriate, bordering on gross. But he's talking about Kornelía's established spirit hunting attire—her dress, her bare feet, and her long hair falling straight down over her shoulders. I'm not sure if it counts as a collection, or if it is simply a personal uniform. Either way, Robbie understands it's something unique to her.

I'm not dressed for the occasion, and neither is

Meander. We're wearing almost the same thing, both of us in jeans and sneakers, our Wanagi sweaters draped over one arm.

"Thanks," Kornelía says. She beams at Robbie, then looks over her shoulder to check the clock in the kitchenette.

"We've got twenty minutes until we're meeting the others," I remind her.

"Relax," Robbie says. "Don't get too anxious about seeing the ghost. It'll make you tense. That's never a good way to begin."

"You're right," Kornelía sighs. She taps her bare foot for a moment, muttering something beneath her breath before going to one of the sofas and plopping down beside Dylan.

"I don't think I've ever seen someone relax so forcefully," Dylan deadpans. Kornelía glares at him, and he smirks. "I like it."

She tries not to look too pleased, since Mim is sitting behind them at the kitchenette's table.

Robbie shakes his head and gives us a final thumbs up. "I'll leave you guys to it," he says, making a last check that we don't need anything before he departs.

When he's gone, Meander sighs. "If we've got twenty minutes, I'm going to grab my book."

He walks off towards the bedroom, and I move to the empty sofa adjacent to Kornelía and Dylan's. As soon as I'm seated, however, Kornelía fixes her eyes on me.

"Do you have the tablet?" she asks.

My mouth twists in aggravation as I shake my head. "No, I forgot," I mutter. "It's on my bed. I'll go grab it now."

I didn't expect that the tablet would be of any further use to us now we don't have any footage to scroll through. But Kornelía thinks that, if the spirit really is as contained as she seems, we might be able to keep the tablet charging in the hall. I'm not sure her theory is valid, but I can't argue that it's worth a shot. As long as we make sure the tablet is safe. If we wind up smashing the screen tonight, I suspect we'll have some serious explaining to do—even if the spirit is to blame for the destruction.

When I approach the bedroom, the door is half-closed. I press a hand to it just as I catch sight of Meander. He's alone in the room, his back to me. He must have decided on a last minute outfit change. The long-sleeved shirt he was wearing a moment ago is off, and a lighter tee is now in Meander's hand.

In Meander's hand, but not yet on his body.

I halt in the doorway, stunned. I've never seen Meander shirtless before. He's always been leaner than I am, but I didn't realize how different his physique would look. Unlike my scrawny frame, his back is rippled with soft peaks of muscle. And while I'm not surprised to find his fair skin unblemished, the few freckles smattered beneath his neck and near the waist of his jeans are an unexpected delight.

Awed-excitement keeps me rooted as I study his back. But before I have a chance to control my elation, Meander turns. His body angles to the right, far enough towards me that I can make out his chest.

And his scars.

For all I knew before, Meander had two scars. The one on his jaw, and the one on his arm. But now I see that at least six short tears of raised flesh mark his front. I can't fathom how he got them. It almost looks like he's been slashed by a pitchfork. No wonder he didn't take his shirt off when we went swimming. He's been living with more scars than any of us knew. And like the other marks marring his skin, I'm sure these are related to his talent.

The scars are fascinating. But knowing how much they must have hurt dampens the enchantment of glimpsing so much of his skin, so I step away from the door before he discovers me gaping. Walking back to the living room, I try not to concoct morbid scenarios for how a spirit could cause such an injury. The scars look old, faded like the mark on his jaw. I wonder if the spirit caused the damage itself, or if it *did* use something like a pitchfork to inflict the cuts. Meander's never even hinted at the existence of these scars. Given how open he is about wound on his arm, I have to believe whatever happened to his chest was intense if he's kept so silent and secretive about it.

I wonder what it's been like for him this summer. Aside from the night at the dock, Meander has only ventured into the water when Althea's made him during Sender Strength and Stamina. His lack of interest in wading through the waves didn't seem at odds with his reserved personality, though. It never occurred to me he stays on the shore because he doesn't want everyone barraging him with questions about his chest.

Realizing how often I've flaunted my unscarred skin opens the gateway for guilt, but I tamp it down, knowing there's no reason for it. Meander's never divulged the truth. I hope someday he will but, for now, beating myself up is pointless. And if I fail to remove my shirt for the rest of the summer, he'll realize I know. Which means I can only pretend I haven't seen anything remarkable tonight.

I take a deep breath and try to be nonchalant as I return to the living room without the tablet. Luckily, the others don't notice the missing device. Mim is too busy berating Kornelía for going out tonight when they are supposed to be travelling to the cave tomorrow.

"I can still go with you," Kornelía insists, twisting so she can keep her friend in sight.

"Not if you release this spirit," Mim says.

I wonder if Kornelía told either Mim or Dylan that we suspect there is more than just a spirit in the treehouse. Robbie doesn't know, nor is he aware Sabeena dragged Sefa and Naasir to the nearby construction site to "borrow" a few tools for our evening's venture.

"There's no guarantee we'll release the spirit," Kornelía reasons, although everyone has to expect she'll do everything she can to clear the house of spiritual activity before the sun comes up.

"But if you do," Mim says, "you'll be knocked out cold. No way will you be conscious enough to go with me."

"*I* could go with you," Dylan mutters from the sofa.

"You can't tell me if the spirit is there," Mim says. Her words are tight, as if she's trying to be civil but finding it a challenge.

"*If* we release the spirit tonight," Kornelía cuts in, "and *if* I'm not able to help you out tomorrow, we can go to the cave in a few days."

Mim huffs. "We're supposed to go *tomorrow*."

"You can stand to wait a few freaking days," Dylan snaps.

The bedroom door creaks open behind me, and I'm relieved to have an excuse to turn around. Meander has changed, and his book is now in hand. For a moment, I prepare to avoid all mention of his outfit, until I realize ignoring his change of attire would be suspicious.

"You changed," I say, making a show of glancing at the others as if to suggest my interest in his clothes is mostly about interrupting the fight brewing a few feet away.

"Yeah." Meander shrugs, the statement void of any distrust. "It might get cold later but, right now, it's too hot."

"Well, we should get going, anyway," Kornelía says, detaching from her argument with Mim when she sees that Meander has reappeared. "I mean, better early than late."

Meander doesn't look pleased to hear we're going after he just retrieved his book, but he puts it on the table next to the nearest sofa and heads for the door.

"Good luck," Dylan says, giving Kornelía's hand a small squeeze while Mim's back is turned.

I follow Meander outside so I don't have to watch the look passing between them, a look they shouldn't be sharing with Mim sitting so close.

"Do you think we're ready?" Meander asks when we're on the path.

Dusk is upon us, but a leftover glimmer of light still stretches across the horizon, the sun's rays lingering over the water as long as they can.

"Are we ever?" I ask.

He laughs. "I suppose it's a foolish question, isn't it?"

His sweater is draped over one arm, while the other hangs down by his side. I reach out my hand, poised to grasp his fingers, until Kornelía throws open the door and nearly whacks me in the back of the head.

"Oh, sorry, Cal!" she squeaks as I duck out of the way.

Meander steadies me, smirking at my near-miss.

"Shall we go?" I ask, eager to move past my embarrassing stumble.

Kornelía nods, patting my head as she steps by as if consoling me for the damage she almost delivered.

# 28



Despite being fifteen minutes early, Sabeena and Isabis are ready to leave as soon as we meet them in the girls' fale. We load up equipment, our tools vastly different than they were last August when our group set off to complete our final project. We lug hammers, crowbars, and even a saw, probably looking like community builders—or making the vacationers we pass fear for the safety of their resort rooms and rental cars.

"So, we know the couple left," I say when we're about halfway to the house. "But are we sure the cleaning staff won't already be tidying up?"

"We aren't," Isabis admits.

"Logically, it makes more sense for them to clean the house tomorrow," Sabeena reasons. Her pale pink sari is trimmed with gold and draped over a gold crop top and flowing pink pants. The crowbar resting on her shoulder and the black sweater tied around her waist make for interesting accessories to the otherwise elegant ensemble.

"Yeah, but this isn't a hotel," Meander reminds her. "Logical maintenance schedules go out the window when the property is privately owned."

"He's right," Isabis agrees. "They might clean up tonight so it's ready for new occupants tomorrow morning."

"They would leave a day between bookings, though, wouldn't they?" Sabeena asks. "What if the people trashed the place? It could take more than a few hours to clean."

"There's no guarantee of that," Meander says.

"And even if there were," I add, "that still doesn't mean they wouldn't start cleaning straight away. Like you said, Sabeena, they might need more than a few hours."

Kornelía steps forward, a sledgehammer dragging along the road behind her."We'll check the camera before we go up to the house," she says, her words curt. "Until we're sure the place is empty, we'll be careful to keep out of sight. But we've always known this is going to be risky. Logically, the cleaning staff will come when its daylight. If the owners use a hired company, standard working hours are likely. Whatever the case, we've made our plans. Now, we have no choice but to hope for the best."

Her declaration brings our conversation to an end, and we walk the rest of the way in silence. When we reach our destination, we pad down the dirt path and push through the foliage to where the video camera is stationed. Kornelía ventures out to check on the house while the rest of us speed through the footage to ensure no one's returned since Isabis changed the memory card this afternoon.

"The house is dark," Kornelía says after her initial assessment.

"No one's come by," Isabis confirms. "We're good to go in."

Kornelía nods. "Then let's go."

Treading with cautious steps, we take the now familiar route up to the porch, each of us searching the windows for signs of life. A dark house and a promising footage reel are no longer enough to banish our fears about startling living inhabitants.

We approach the front door, and Kornelía places a hand on the doorknob before whipping around so fast her long hair hits me in the face.

"I forgot the bobby pins," she groans, leaning back against the door.

I blink in disoriented surprise, while Kornelía settles her gaze on Sabeena and Isabis. "Do either of you have a hairpin I can borrow?" she asks.

The girls shake their heads, and Kornelía sighs, looking at me.

"I can't help you, either," I say with half a laugh as I point to my short, pin-free hairstyle.

She nods as if she was expecting the response. Her questioning gaze flits to Meander, only to be greeted by a small shake of the head.

"I'll have to go back and find one," she says, glancing up at the house. "Sorry, everyone. I'll run as fast as I can."

She starts forward, but Isabis signals for her to stop.

"Hold on," she says, taking slow steps towards the house. "You may not need to leave."

"Do you know another way to get inside?" Sabeena

asks, following her movements.

Isabis smiles. "You're forgetting my ability," she says. "I can't see ghosts, but I can manipulate them. I might be able to get the girl to open the door."

Kornelía beams for about a second before her face falls into a troubled frown. "The spirit won't leave the room," she says. "I mean, I'm fairly certain she won't."

"She must be able to," Isabis says as she considers the house. "I felt her once, from all the way down at the path, remember? Still… I don't feel her now, so maybe you're right."

"We could climb up the back again," Sabeena suggests. "The girl's presence is stronger there. Isabis, you can try to get her to open the window."

This time Kornelía's grin doesn't diminish. "That's a great idea!" she exclaims.

The girls walk together around the house, and I prepare for the pain of having Sabeena stand on my shoulders again. When we reach the back wall, however, Kornelía has other plans.

"We need to be as efficient as possible," she says, staring up at the window. "I'm tall, and I won't be in pain when I enter the room. So, I should be the first one up. I can run through the room and go downstairs to unlock the front door for the rest of you." She turns to me and smiles. "Sorry, Cal, but Meander's taller than you. He should be my base."

Meander scrunches his nose in distaste, and I smirk.

"See? You're already more useful than I am," I whisper.

"Being useful is highly overrated," he replies, crossing to the wall and positioning himself under the window.

"Cal, when you get inside the house, place the tablet out in the hall before you come into the room," Kornelía instructs.

The smile slides off my face, my lips falling in time to the flush rising in my cheeks. "I, uh… forgot the tablet," I admit.

"You *forgot* it?" Kornelía looks like she's about to swat me, so I put my hands up in surrender.

"You forgot the bobby pins," I remind her.

"And I came to the rescue," Isabis says. "Which I'll do again." She pulls out her phone and waggles it in the air. "I've got a good data plan. I don't mind using it for research."

"Thanks." Kornelía gives her a grateful smile. "You can place it out in the hall when we get inside. If we're lucky, the battery won't drain out there."

She walks over to Meander and places her hands on his shoulders, prepared to start her climb.

"Wait!" Sabeena calls, her gaze stern. "You're *still* wearing a dress."

Kornelía eyes the sky in annoyance before surveying us with arched brows. "Meander, don't look up my dress," she instructs.

"Sure thing," he mutters, looking mortified by the implication he'd use a moment like this to be a creep.

He braces himself against the wall while Sabeena and I help Kornelía up. I'm glad I'm not the support this time, though I feel for Meander as he struggles under the pressure of Kornelía's weight.

While the rest of us focus on getting Kornelía up to the second storey, Isabis tries to connect with the spirit.

"Open the window," she mumbles as we propel Kornelía up to the room. "Open the window."

She pauses, then repeats the phrase a third time in the language I've now learned is Zulu. The change in her speech has an effect. Above us, a mass appears by the window, and a fetid vanilla scent drifts down from its sill, growing stronger as the window creaks open.

"You did it," Sabeena says, sounding relieved.

The window inches up, the movement slow and jerky. It slides, pauses, and twitches up another inch before it pauses once more.

"I've reached it!" Kornelía calls, sliding her fingers into the open space and heaving the window up. She braces herself against the frame before kicking off Meander's shoulders and tumbling head first into the room.

"You okay?" I yell after we hear the heavy thud of her landing.

"Yes," she moans. Her head appears out the window. "I'll let you in."

We meet Kornelía at the front of the house, where she stands in the open doorway waiting to welcome us inside. The entryway is as dark as it was last night when the two of us were here, but Sabeena's flashlight beam is far stronger than the light on my phone. She shines it around the first floor before directing it up the staircase.

"I think I'll stay out in the hall with the phone," Isabis says, lifting one of her crutches onto the bottom stair.

"Are you sure?" Sabeena turns the light onto her face, lowering it when Isabis squints away from the beam.

"Yes," Isabis says. "I can't see the ghost. And this way, I can keep an eye on the battery level. I'll keep watch, too, and let you know if anyone is coming."

"Not that it matters," Meander scoffs. "We're about to knock down walls. I think the owner's going to know someone broke in."

Sabeena falters, stepping back as she considers him. But then she shakes her head and moves forward again. "Freeing a trapped soul is more important than abiding the law," she says in a determined tone.

"How far does that logic extend?" I muse a third of the way up the steps.

"What do you mean?" Sabeena asks in confusion.

"Like, what if someone was killed, and the only thing that could release them was, you know, to *off* their killer?"

Sabeena stops on the stair ahead of me and looks back over her shoulder. "Why would you even think of something so grotesque?" she asks, her eyes crinkled with distaste.

"He sees the ghosts of murder victims," Meander offers. "It's kind of his territory."

"We're wasting time," Kornelía cuts in from the upstairs hallway.

We mumble our apologies and hurry up the remaining steps. Sabeena ensures Isabis is set up on her phone, then we head to the room.

I'm not looking forward to seeing the spirit—or rather, *feeling* the spirit again. But having more people here makes it better. Although, to be honest, it's not about having *more* people—it's about having the *right* people.

The right *person*.

Meander's quiet, the way he's always quiet when it's not just me and him talking about the most—and least—important things in the world. But he's here, and his presence is like a pillar I can lean against. This is, in the bizarre reality of our lives, what we do. Our friendship began in this world and, while I'd love to be at the beach, on a boat, or in the library playing my violin for him, facing this spirit together feels right.

"She hits hard," I warn him as we approach the door.

He takes a deep breath and nods. "Then let's not prolong the anticipation."

He steps into the room and I follow behind, the pain and sickness engulfing me as soon as I've once again crossed the threshold. The effects are worse than they were yesterday; Meander spikes her anger the instant she feels him close.

I try to withstand the shock, but having experienced it before doesn't numb the impact. Gritting my teeth against the punch of pain, I remind myself that the girl here needs our help. She doesn't try to throw things, at least. Her anger is directed not at us but at the wall, her fist ramming it over and over again.

"Oh my…" Sabeena gulps, dropping to her knees in the middle of the room.

"Are you all right, Sabeena?" I ask, pressing a hand to my roiling stomach.

"Yes," Sabeena says, her voice shaking. She folds into herself with a groan before pulling herself up to her knees and shaking her head. "She… she starved to death."

"What?" Kornelía had been studying the wall, but now she stares at Sabeena, her eyes big with surprise.

"This spirit," Sabeena repeats. She wipes matted hair off her forehead and collapses back to all fours. "This poor girl died of starvation."

The spirit doesn't react to Sabeena's statement, other than to use the power Meander's provided to hit the wall with as much force as she can muster.

"She's suffered long enough," Kornelía says, staring at the shaking frame of the picture above the spirit's wispy head. "We need to help her."

"And how do we do that?" Sabeena asks. "Do you really think bringing down the wall will help?"

"What do you think?" Meander asks. He sounds annoyed, probably because of the icy pain making him hold his head while his teeth chatter with cold.

I step beside him, and a spark of warmth breaks through the chilled air when he leans into me.

"She seems hell bent on that bloody wall," he mutters. "Must be *something* important behind it."

Kornelía hefts her sledgehammer over one shoulder. She surveys the rest of us, her expression struggling between pity and frustration over our sorry states. Then she nods.

"Let's not waste anymore time, then," she says.

She pulls the hammer back, swinging it through the spirit's torso before it collides with the wall.

I'M GLAD THE SPIRIT ISN'T ANGRY WITH US. I'D HATE TO SEE WHAT KIND of destruction she could cause with abnormal strength and a few hammers at her disposal, especially once one such hammer has gone through her misty middle.

I don't think Kornelía is aware of what she just did. Her eyes are open and no glasses adorn her face, which means she can't see the living *or* the dead. She's lucky the little girl doesn't seem bothered by the strike. I guess if she can slip through walls with no concern, a bit of metal isn't a big deal.

Still, even if the spirit doesn't find Kornelía's actions problematic, I cringe as the hammer vaults forward, smashing into the wall with a thud muffled only slightly by the static in my head. Kornelía doesn't hesitate once the sledgehammer is wedged into the plaster. She pries it out like she's a construction pro while the rest of us watch, too stunned and weak to attempt any help.

"What's wrong with you?" Isabis asks from the doorway after a moment. I think she's talking to Kornelía but, when I swivel my head, I see she's watching the three of us struggling to keep on our feet. Or, I should say the two of us—Sabeena is still on her knees, and she doesn't look like she's going to pull herself up anytime soon.

"The spirit's affecting them," Kornelía exclaims, huffing with the effort of hitting the wall a second time.

"You're pathetic," Isabis says in her dry, breathy voice.

My eyes narrow as I focus on the doorway. "It hurts," I say, annoyed she's so callous when even her friend is convulsing with cold and gripping her head.

Isabis fixes me with a hard stare. "Think I don't know what pain feels like?" she asks, stepping into the room. She looks around and sighs, her tone softening. "Maybe I can help."

Closing her eyes, she utters a command in Zulu. Only one sentence is needed to catch the spirit's attention. The little girl turns her head to the pile of tools on the floor by the bed. She leaves off hitting her fist against the wall as she goes for the pile, swooping down and lifting a hammer.

"Are you *insane*?" Meander hisses, backing up several steps and nearly stumbling into her. "Do you have any idea what she could do with that?"

"Yeah, help," Isabis says, eyes still closed. "If you don't interrupt."

Meander shakes his head and moves to the door, ready to bolt if the spirit decides to use the hammer on the five of us. But she doesn't. She takes the tool and, with a gentle glide, returns to her former position. Kornelía is forced to move aside as the spirit pulls her fist back, the same motion she's made dozens of times. The hammer in that wispy fist alters the impact, though, and the heavy metal slams straight through the plaster.

"You're brilliant!" Sabeena says, gasping through her pain. She looks over her shoulder at Isabis with a smile that would be kind and grateful, if it weren't for the gleam of sweat and feverish discoloring of her skin that makes the expression appear almost delirious.

"You don't know what you're doing," Meander utters in a low, dangerous voice.

"She's helping," Sabeena says.

"Without understanding the risks," he shoots back.

They're both aggravated, and my guess is that the pain and over-sweet vanilla scent aren't helping matters.

"What are you talking about?" Sabeena asks, her brows furrowing in genuine confusion.

The question is a surprise. We've known Sabeena for over a year but, in all that time, neither me nor Meander have been this close to a spirit with her. Realizing she doesn't understand his talent sends a shock of incredulity through my shivering limbs.

"It's okay," Kornelía snaps, pausing to scold us all. "She didn't consider the risks but, turns out, she didn't need to worry. Isabis—and the *ghost*—are helping far more than you three."

"I can't go near her," Meanders says, shaking his head. "I'll stay out in the hall, do the research."

He steps across the threshold, disappearing around the side of the door. As soon as he's gone, the spirit's hold on the hammer diminishes. The wood handle wobbles in the blue-white smoke of her hand until it falls to the floor next to Kornelía's foot.

Kornelía squeaks, hopping out of the hammer's way in a brief moment of mousy fright.

"What happened?" Isabis asks, opening her eyes. "I had such a good connection."

Kornelía's confidence returns in a blink. She rounds on me, the billowing motion of her dress and hair making her share, for one astonishing moment, a surreal similarity with the dead girl floating beside her.

"Get him back in here!" she demands, and her dark tone—not to mention the fact I know I'll have a nice break from the pain as soon as I'm out of this room—sets me walking.

Meander sits on the top step of the staircase. I drag a deep, almost stench-free breath into my lungs as I pass the closed doorways between us. When I reach the curved steps dropping to the dark foyer below, I sit down as he sighs.

"Sorry," he mutters.

I smile, glad for the excuse to return his earlier favor by rubbing his back. "She can't hold the hammer without you," I tell him as my hand makes smooth circles against his sweater. "Kornelía was quite insistent you return."

Meander groans, running his fingers through his curls. Then he drops his hands onto his knees and remains silent for a long moment, as if he's weighing the options of returning to the room versus hightailing it back to camp.

At length, he turns to me.

"If the spirit goes off," he says, his expression serious, "you get out of the way."

"Deal," I agree.

Remaining on the stairs, we stretch our peace as far as we can, my hand on his back and his shoulder leaning against my own. The break lasts for less than a minute, but the slip of time is enough to invigorate my nerve and settle my stomach before we venture back.

By the time we return, Sabeena has struggled to her feet. She holds her crowbar again, though she hasn't made it to the wall to start prying away the plaster Kornelía and the spirit have smashed through. Kornelía is back at work, and the girl—without Meander's strength and Isabis's manipulation—has returned to the ineffective task of hitting the wall with her fist.

Re-entering the room is like walking into brick. I mutter a few curses and do my best to breathe through the swell of sickness as we pass through the doorway.

"What happened?" Isabis asks again, looking between us.

"Just get her to pick up the damned hammer," Meander mutters. He grabs my arm and guides me over to the tools, wincing as Isabis once more manipulates the spirit.

"What are you doing?" I ask, speaking loud to cover the noise bouncing between my ears.

"Let's get this over with as fast as possible," he says, the words brusque.

I nod, recognizing the pain in his voice and wanting to put an end to it. I may not have the will to push through the discomfort for my own sake, but I sure as hell have it when it comes to helping him.

The static thrum rises in a sudden spike as I pick another hammer out of the pile.

*"Bean?"*

"We're not far away from whatever is on the other side of that wall," I say. "If we keep going, it won't take long to reach it… or her."

Kornelía moves into the closet, leaving me nowhere else to stand except next to the dead girl pounding through the wall. I stare at the plaster as I approach, trying my best to pretend the spirit is not so close. My arm is shaking when I lift the hammer, but I breathe out and swing with as much power as I can.

For the next few minutes, we work. Kornelía takes the lead, sledging through the wall with apparent ease. I try to hammer at the edges of where the spirit is to make her hole bigger, while Meander and Sabeena use crowbars to pry away the plaster and the lathing beneath. Isabis stands behind us, her energy focused on the girl.

The reality of breaking into someone's house and knocking down walls has become so skewed it feels almost imaginary. I don't want to think about what's going to happen once the Oracle finds out what we've done, spirit or no. So, I block out all thoughts that don't pertain to my current task. I want to get this finished so the pain, cold, and smell disappear. Plus, the sooner this task is complete, the sooner I can stop standing next to a spirit holding a hammer, worrying Isabis's connection will slip and the anger brought out by Meander will have a deadly effect.

"I see something!" Kornelía says after she's tugged a large portion of the wall away. She steps out from the closet and glances around the room. "Do we have a working flashlight?"

*"Bean."*

"By the tools," Sabeena says, her breath shallow.

Kornelía's steps are light as she walks barefoot over to the pile by the bed. I don't know how she doesn't feel the cold in her dress. Every part of me is shaking, and each time I breathe out I'm surprised there isn't a visible cloud. She doesn't seem to feel it, though. She looks content as she bends to retrieve a flashlight, flicking it on and hitting it twice before a fluctuating beam of light shines out.

"She's draining it," Sabeena says, eyeing the flickering glow.

"It'll have to do," Kornelía mutters. She returns to the closet and shines the light inside. "There's definitely something here," she says, coughing through the dust. "I think we were right. It might be a room. It might—"

*"Bean!"*

I cry out, the sharp attack on my eardrums unexpected and fierce.

"Cal, are you all right?"

Meander is at my side, but I put a hand on his arm and stare at the spirit instead. Her vacant gaze is on the wall, the same as it has been since Isabis took control. Her face remains motionless and, for the first time, I understand that she's not speaking, that she never spoke at all. Because Sabeena is watching me, and Meander is checking to see if I'm okay. They didn't hear what I did. They haven't been hearing it this entire time.

The others don't hear her speak because she's not the one speaking.

*"You're* Bean," I mutter, and the spirit turns to me.

She raises the hammer, which makes Meander grip my arm in anticipation. But then she drops the tool and disappears through the wall.

"Kornelía, give me that light," I say, dropping my own hammer and stepping over to the hole in the closet.

I grab the flashlight and shine the beam through the opening. The room beyond is dark and dusty, and the light's failing. But a good kick to a loose piece of wood opens the space enough for me to see what—and who—is inside.

*"Bean."*

The static rustles, painful but quiet as the spirit of a small boy watches me and then looks to his silent sister. They're related, I'm certain of that. And while the girl—Bean—had indistinguishable death marks, this boy's murder is easy to pinpoint. A dark tendril cuts across his throat, like the knife someone slashed him with. I'm sure he's younger than his sister—he can't have been more than six or seven when he died.

"Cal, do you see anything?" Sabeena asks, stepping in behind me.

Her eyes flit to Bean, and there they stay, unaware of the other spirit clinging to her arm. I pull my gaze away from the smoky masses and shine the beam towards the far wall, where a cobwebbed mound rests, ominous and sickening.

"Is that a… bed?" Sabeena asks, placing a hand over her mouth in shock.

A lump, covered by what I think are blankets, lies on the bed, its shape small and human. And beside it, near the wall, there's a second thing next to the mound, a spread of hair catching in the light.

"T-two," Sabeena cries. "There are two."

I look back at the spirits and nod. "We'll make sure someone knows," I say, looking between brother and sister.

The boy hugs his sister tight, their misty masses ebbing together like tangled weeds blowing in the wind. No wonder Kornelía thought Bean's energy was muddled. When they're together, the two sink into one another like they are parts of a single entity.

"We'll take you out of here," I promise.

"What's going on?" Kornelía asks.

She presses behind us, but I push back against her, forcing her out of the space. The spirit of the boy is starting to turn, his light growing bright. A beat behind him, Bean's light tremors, too, like her sole purpose for hanging around has been to wait for his release.

I don't want to pass out here, stuck between walls with two corpses before me and rusted nails on either side.

"Get out, before they cross," I say, my voice sharp.

Sabeena must realize the girl is changing. She turns around and pushes Kornelía out of the way, and I stumble out behind them, my head twisting with dizziness. Two spirits, both of them crossing over at the same time. I'm disoriented as I fall back into the room, my senses swaying like I've been drugged. I trip over the sledgehammer and land hard on my knees, but Meander's quick to pull me up again. His eyes fix on the white light streaming out from the hidden room even while we both head for the door. My feet trip over themselves and, across from me, Isabis staggers backwards.

"What's g-going on?" she mumbles, her face a

grimace of confusion and pain.

"It's good," Sabeena gasps from behind me.

"We can't make it out," Meander mumbles, grabbing my shirt and twisting me around. "We don't have time to get out of the room."

I think we're going to fall onto the heap of remaining tools, but he gets us to the bed. We land atop the covers at the same moment as Kornelía. My head is cushioned by the softness of the duvet, and I roll onto my back to watch the light streaming through the room. The thrum in my head grows loud, white noise twisting to its peak volume. I inhale the sugary scent of sweet vanilla bean frosting and close my eyes against the now too-intense brightness.

My eyelids are far too thin to block the light as it bursts. Whiteness explodes in my head, and the siblings drain my energy until I'm no longer aware of anything.

I DON'T KNOW WHO RETRIEVES US. ROBBIE'S MY BEST GUESS, SINCE HE'S the one unofficially overseeing the project. Whoever it is, they get us out the next morning.

Unlike last year, when my post-release trips were made unconsciously, this time I have a few blurry moments of half-wakefulness. Mostly, I remember flinching from the brightness of the sun, and the dizziness of the twirling descent around the trunk of the tree.

I'm not out for as long this time, either. We reach our beds Thursday morning and, by the evening, I'm up long enough to make sense of my trips to the kitchen and bathroom before I shuffle back to my bunk. Friday is spotty, but there's a good half hour during which I lay in bed, too tired to stand, but awake enough to grab my earbuds and listen to Bruch's "Scottish Fantasy" before I pass out again.

By Saturday, I'm tired but awake, dragging my feet

around the fale and dozing on the couch until Robbie summons me to the dining hall to ask about what happened. I'm not sure what the others are saying, but I maintain a half-lie, claiming we went to the house to knock down the wall expecting to find only a doll or a trinket. At least my shock at discovering two bodies is not fake. As far as I know, I'm the only one who saw the second ghost, and he was not a spirit I was anticipating.

The questions are tense at first but, by the time I leave, Robbie, Alex, and Mrs. Buxley offer only a mild scolding about the fact that we should have obtained proper permission to go into the house and complete the task. If we hadn't found anything more than a dead child's toy, I'm sure the lecture would have been worse. But we uncovered a hidden double-murder, and it's hard for them to deny the implications of what we found.

When I return to the fale, Meander is awake. Robbie drops me off and gathers him for questioning next, taking him from the fale before he even has a chance to make tea. I get the kettle ready in his absence. When he's back twenty minutes later, I fill two mugs and join him on one of the couches, while Dylan puts a movie on his laptop and angles the screen so we're able to watch.

Mim and Kornelía make their way over after dinner Saturday night. Kornelía yawns as she plops down beside me on the sofa, but she's pretty with it, all things considered.

"How are you feeling?" she asks, looking first at Meander then at me.

"Tired," I say. Meander nods in agreement. "Did

they talk to you?"

"Yes." Kornelía smiles, pulling her hair into a sloppy ponytail. "They didn't seem too concerned."

"Kind of hard for them to be," Mim laughs. "You found *bodies*. They can't fault you for that."

"Have they figured out what happened?" Meander asks. "To the kids? We never did locate any records."

"The Oracle found them," Kornelía informs us. "They were siblings. Reported missing in the 70s. I don't know what happened to them, but…"

"His throat was slit," I say with a hard swallow. All eyes turn to me, and I shrug. "His death was quick, at least. Hers… I couldn't pinpoint how she died, but Sabeena said she starved to death. He was dead when those walls went up. She probably wasn't."

"Why would you do that? Kill one quickly, and let the other one suffer?" Mim asks, her voice pinched with disgust.

"Maybe it was an accident," Dylan offers. "They meant to commit one murder but didn't realize the other kid was still in the room."

"Even if that was true, they found out at some point," I say. "I saw two spirits, which means both of them were murdered. If she was walled up by accident, someone figured it out and decided to leave her, anyway."

I wonder how long she knocked on the walls while she was still alive, pounding the plaster with her weakening fist. A shiver of revulsion and pity snakes up my spine. I push against the sofa cushion to quash it.

The five of us—the only current occupants of the fale—are quiet for a moment before Kornelía speaks again.

"We were pretty awful, though," she says with a sigh. "We never warned Isabis what would happen. She's left camp."

"What?" I say with a start. "The release freaked her out that much?"

"No." Kornelía shakes her head, a small smile lifting her lips. "She's coming back, at least I assume she is. Next year. But when the spirits crossed, she fell. She hit her crutches pretty hard and injured her leg. She's gone home to recuperate with proper medical attention. We were so wrapped up, we didn't think about what a fall might do."

"In our defense, it happened quick," Meander sighs. "We didn't even talk to the girl, or…" he looks at me, "the boy. We barely managed to make a hole before they were crossing over."

"We should have been prepared," Kornelía argues. "Well beforehand."

"Yeah, I suppose we should have," Meander concedes. He takes a sip from his fourth mug of tea. "Is she okay?" he asks.

"I think so," Kornelía nods. "They just want to make sure she gets the rest she needs."

"Yes, preparation is key," Mim interjects, her transition about as subtle as Bean with her hammer. "Which is why we should start preparing for Anjelo."

"Who is Anjelo?" Dylan asks, his words sharp.

"The ghost in Swallow's Cave," Mim explains.

Kornelía gives her friend a disappointed frown. "Mim, you didn't go out there by yourself, did you?" she asks.

"Of course I did," Mim sighs, twisting her finger around one of the now-faded pink strands peeking out from beneath her dark hair. "I didn't want to waste any time. So, I didn't."

"You could have been hurt, Mim," Dylan snaps. The anger is evident in his harsh tone, but I suspect more than anything he's hurt she didn't take him along.

"I wasn't alone," she says, eyeing him before turning back to the rest of us. "I went with a tour group. Lots of people, and I was the only one who noticed anything unusual. I *did* see him, though. His presence was subdued, but clear enough. He's waiting, and I'm eager to meet him."

Faster recovery or no, I'm not ready to deal with this. I tilt my head back and close my eyes, listening to the others bicker about when and how we're going to face this new spirit.

"We'll do it in a week," Mim says, her voice more serious—and stubborn—than it was last year. "Next Saturday. It's the night of the party, so everyone will be preoccupied."

I'm tempted to ask why she doesn't think we want to attend the annual Camp Wanagi year-end party as well. But, considering we only stayed at last summer's shindig for half an hour, using it as an excuse would be pointless. I don't care about missing it. What bothers me is the idea of going to the cave at night when everyone else is too busy with their own fun to even notice our absence.

"You can't do this, Mim," Dylan says with a weary breath. "It's too dangerous."

"I know what I'm getting myself into," Mim replies. "And that's why I'm planning ahead. For the next six days I'll be preparing, practicing what I'll say, and working out the sequence for the actions I'll take. I already know the ghost's name, when he died, and how. If it makes you feel any better, know that when we go to the cave, I'll talk to Anjelo and see if I can figure out what he needs without resorting to more *forceful* measures."

"Have you stopped to think about just how *forceful* you're being, Mim?" Kornelía asks, drawing her knees onto the sofa. "Aren't those methods of release controversial?"

Mim snorts away the question, although I'm not sure it's worth such a careless dismissal. I didn't take Resistive Spirits, so I don't understand the intricacies of exorcism and the beliefs surrounding it. But I remember last summer, when Mr. Bujak—an instructor I have been lucky enough not to see this year—made a vague reference to other methods of releasing the dead. Not all the campers were happy about the idea. Even from that brief experience, I've gathered this kind of release is not something to approach lightly.

"Spirits are not meant to stay here," Mim says with confidence. "They are lost souls, and they need help. All reports of exorcism and other manipulated releases have stated that nothing is different. The crossing over remains the same, whether the spirit decides to go on its own, or a Sender intervenes."

She's convinced of herself, at any rate, an attitude I'm sure will help in the cave. I can't imagine performing an exorcism would be easy with jittery nerves and uncertain motives.

I lift my head and open my eyes to see Kornelía and Dylan exchanging a glance, one Mim definitely notices. She looks like she might say something and, although I don't want to be involved in *that* argument,

I kind of wish she would force everything out in the open. Watching the dance these three are fumbling through is tiring—being a participant must be as exhausting as waking up after a spiritual release.

A tense moment passes before it becomes obvious Mim isn't going to speak. The others remain quiet as well, and the conversation fizzles into awkward silence. Part of me wants to change the topic and lighten the mood, but I'm too tired to bother. Plus, if I did have the energy to get off this couch and do something productive, I'd rather go out to the beach with Meander—without the others tagging along.

"I'm going to head back to our room," Kornelía says after a few minutes, patting my knee as she stands. "See how Sabeena's doing."

"She didn't get hurt, too, did she?" I ask, putting a hand to my mouth to stifle a yawn.

"No," Kornelía says. "She's okay. Good, in fact. She's happy we were so successful. I am, too." She turns away and heads for the door without waiting for Mim. "Night, everyone," she calls, waving as she leaves.

"We were going to start a movie," Dylan says, glancing at Mim uncertainly. "Want to join us?"

She considers the offer, but shakes her head. "No, I've got tutoring," she says.

Her eyes are regretful, and she lingers a moment as if she's waiting for Dylan to insist she stay put. When he fails to repeat his offer, she pushes off the sofa and leaves the fale, her sandals smacking against the tiled floor.

Dylan watches her go, but he doesn't say anything. Once she disappears from view, he flips up his computer screen and resumes the sci-fi marathon we started this morning.

I relax into the sofa cushion and zone out, exhausted enough to pretend the ordeal Mim is planning for Swallow's Cave is still ages away.

WE'RE EXEMPT FROM STRENGTH AND STAMINA ON TUESDAY, A REWARD we probably don't deserve after all the trouble we've caused. Sefa tells us afterward that authorities have swarmed the treehouse, as have news reporters looking for a morbid glimpse of the details unfolding inside. But even with the frenzy occurring so close, I don't see any of it until Thursday, when I'm restored enough to walk further than a block without getting winded.

Visiting the treehouse is not intentional. I only plan to walk through the neighborhood close to the resort, taking in the warmth of the sun while trying to think about the talk I'm supposed to give in tonight's Introduction to Communication Techniques. We've been tasked with giving an oral presentation about a method for communicating with spirits that ties into our own abilities. I was going to explore dowsing rods, following up on the experience I had at the beginning of the summer with Daniel and the other leads. But the unexpected project in the treehouse—followed by the sooner than expected release of the two spirits within—means I haven't spent enough time researching.

After breakfast, I go for a stroll to brainstorm a lazy idea for my assignment. But even as I wander, my thoughts focus less on homework and more on the lightness of being wide awake and uninjured post-release. For the past year, I've been paranoid about spirits guiding my will. The events at the treehouse happened in such a whirlwind, it didn't occur to me until afterwards that the siblings were harmless. I spent weeks familiar with at least one spirit's existence, and knowing I was never trapped under her influence is a relief far greater than I expected.

My mind is easy as I walk past a restaurant patio. In my hazy happiness, I almost miss Mim and Reed huddled close at a table. They must be having another tutoring session. Two books are open before them, and they each sip from pale yellow drinks while they read and mumble comments in turn.

I'm not surprised to see them until I notice how comfortable they are together, sitting close and smiling each time they share a glance. A few weeks ago, Mim thought Reed's eagerness to learn more about his ability was an amusing nuisance. Now, she looks like she's enjoying his company more than she has enjoyed Dylan's for a long while.

I walk by without stopping, but Mim catches me before I'm out of sight. "Hey, Cal," she calls, her voice cheerful.

I glance back with a wave, not planning to disturb

them. But Reed says something to Mim, checking his watch as he pushes his chair back. She sees him off before beckoning me over.

"Tutoring going well?" I ask, eyeing the books as I approach the table.

She pats the empty seat beside her and waits for me to sit. "We were talking about our group's project," she explains.

Mim and Dylan, along with Reed, Sefa, and Naasir, are working together for their final task this summer. I don't know much about it, other than their spirit is an elderly woman on the other side of the island. Neither Mim nor Dylan seem too enthusiastic about it, which isn't surprising given how invested Mim is in her secret plan.

"To be honest, I'm hoping I won't be able to go with the others," Mim continues. "I'll be at the cave the night before Sefa's decided we should tackle the old woman. But Reed doesn't know that, so we were just going over the details. He'll be taking notes during the event, and he wants to make sure he's got the terminology all correct."

She laughs, her smile fond. But then her eyes turn serious as she looks at me. "Meanwhile, I'm trying to make sure I have every detail ready for Saturday," she says. She pauses, licking her lips before she speaks again. "I know you all think I'm a lunatic for doing this."

"No we—" I start shaking my head, but then stop and shrug instead. "Well..."

Mim laughs. "I *am* a lunatic, I think," she admits. "But this is something I want to do. Our second summer is almost over. We only have what—about twenty weeks left? And that's all the training we get. If I'm going to mess up, I'd rather do it here." She closes the books, her fingers outspread on the covers. "Not that I plan on messing up."

"Well, maybe you are loony," I say, staring at the ragged state of her nails as I think about the summer that's gone by. "But at least you're being productive. I get it—we're only a part of Camp Wanagi for a short time, and we should be utilizing that time as best we can. I wish I was more like you. I didn't take enough risks this summer... I didn't even take any challenging courses."

My summer has been anything but boring. But all of my involvement has been the result of someone else's decision-making. If it weren't for Kornelía or even Isabis, I never would have ventured to solve the mystery at the treehouse. I don't agree with the plans Mim has made. But I can't fault her initiative.

"Why?" Mim asks.

Her gaze is full of curiosity, and I swallow my excuses, knowing she wouldn't believe them, anyway. "I was afraid," I admit.

I glance around, always nervous to talk about spirits when others are close. Mim follows my eyes and catches my drift. She motions for us to leave, and we pack up and head for the road.

"Why were you afraid?" she asks once we're a safe distance from any passersby.

I hunch my shoulders forward and stuff my hands into the pockets of my shorts. "I thought if I let my guard down, even for a second, I'd be—*guided*—by a spirit again," I sigh. "So, I tried to hide."

Mim studies me, her expression thoughtful and

understanding. When we first arrived in Tonga, I thought Mim would be as vivacious and outgoing as she'd been last year. But she's no longer the hot tempered, self-centered girl she showed herself to be when we first met. At least not totally. Perhaps her choices haven't been the most altruistic. But while she once led our group just so she could be in charge, now she's taking risks for a different purpose—to make herself a better Sender.

"We're very different," she says after a moment. "You steer clear of danger. I run to it."

"I don't steer clear," I say, feeling sheepish. "I just… I don't want to put myself in danger unless it's necessary—or important. I'll risk danger if it's important."

She tilts her head to one side. "But aren't all ghosts important?" she asks. "Isn't helping them always worth the risk?"

I consider what she says, but I can't view things from her perspective. "They've lived their lives," I say with a shrug I suspect looks more callous than I intend. "I'd like to live mine, too. The lengths to which I'm willing to go in order to help a spirit depend on what I have to risk and who I'm risking it for. Don't you think there are things more important than spirits? *People* more important? Maybe I'm selfish but, if it comes down to a spirit's release or my life, I'm going to save myself. If it's between a spirit and someone else's life, the living will always take priority over the dead."

"A spirit suffers, though!" Mim exclaims in a sudden passion, before her lips draw tight like she didn't mean to have such an outburst.

"But the living person would be *dead*," I finish. "And

there's always another shot with spirits… They're not going anywhere, are they?"

Mim watches a family cross the road as she shakes her head. "We don't agree," she mumbles. "I believe that things will work out, as they're supposed to."

I scoff, and she turns to me, her gaze questioning. With one brow quirked, I meet her stare. "If things worked out the way they were supposed to, I wouldn't see spirits," I say.

"Events happen for a reason, Cal," she insists, searching my face before she looks at the street once more. "If you didn't see ghosts, your whole life would be different. Different personality, different friends… You wouldn't have the same experiences or see the same places. You wouldn't know me or anyone else here. Would you honestly be okay with that?"

I know the answer before the question's finished being asked. Maybe if everything was different, if I was another person altogether, I wouldn't care about not having this alternate life. But as things stand, the idea of not meeting my fellow camp mates ranges from unpleasant to unthinkable.

"No, I wouldn't be okay with it," I say in a hushed voice.

Ahead of us, a line of police tape cordons off the path leading to the treehouse. I didn't notice this is where we were heading. I'm not sure if Mim had a direction in mind, but she doesn't seem too surprised to find us approaching the site of my latest encounter with spirits.

"You do risk the danger," she muses, staring at the tape wriggling in the breeze. "This is the place, isn't it? You helped those souls."

"I didn't do much," I say. The house is not visible from here, but I peer through the thick plant life, trying to work out the architecture beyond the trees. "It was mostly Kornelía. This was her project."

Mim gives me a little push. "No, it wasn't," she says, smiling. "Korni wanted to go there, but she can't communicate. You did that part."

"Yeah, but I wouldn't have gone if she hadn't made me. Plus, she was the one who knocked down most of the wall."

Mim is still unconvinced. "We all play our part. You're the one who told me that," she says. "Kornelía wanted to go. You communicated. You all worked on the walls. And I think I heard something about that other camper… She made the spirit help, too?"

I laugh. "She got her swinging a hammer."

"And that wasn't a risk?" Mim says, her smile spreading into a grin. "Meander was there, wasn't he? I thought spirits were always stronger around him."

"Not stronger, exactly. Angrier, which sometimes has the same effect," I correct.

"Even better," Mim snorts. "An angry ghost with a hammer. What wasn't dangerous about that?"

The pieces connect, just like last year. But the truth of it still amazes me. Even in the aftermath of what occurred, Sabeena's ability to identify how the girl died— combined with my identification of the boy's slit throat—means the investigation got off to a strong start well before forensic forces became involved.

"It's amazing, what we do without even realizing it," Mim says. She loops her arm around mine and pulls me away from the house, back towards camp. "Just remember that on Saturday. I will do everything, but you should still be prepared. Danger might not stay away."

Danger is what I'm afraid of, and it's the reason I want to tell Mim to give up her entire plan for Swallow's Cave. But if I turned my back every time a dangerous situation presented itself at Camp Wanagi, I'd never have made it beyond my first night as a Shade.

Besides, Mim is right about one thing—if she's going to mess up, it's better she do it here. I don't want her to take this risk. But I know her well enough to understand this is not something I can talk her out of. Even if we go behind her back and get the Oracle involved, there'll be no stopping her once she's at home.

Once she's alone to face the danger without any help.

"Yeah, I've figured that out," I say.

I swallow my misgivings, and once more pin my hopes on someone else having this whole *Sender* thing under control.

SATURDAY ROLLS AROUND WITH UNBELIEVABLE SPEED. BUT EVEN WHEN I realize Mim's chosen date to sneak to the cave has arrived, it's difficult not to enjoy the bright light and happy noises filtering through the bedroom window. The morning is a relaxing one. I spend a few hours at the beach, followed by a late lunch and a long shower. By four o'clock, the plan for later has escaped my notice entirely. Feeling refreshed and calm, I grab the last bag of ketchup chips from my backpack and head to the fale's courtyard hammock, unraveling my earbuds along the way.

I listen to the summer movement of Glazunov's "The Seasons" as I flip through photos on my phone. I relive memories of the summer, lamenting that in the few pictures I have managed to snap, I've failed to capture the face I'd most like to have close once I'm back at home. I run through the set of pictures three times before I lay back to enjoy my music, pulling open my chips and savoring the tangy taste.

"Ketchup crisps? You've been holding out on me, Silver."

My earbuds are out before the smile is finished spreading across my face, and I lay the phone to my left as Meander falls into the hammock on my right. We droop into the middle together, our bodies nestled close.

"Like I don't know you've got a whole package of lemon custards buried under your blankets, *Rhoades*," I say, handing him the bag. He pulls out a chip and rests his head against the hammock as he takes a bite. I lean my head back, too, and let out a quiet laugh. "By the way, have I ever mentioned that you have a fantastic name?"

Meander groans. "It's an awful name," he mumbles as he chews.

I turn my head so I can see him. "Are you kidding? It's amazing."

"It was my father's idea," he says with a soft shake of his dark golden curls. "Rhoades is his last name, not Mum's. He thought it'd be funny… I don't even know if he was serious about it. Seems likely the suggestion was a joke Mum didn't understand. In the end, she used the name to entice him to come back. Obviously, it didn't work."

I'm not familiar with all of Meander's history, but I know enough. According to what he's been told, when his mom found herself accidentally with child, it was his dad who convinced her to see the pregnancy through. Then, seven months in, Meander's father changed his mind and disappeared, leaving her a single mother of two—this time with a child she never wanted in the first place.

"Well, it's still a good name, whatever you say," I tell him, feeling like an idiot for bringing the subject up. I offer him another chip and clear my throat, glad I know the perfect way to change the topic at hand. "Much better than mine."

"I like your name," he smirks.

"It's not real, you know," I say with a frown. "Well, it *is* real. *Now*. But Silver's not my family's original surname."

"It's not?" Meander shifts to see me better. "So, what is?"

"No idea," I shrug. I take a deep breath and brace myself to share a story I've never before admitted to anyone. "When my great-great-grandfather immigrated to Canada, he decided to change his name. I'm not sure why, but he must have had his reasons. Anyway, when he was thinking about what to call himself, he decided to turn to his favorite story... A fan of Robert Louis Stevenson, he was."

Meander blinks, and his lips twist into a wide, teasing smile as he makes the connection I knew he'd be quick to understand.

"Are you saying..."

"I guess he fancied himself a bit of a pirate." I nod. "So, he changed his name to Silver."

"You're sure of this?" Meander asks, the question broken by laughter.

I nod again, my cheeks hot with amusement and embarrassment.

"The day he got his name changed he bought himself a copy of *Treasure Island*. He wrote the date on the title page, and then added: *From This Date Forth,*

*This Book Belongs to Henry Jonathon Silver.* I don't know if he made the middle name up, too. But at any rate, my dad still has the book in his study."

"Wait," Meander interjects with happy incredulity. "Middle name? Like *your* middle name? Callum *Jonathon* Silver. How have I never noticed that before?"

I groan, and he laughs, his crooked bottom teeth on brief display in his joy.

"My dad wanted to name me Jonathon," I mumble. "Thankfully Mom refused, so they named me after her father instead."

"I've read a lot of stories in my life," Meander grins. "But that is the *best* one. I've never been happier not to have a middle name." His eyes are mischievous when they meet mine. "Will you stop talking to me if I call you 'Long John'?"

"Immediately and without hesitation," I say.

He laughs again as he lays back against the hammock. I watch his lips settle into a smile, and I try not to think about how much I'm going to miss being here to study the details of his face, all while enjoying the press of his side against mine. At home we talk over video, but video is not the same. He's not close enough, stuck behind a cold computer screen thousands of miles away.

I pick up my phone and pull up my photo app, determined to capture this closeness, even if only through a still shot.

"Hey, you know I don't have a single photo of you?" I say.

He crinkles his nose, shaking his head. "I don't do photos."

"You can't say you 'don't do photos'," I smirk,

elbowing him in the stomach.

He quirks a brow. "Why not?"

"For one, it's like being a walking cliché," I tell him as I lay the phone on my chest. "For two, if I can look at you over video, you shouldn't have a problem being captured in a picture. And for three, you've got…" I stop, blushing when I realize he's watching me.

"What have I got?" he asks, his voice a tease.

I sigh, staring up at the sky and hoping my face doesn't turn as pink as the sunburns a few campers have suffered over the last eight weeks.

"You've got too nice a face to keep it hidden from the lens," I mumble.

He doesn't respond and, when I get the nerve to look back at him, his expression is unreadable. His eyes search mine for a few seconds, then he rakes in a deep breath before grabbing the phone from my chest.

"One picture," he says, shifting so his head is close to mine. "But I'm *not* smiling."

"I wouldn't dream of making you," I say, taking the phone and holding it above us.

He doesn't smile at the camera but, lucky for me, he can pull off the smoldering look in a way I'd never be able to. Not that I try. I think I could bite the inside of my cheek until it bled, and still my grin would be obvious.

The picture, when we view it, is excellent, one I'm sure I'll spend way too long staring at over the next few months. I text him a copy, and then I put the phone to my side and drop the bag of chips to the ground before shifting back towards him.

We lay against the hammock with one another in view, neither of us speaking. Admitting out loud that Meander looks good was difficult. But studying his features in full sight of his watching eyes is not. I work at memorizing every mark, line, and freckle, not ready for him to return home in ten days' time. This camp could stretch into an infinity of spirit sightings and dangerous missions and, still, as easily as I can envision wanting to get away from the ghosts, I don't think even the worst events could ease the blow of leaving Meander behind.

Our eyes catch, the light chestnut starburst close to his pupil taking prominence in the shaded light of the courtyard. His gaze is searching again, and I let him explore until his stare flits down to my lips. When his hand touches mine, I almost start. But while my heart picks up speed, I force my limbs to stay steady. Our fingers entwine like puzzle pieces sliding together, the motion smooth and resulting in a perfect fit.

His skin is warm, his cheeks are pink, and the air around us is sweltering as our faces inch closer. Curls brush against my neck, the smell of his sandalwood shampoo kicking my heart up another notch as the hammock sways in a hot, tropical breeze. Everything swims with heat, my temperature rising until I feel like I'm going to burn up with anticipation—a crisp edge that begins to melt into blissful delirium when Meander's lips wisp against mine.

"Oh, no. I'm too late. I'm so, *so* sorry!"

Kornelía steps into the courtyard, a hand over her eyes and an apologetic squeak in her voice. Meander and I jolt back, the hammock rocking with such violence we have to hold onto each other to keep from spilling out of it.

"*What the hell*, Kornelía," Meander snaps, breathless

and pissed.

"I tried to wait," Kornelía begins. She peeks through her fingers and drops her hand when she finds us both watching her. "I could sense you were having an… important conversation," she mumbles. "So, I tried to wait until it was done. But then you stopped, and well, I didn't want to risk you getting too *preoccupied*."

My heart feels like it's going to crack with the effort of beating so fast. I close my eyes, but the swaying of the hammock makes my head swim without a fixed point to focus on.

"Why are you interrupting us in the first place?" I ask, opening my eyes to glare at her before staring instead at the hammock's sturdy, unmoving wood post.

Kornelía lets a long breath whistle through her teeth. "Mim's ready to go," she says.

"Are you serious? It's not even dark yet," Meander complains.

His hand is still clasped with mine, and I hold it tight as my vision works to regain its balance.

"I know, but she wants us to have dinner together," Kornelía explains. "She's planned a whole meal as part of the exorcism process. She sent me to fetch you right away."

I don't want to leave this hammock. But since I can't rewind time and stop Kornelía from interrupting what should have been the greatest moment of my life, I give Meander's hand a squeeze before I let go and swing my feet to the ground.

He follows my movement, and the three of us walk back into the fale. We make it to the sofas before I realize my phone is still outside.

"I left my phone on the hammock," I say, turning

back.

Meander smiles. "I'll get it," he says, heading back outside before I can refuse.

Kornelía's entire countenance changes the second Meander's back is turned. The expression of morose regret brightens into a teasing smirk as she eyes me.

"Shut up," I grumble, my face still hot.

She laughs. "I didn't say anything," she points out, her voice full of unconvincing innocence.

"Yeah, but you were thinking it," I say with a sideways glance.

She grins. "Oh, can you read minds now, too?"

She pats my shoulder like a pleased, doting sister, her arm dropping back to her side a half-second before Meander returns. He hands me my phone and tosses the half-empty bag of chips onto the table, saving me from having to endure any further knowing looks as Kornelía steps ahead to lead us out of the fale.

We collect our sweaters and step outside, starting towards wherever it is we're meeting Mim. The trip is quiet with nervous unease, my thoughts bouncing between what I didn't get to experience on the hammock and what I might be forced to participate in at the cave. But when we've pushed through the initial crowd of people hanging around camp, Meander steps close to me, looping his pinkie around mine as we walk. I smile, my discomfort vanishing as we turn onto the main road beyond the resort.

Trying to anticipate the horrors of Swallow's Cave is pointless. So, I leave all thoughts of today aside and let my mind wander instead over the vast possibilities of what fantastic moments are waiting once this night is over.

WE JOIN MIM AND DYLAN AT A RESTAURANT NEAR THE RESORT. MIM DOES all of the ordering, loading us up with heavy breads and pastas. The thought of facing a spirit after this huge meal makes my stomach churn, but Mim insists we eat a ton.

"You need energy and sustenance," she says. "If things go as planned, the cross-over will be intense."

No one talks much during the meal. Dylan is sullen, splitting his glances between Mim and Kornelía like he's not sure which girl he's supposed to be gazing at. Meander and I sit together against the wall, sharing the frivolous delight of holding hands under the table like we're five. But still, his muscles are rigid, his grip tight against mine. Mim's warning about the intensity of what's to come tonight has him on edge. He takes careful bites of his food, as if he wants to make sure everything is properly chewed and swallowed, lest something make a reappearance later.

When we finish eating, Mim pays the bill, claiming the Oracle will reimburse her after they find out about tonight's events. I don't believe the excuse, but she's steadfast in her explanation, staunchly refusing to let us pay.

Outside, we walk to the same dock Meander and I took a boat from weeks ago. A small vessel bobs in the water, a pink crocheted bag is tucked under its rear bench seat. I wonder if Mim got this boat from the same man who so carelessly sent Meander and me on our way to the cave, or if she obtained the proper permit to borrow a registered watercraft.

Mim climbs on board and glances through the contents in the bag to ensure she has everything she'll need.

"Are you going to the party?" Kornelía asks Dylan as Meander and I climb aboard as well.

Dylan helps Kornelía into the boat before he steps back. "I might go for a walk," he says, glancing up at the road. "Or a run."

"Be safe," Mim tells him.

He hesitates, like he wasn't expecting her to say it and doesn't know how to respond. The way he eyes the road before his startled gaze shifts back to her, it's like she's guessed he is up to something he hasn't told anyone else about.

"Same to you," he says after a beat. "All of you."

Mim pulls an old pocket watch from her bag and checks the time. The watch must be a wind-up model, a way for us to keep track of the hours without worrying about dead batteries. I'm impressed she thought of it.

"It's a quarter past seven," she says, snapping the

watch closed. "If we're not back by two, send for help."

"Two in the morning?" Dylan asks, his eyes wide. "I know these things take a while, but that's way too long to wait."

Mim starts the boat's motor. I wonder if this is another talent she's been hiding or if she's learned how to operate the boat strictly for tonight's adventure.

"Two o'clock," she says again, her voice firm. "Don't tell anyone where we are before then."

Dylan sighs, taking another step back. "If you say so," he mumbles. "Good luck."

He eyes Kornelía as Mim starts to guide the boat away from the dock, and I look away before the lingering gaze ends.

Mim steers with ease, the boat's light brightening the way ahead of us so it's easy to see when we near the cave. We coast between the rocks, everything not illuminated by the boat's light cast in dark shadow. The cave is vastly different now than it was the day I came here with Meander. The warm blue waters have turned eerily black, and an unnerving void has replaced the open pocket of light above our heads.

I take a shaky breath as Mim brings the boat to the rocky shore of the dark recess deep inside the cave.

"Okay, Mim," Kornelía says in a hushed voice once the boat is stopped. "We're here. Now it's time to tell us what you've got planned."

Mim faces us, although it's hard to make out her features in the dark. "He's here," she says, grabbing her bag and pulling it onto her lap. She holds the fabric close, as if she's clutching it for warmth. "I can feel him. Which means it shouldn't take long for us to get to work. I'll talk to him, ask him questions, and make an effort to release him in a natural way. But—the Oracle's attempted that before. So far it hasn't worked. And so… I'm prepared for the next step."

"Give us the details," Meander says, his voice tight. "If we're going to be here, we need to know every move you're going to make."

Mim nods, bending over her bag as she starts to dig through it.

"The first step of a Sender exorcism is conviction," she says, lifting out a flashlight and switching it on. "This is different for everyone. For me, it means—"

She pauses, staring at us for a long moment before she grabs the wooden beads tucked into her yellow shirt and pulls them free. I never realized the necklace is a rosary. By the determined look on her face, I'm guessing Mim's been careful to ensure none of us did.

"I'll say a prayer," she continues. "Words to reflect my belief and state my intent."

"Wait… Are you saying it's not a standard ritual?" I ask, confused. I haven't given exorcism much thought, but I figured there'd be some kind of instruction set.

"No," Meander says from beside me. "I read about this. The power of an exorcism is drawn largely from the Sender's core beliefs about what is happening and why. You can't perform an exorcism if you don't believe in what you're doing. It's one of the reasons they're so difficult to achieve. The energy needed to take over the spirit doesn't come from outside sources. It comes from within."

Mim shifts in her seat, her expression briefly visible in the glow of the flashlight. Her lips are pursed, like she's restraining herself from starting an argument.

Maybe about Meander's remark that the energy doesn't come from any outside force.

She holds her cross tight in her fist as she nods, not bothering to fight the point. "The steps of an exorcism are not complicated," she says, resuming her role as speaker. "It is only the conviction and the strength of the Sender's ability that make it a complex and tough process. For me, the event will involve dousing the spirit with holy water, reading texts, saying prayers, and holding a strong trust that my… my faith will see it through." She pauses again and sighs. "That the angels who oversee me will help guide this spirit away from our realm."

An awkward silence follows Mim's words, the reality striking us with uncertainty. I'm not surprised—at least not wholly shocked—to hear her mention angels. But Mim's belief is not one I share and, judging by the shadowed faces of the other two, I'm guessing they don't, either.

Of course, it doesn't matter whether we think there are angels nearby, or even believe in angels at all. Mim does, and she's the one performing the exorcism. Still, it makes me wonder what my conviction would be if I was going to attempt a feat like this. Do I have a strong enough conviction in *anything* to exorcise a spirit?

"You're missing a step," Meander says, bringing the conversation back into focus.

"I was getting to it," Mim says, although I suspect it's a lie. She starts climbing out of the boat, keeping her back to us as she talks. "When a person dies, their soul crosses over immediately. Or, at least, it's supposed to. This crossing, when it happens, is not usually noticed by anyone else. Those nearby don't lose their energy, and no one passes out."

The boat rocks as she stumbles onto the shore, her legs too short to make a graceful exit.

"There's a reason for this," she says as she catches her balance. "The soul uses the last remaining energy of its own body to make its exit from our world. Everything it needs to cross over is contained within the walls of its personal temple."

I eye Meander at her use of the word 'temple', and he smirks.

"When a soul stays as a ghost, it needs to collect energy from other sources to cross over," Mim continues, turning back to help Kornelía out of the boat. "But during an exorcism, the spirit is not in control. The Sender *forces* it to cross over. So, the Sender needs to provide the necessary energy."

Kornelía makes easy work of getting onto the rock. Once she's standing, she holds a hand out in front of her.

"Hold on," she interjects. "*You* need to provide the energy? Mim, are you talking about your… your body?"

Mim gives a terse nod.

"The whole process will be about drawing Anjelo to me, and opening myself to him. Only for a second. When the ghost is weak enough to obey my command, he will move into the comfort of my energy. Then, the force of my own spirit will be enough to push him across the divide."

"Mim, that is crazy," I say, standing in the boat.

"It's an exorcism," Mim retorts. "I hope you weren't counting on a quiet evening."

I wasn't planning for a night of sing-songing around

a campfire, but I didn't expect Mim to let a spirit overcome her. At least Kornelía looks as surprised as I am. Meander's the one who brought the topic up, so he clearly knows what's going on better than we do.

The two of us get out of the boat and follow Mim to a flat expanse of rock next to the water.

"So, what do you want from us?" Meander asks.

Mim passes around flashlights and lays out the books she's going to read from before she answers him. "I don't know," she admits.

She sounds more uncomfortable now that she's closer to the spirit's earthly residence. I don't feel cold or smell anything other than the normal scents of the cave, at least. Meander doesn't seem to be affected, either, and I'm glad. Despite what Mim's proposing, he smiles when I step close to him and, with a discreet shift of position, his hand finds mine again.

"Because exorcism is such an individual process," Mim says as she unstops a vial of what must be holy water, "it's impossible to guess at what could go wrong. I might need someone to hold the light while I read. I might need someone to hold me up, if I get too weak." She glances at Meander, her gaze serious. "I might need assistance getting the spirit's attention. In case you haven't noticed, he's shy. He might need some *coaxing*."

"I don't feel anything," Meander says. "He's not angry."

"Not yet," Mim agrees. "This ghost is a weak one, most of the time. But I haven't opened its old wounds yet."

"Mim, is this spirit dangerous?" Kornelía asks, before amending her own words with a shake of her head. "I mean, under normal circumstances? You said he drowned after throwing himself into the water. Is that the end of his story?"

She senses something, and Mim bristles with aggravation that another of her sidekicks is calling out what she's avoided revealing.

"He has a trigger point," Mim says with a sigh. "And when it's reached, he's known to seek revenge for what happened to him."

"Revenge?" I repeat. I remember our first camp assignment, when I discovered that one Wanagi sector is named after ghosts seeking vengeful retribution for some perceived wrong. "But doesn't that mean… Mim, is this spirit a *revenant*?" I finish, my stomach plunging with alarm.

"Oh, Mim." Kornelía shudders. "This is a bad idea. Why didn't you tell us?"

"He is only a revenant in the broadest sense of the word," Mim assures us, which isn't reassuring at all. "You don't have to worry. His trigger point is specific, and it's not going to come into play tonight. Anjelo is usually a meek soul. His anger, if it comes, won't be because of his past. And it won't be vengeful. Any fury that emerges will be directed at me, when I demand he leave the place he's called home for the past ninety years."

The water lapping against the rocks of the cave amplifies in my head, and I take deep breaths to keep the panic at bay. Squeezing Meander's hand helps. Especially when he laces his fingers with mine and holds tight.

"Let's start then, shall we?" he says, nodding to Mim. "No point giving him any more time to hide."

"Agreed," Mim says. She kneels down, glancing up at Kornelía and then over to me. "Ready?"

"Yes," Kornelía says, her voice quiet but not afraid.

My eyes flick to Meander as I work to keep the nerves from setting my arm shaking. Whatever happens tonight, I don't intend to let him out of grasping distance.

"Go ahead," I say, swallowing as I meet Mim's gaze.

She nods, then bows her head in prayer.

# 34

As Mim finishes her prayer and begins a louder incantation in Spanish, small tapping noises echo across the cave. When Kornelía kicks something by her foot, I realize the sound comes from tiny fragments of stone chipping off the cliffs and rolling towards us. The action is unobtrusive, only alarming in its potential to distract Mim from her task. Still, my head throbs with phantom pain, an involuntary image of a spirit throwing one of those rocks swimming behind my eyes.

I bite back a panicked warning to watch out for flying objects and force myself to focus on Mim. Her breathing is shallow by the time her incantation is complete, but she smiles, watching the shadowy recess with satisfaction.

"He's coming closer," Kornelía says, her back to the pocket of darkness. Her eyes are closed, her brow creased. "He's so sad," she says with pity.

"He's heartbroken," Mim agrees in English. "He ended his life because he didn't think he could face the world after the woman he loved spurned him for someone else. He doesn't think he can face the realm beyond this, either. So, he keeps himself hidden. Unless someone makes him come out and talk."

She twists her head, a sudden groan escaping her lips as the spirit moves closer—at least, I'm guessing that's why. I feel nothing, see nothing, and have only residual worry based on past experience. Vague dread lingers in the back of my mind, but even that fades once Mim begins speaking to Anjelo.

The rocks stop rolling once the incantation is over, and the cave is quiet while Mim mumbles questions in a mix of Spanish and English. I stand by the water's edge, my hand still clasped with Meander's. His eyes are watchful, his expression shifting from curious to annoyed as the questions continue without Mim making any headway.

"Same story he's told before," Mim says after she's asked the spirit about twenty questions and reiterated that he's free to cross over four or five times. "He knows he's dead. He knows the girl who betrayed his heart is dead, too. But he won't cross. He doesn't have any unfinished business. He only wants to stay here and mourn."

"Mourn?" Meander scoffs. "Ninety years feeling sorry for yourself should be enough mourning for anyone."

Mim glares at him. "Do *not* disrespect the dead," she warns, her voice low.

Meander takes a step towards her, his hand dropping away from mine in the process. The air is damp and cool compared to his touch.

"Respect is not a given," he replies, staring in the general direction the spirit must be hovering in. "It's earned, whether you're alive or dead. I don't feel sorry for someone who knows there's nothing left to do but move on, and won't. He's not waiting for someone to find him, and he's not trying to relay a message to anyone he left behind."

"Maybe he's afraid to cross-over," Kornelía offers, but then she shakes her head. "I don't sense fear, though. Just sadness."

"Exactly. He's nothing but a sorry sap, who needs to be told to cross over like a bloody child," Meander huffs. "So, let's get on with it and make him leave."

"This is not your…" Mim begins, but then she closes her mouth and takes a deep breath, keeping herself calm. "You're right, we should get started."

He nods and turns back to me.

"You know, there *is* a reason people call you standoffish," I say, caught between laughing at his tantrum and scolding him for it.

He sighs, running a hand through his curls. "Sorry," he mutters, offering me a small smile. "I just want to be done here. No point wasting time on something that's not going to work."

He returns to his spot beside me, his stormy look clearing as I begin to rub his back.

"If you're so impatient, then stop talking and listen," Mim says, glowering at Meander as she stoops to her bag. She pulls out a wooden cross far bigger than the adornment around her neck. She grips it in one hand and picks up a book with the other.

"This is where it gets difficult," she explains. "I will

say a prayer, and tell Anjelo what I'm going to do. I need you all to be prepared for what might happen next."

Kornelía steps closer to Mim and shines her flashlight over the shorter girl's shoulder so she can see the text.

"Anjelo Savou," Mim says aloud, "we are here tonight to help you cross over, to guide your spirit and set you free." She speaks in English, more for our benefit than for his. "You have suffered too long. You are not meant to be here, and I cannot let you remain. Go to the light, Anjelo. Let the angels take you. If you don't—if you cannot leave of your own accord, I will guide you myself."

"Shit."

Meander mumbles the word in a low, tired voice. He crosses his arms over his chest like he's warding off a cool breeze while, a few feet away, Mim winces. Clearing her throat, she pauses to let out a long, slow breath before she looks down at her book. When she starts speaking again, I think her words are in Spanish, but then I realize they're a third language which must be the Latin she was trying to study earlier this summer. Maybe she discovered reading the passages in their intended language is more powerful than a translation would be.

She fumbles over her words, but that doesn't seem to matter. The rocks start rolling again and, this time, I don't think my panic is ill-founded. Meander's breath hitches, and he groans, staggering back a step. His foot tips over the edge of the recess, and I grab him to keep him from falling into the water.

Mim was right. Now that she's told the spirit to take

a hike, his anger is starting to appear from beneath the folds of his meekness. He didn't show any sign of fury before and, if we're lucky, that means something good for us now—if it took the threat of an exorcism to spark his anger, I'm clinging to the hope it's not strong enough to keep up this show of malice for long.

Mim steps forward, her cross now exchanged for the vial of holy water. She says a prayer in Spanish and crosses herself with the hand holding the small bottle.

"With this water, I weaken your strength," she says, switching back to English to keep us informed.

She splashes a bit of water into the air. At the same time, Meander grabs hold of his arm, pressing a palm to his scar as if the wound has flared with pain. I give him a questioning look, but he shakes it away, lowering his hand back to his side.

"It's working," Kornelía says.

Her glasses are off, her hair is down, and she's wearing the same dress she's worn each time she's been around spirits this summer. But unlike the treehouse or the village home with the burned man, here she doesn't have a starring role. She holds the flashlight, and her stance is awkward, stuck between wanting to take command and knowing she can't. Sensing so much but interacting so little must be frustrating. As advanced as her talents are, I'm sure she's bothered she can't lead the way as the spirit crosses over.

"With this water, I lower your defenses," Mim continues, shaking the bottle a second time.

Meander winces, his hand jerking. He grips his leg, though I suspect what he wants is to grab his scar again. The events are obviously related, Mim dousing the spirit with holy water and Meander feeling a shot of pain in his arm, but I don't understand how. And I don't like being so helpless. Wondering whether Kornelía is bothered by the limitations of her talents is idiotic. I'm frustrated by my lack of ability to interact with this spirit, too.

Things have changed so much since my introduction to the world of the Oracle. I've spent most of my life wishing I could stop seeing spirits. Never before this moment have I wished I could see more ghosts than I already do.

I don't need to take charge, like I suspect Kornelía wishes she could. But I do want to help. Standing here watching the rocks roll past our feet and drop into the water is like witnessing a convincing magic act. I don't see this spirit, don't even feel the cold, or smell whatever scent is wafting over one half of our quartet. If I did, I could at least try to assist with Mim's process or help divert the spirit's attention in an effort to push his anger back.

Mim takes another step forward and empties the vial. Meander hisses with pain, doubling over as something like wind kicks up the rocks and blows them into the air. A chill sweeps across my face and, with it, the smell of the water becomes stronger—saltier—as if the entire ocean is full of nothing but crystal-white grains. My tastebuds tingle with the suggestion of such a brackish tang.

Holding a hand over my nose, I glance at the others. Kornelía is still gripping the flashlight, her long hair fluttering in the soft wind. Mim continues to read passages from the book, but she's speaking in a quiet, weak voice now, her syllables shaking and hard to distinguish. She slumps forward, and Kornelía loops an arm around her waist to help keep her upright.

Meander is still beside me, his eyes focused on a single spot, the place I imagine the spirit stands. His jaw is set and his feet are planted like he's bracing himself for what's going to come. His hand is shaking against his side. I want to hold it, but I don't think I should just now. He needs to focus all of his attention on the ghost.

"A-Anjelo," Mim stammers. She leans forward with a groan, resting her weight against Kornelía's arm for five or ten seconds before she forces herself to stand up straight. "Anjelo Savou," she begins again, her chin raised in the spirit's direction, "I command you to come to me. The angels are waiting. Come to me now, and all will be well."

I can't see what's happening but, judging by the smash of rock against rock on the cave walls around us, I'm guessing Anjelo doesn't listen to Mim's instructions.

"No," Meander breathes, the word full of dread. He takes a step back, and I reach for him again, keeping him once more on dry land. "You have to go," he says in a quiet voice. I think he's talking to the spirit, affirming Mim's commands by telling him the same thing. But when he turns, I realize he's speaking to me.

"I'm not going anywhere," I say, surprised. And hurt. No wonder Dylan's been so solemn. Being singled out as useless isn't much fun.

"He knows," Meander says, his gaze pleading.

Brows furrowed, I follow the shift of his head as he turns back to the spot where the spirit must be.

"Anjelo," Mim gasps. She falls to her knees, Kornelía

no longer able to bear the force of her weight. "Follow the light. Follow the light into me. Follow the angels."

The rocks smash again, the wind begins to whip, and the water behind us sloshes and crashes against the stony shore.

"Get in the boat," Meander says, reaching up to nudge me away from him.

I move a step towards the boat, unsure why he wants me to leave but trying not to let petty feelings get in the way of Mim's task. I don't want to go, and I couldn't drive the boat even if I did think it best to escape. But Mim is on all fours now, her head bent and her breath ragged. The exorcism is in full swing, and I don't intend to add more trouble to the scene—even if that entails sitting uselessly in the boat watching everything unfold.

Mim struggles to her feet, slipping twice before Kornelía manages to help her find a steady footing. I pause after a couple of steps to watch as she faces the spirit, mustering every bit of energy she can.

"*Anjelo Savou*," she yells, her voice echoing through the cave, piercing the loud winds and rising even over the crashing stones and splashing waves, "*sutiempo se ha terminado.* Your time is up."

A flare of static enters my head, mingling with the wind rushing between my ears. I raise my hands to block the noise but, when they're only halfway up, they freeze. A sharp chunk of rock has made its way into the whirlwind surrounding a vaguely human-shaped cloud. The rock bounces, twists, and hurtles forward. I lower my arms and prepare to push Meander out of the way. But far too late, I realize the rock is not headed towards him—it's coming for me.

"Callum!"

Meander is quick to react, which is good because I am not. The shock of his weight against mine as he pushes me into the water barely even registers. Only once I'm submerged—and my body has enough sense to make me hold my breath—do I break out of my stupor.

The water is dark and cold, and the force of our fall pushes me with enough momentum that, when my arm hits the wet rock beneath the shoreline, I feel the crack a full beat before the burn of pain rattles through the bone. My head is muddy with strange certainty that this is the place—the very spot—Anjelo hit his head when he crashed into the water ninety years ago. Crazed panic skitters across my nerves as I think my head's been hit, too. But then the pain pools in my arm, and my relief is as great as the agony.

I cry out as best I can while keeping my mouth closed, and around me the water goes hazy. I think I might be sinking, but then there is pressure under my arms as I'm pulled to the surface.

When I break through, I rake in a gasping breath and let it out as a proper, gritted cry. I clutch my arm as Meander pushes his hair back, then surveys the damage, his expression probably more pained than mine.

Getting an explanation for what just occurred is not a priority. But the spirit's influence, combined with the despair I catch in Meander's eyes, gifts me a moment of total clarity about why he told me to leave. Anjelo Savou was heartbroken. And as much as Mim was sure his trigger point wouldn't be reached, he is—at his spiritual core—a jilted lover seeking revenge. His anger was strengthened by Meander. But, instead of attacking Meander directly, he decided to attack me.

Because he *knew*.

I manage a fleeting smile, a bit of warmth shining through the shadows as Meander pulls me in and holds me against him to keep me from sinking. I wrap my uninjured arm around his shoulder and bury my face in his neck. For a short second, we bob in the water as if we were only enjoying a carefree, late-night swim.

"Mim!"

Kornelía's voice snaps me out of my daze before I've even had time to assure Meander I'm okay. I can't make out the shore, but he guides us to the stone and helps me onto the rock before he hauls himself up. When we're back in the light of the flashlights we dropped before the attack—beams that should *not* still be lit—we find Kornelía bent over Mim, the shorter girl flat on her back, convulsing.

"What the hell happened?" Meander asks as we both hurry over. Fiery pain shoots through my arm when I take a quick step, so I slow my movements to minimize the aggravation.

"The spirit couldn't resist anymore," Kornelía says. She eyes me, her gaze shifting to my arm before she looks back at Mim. "I think the whirlwind and the rock were too much. He dissipated within her, and then she fell. I caught her before her head hit the stone, but… She started convulsing."

"We've seen this before," Meander says, looking at me.

I nod, remembering last summer when a boy named Tomas was momentarily possessed by a spirit in a French café.

"Isn't this what's supposed to happen?" I ask, my voice unsure. Like Tomas, Mim's skin has turned a bruised sort of purple, and a soft, high-pitched whine emanates from her throat.

"I don't think so," Meander says, wiping water off his face with the back of his hand. He runs his teeth over his bottom lip in thought. Then he turns back to me. "From what I read, there should be a light. Mim should only have harbored him for a short time. Like, a few seconds. Then there should have been a light as he crossed over."

"There hasn't been any light," Kornelía whispers. "Maybe it's taking longer? Or—"

"Look," I say, cutting her off.

Mim's skin is fading back to its normal shade, and the convulsions are slowing down. The whine turns into a thin, reedy whistle, then one final, gasping sob issues forth before she falls silent.

The three of us look at each other, and Kornelía gives Mim's shoulder a gentle shake. "Mim?" she says, her voice grave.

Mim doesn't stir, and Kornelía bends down, her ear close to the girl's open mouth. "She's still breathing," she says with some relief.

I nod, able to see the slow, rhythmic rise and fall of Mim's torso.

Kornelía tries again to shake her, but Mim doesn't react.

"She's cold," Kornelía says after a moment. She closes her eyes, looking like she's working to keep herself from crying. "She's frozen."

"I don't think the spirit crossed over," Meander says. "I think it's still in her."

"Can that happen?" I ask, alarmed. "I know possession is possible, but… Can a spirit last inside of a living body?"

"I have no idea," Meander sighs. He considers me for a moment, looking at my right hand holding my injured left arm against my body. "We have to get back to camp." He glances at Mim, then over at the boat. "We need to get you both back."

"Agreed," Kornelía says.

She doesn't bother to collect Mim's things. With Meander's help, she lifts Mim and lays her down in the bottom of the boat, a boat which should be dead but still starts without hesitation. I'm glad Meander knows how to work it. Once we're all on board, he eases us out of the cave before working the boat up to a speed that would be too fast, if we weren't in dire need of help.

I slump into the seat, my eyes fixed on Mim, my head swimming with the throbbing pain in my arm. Meander steers the boat, and Kornelía keeps watch for the dock as we leave the cave behind—possibly taking the spirit of Anjelo Savou with us.

Getting back to camp is chaotic. Mim left her phone in the boat, and it still has one bar remaining when we zoom into open water. Kornelía uses it to call Dylan, telling him to get help. I can't hear his half of the conversation, but Kornelía's voice is loud and impatient.

"You *will* see her," she says, glancing down at Mim. "But we need assistance." She pauses, heaving an inaudible sigh as she listens to Dylan's response. "So *run*," she says at length. "You're good at that. Run fast, and you'll be back by the time we arrive."

Dylan *is* fast. When we pull into the dock, a car is parked on the road, and Robbie, Alex, and an instructor I don't know are waiting for us. They lift Mim's body out of the boat and carry it to the car while Dylan badgers us about what happened. He looks frenzied, his hair wild and his eyes shining. He bounces between us, asking questions that receive no answers until the instructor orders him to be quiet and he shies away like a reprimanded dog.

I try to stay close to Meander, but the effort is fruitless. As soon as they notice me clutching my arm, I'm ushered into the car with the instructor and Mim, while Robbie and Alex escort the others on foot.

They take me into the resort's first-aid room, where someone who works for the hotel looks at my arm. Under the indoor lighting, it's easy to see the swelling, and the attendant loads me up with pain killers before I'm put in another car and transported to the airport. I'm pretty out of it when I board a small plane, but I'm conscious enough to understand the flight's purpose is to take Mim and I away from Vava'u—so we can check into a hospital on the mainland.

Being ordered around by people I don't know is frightening. Especially since Mim, still unconscious, is separated from me as soon as we're inside the hospital walls. Someone must have my details because, after a short stint in the waiting room, I'm examined and x-rayed. They determine I've got a small ulnar fracture in my forearm, but no bones are sticking out through my skin, so I don't think it's too bad. Once it's set, casted, and put in a temporary sling, they more or less leave me alone.

I don't see anyone from the Oracle for three days, and I worry that means they're going to send me straight back home, like they did with Isabis. But on Wednesday, while I'm going stir-crazy in a small room with a bunch of people who don't speak my language, Robbie appears to fill me in. His tall hair is like a cool fan for my overheated nerves, his familiar face a much needed comfort. Knowing I haven't been forgotten amidst the calamity surrounding Mim's condition is reassuring.

Robbie sinks into the chair beside my bed and cracks his knuckles before he looks up at me.

"You know, people are going to start thinking I'm an incompetent lead," he says, his lips slowly spreading into a smile.

"Well, you did set a bad example for us last year, nearly getting us killed in that old house," I reply, unable to mask the pain and weariness in my voice.

He eyes my cast, his smile fading into a more neutral expression. "How's the arm?"

"Hurts," I say, shrugging with my uninjured side. "But I'm okay. How's Mim?"

"No change," he says.

I like how direct he is and appreciate that he doesn't try to avoid the topic.

"What happened to her?" I ask.

I've had a lot of time to think about the cave over the last few days, but I still can't make sense of the quick, downward spiral of events. Maybe it would seem more logical if I hadn't been underwater breaking my arm while the spirit overtook her.

Robbie runs his hands up the length of his mohawk as he leans back in the chair. "I've never performed an exorcism," he says. "But from what I gather, they're hella tricky. Now, usually if something goes wrong, it happens *outside* of anyone's body. Destruction of property and a few cuts or bruises is expected. But what happened to Mim…"

He stretches out his legs, crossing his ankles and staring at his sandals as he continues. "The ghost got inside of her. Which, fair enough, is what's supposed to happen. But Mim was too weak—or it was too strong. However you look at it, the ghost got inside of her, and it took hold. The problem, of course, is that two spirits can't reside within the same functioning body. Mim's still alive, but her spirit is being held hostage."

"So… she's stuck?"

Robbie nods. "For now, anyway," he sighs. "They're taking her home to Guatemala while the Oracle works on solutions. But there's nothing more we can do for her right now. So, yeah. She's stuck."

My hair is a mess, but I attempt to smooth it back with one palm as I think about Mim lying comatose on a plane ride back to her homeland.

"Are we in trouble?" I ask after a moment, wondering what this means for all five of our futures at Camp Wanagi. "*Of course* we're in trouble. But are we, you know, in *big* trouble?"

"No one's about to give you a medal of honor," Robbie says, the smile creeping back onto his lips. "But no one's getting ready to dole out punishment, either. You were stupid not to tell anyone what you were planning. But to be honest, you're not as stupid as some of us have been."

"Some of *us*?" I ask, one eyebrow quirked.

Robbie grins. "During my third summer, I *may* have been present while one Shade shattered her leg in an unfortunate spirit-related rock climbing incident."

I laugh, which turns into a groan halfway through. We shouldn't be making light of people getting hurt, and Mim's condition is unquestionably more serious than my broken arm or someone else's shattered leg. But it does make me feel good to know my friends and I are not the only foolish campers. Maybe it's a Shade thing. More likely, it's a Sender one.

"Anyway," Robbie says, drawing his legs in. "It was Mim's idea. If anyone was going to get hell for what happened, it'd be her. But if she wakes up, I'm sure she'll be forgiven."

He stands, eyeing my arm before he turns towards the door. "I bet you're starved for some decent food," he says. "I'm going to go scrounge for something good. I'll be back."

Worry sinks into my pores as soon as Robbie leaves me to obsess over what he's said.

*If* Mim wakes up. Which means it's not a guarantee she will.

Up to this point, my fears have been centered around Mim's present, and my future. I figured the Oracle would have a way to fix her, that post-exorcism possession is something they were at least somewhat familiar with. The situation wasn't good, but I didn't honestly believe Mim's failure could result in indefinite stasis—with potentially life-threatening consequences.

Living and dead energy can't exist together forever. And even if they could remain mingled while Mim's body is a *temple* of living flesh, being in a coma for the rest of her life is no better than being dead. She's not at peace. If Anjelo Savou is clinging to her spirit, she's fighting an unimaginable battle.

But she can't fight forever. If the Oracle can't save her, and Mim's unable to save herself, what will happen then?

# 36

 behalf) in getting the hospital to release me the next morning.

We fly back to Vava'u through rain, the flight turbulent as the small plane fights with the wind. The motion doesn't mix well with my medication, and my stomach bucks with every bounce of the cabin. The amount of times I've felt sick to my stomach over the course of my life is numerous, but nausea isn't something I've ever grown accustomed to—regardless of whether it's brought on by a spirit or a shaking plane.

Once we've landed and trudged through the resort, I'm not surprised to see that the beach is empty, the rain keeping everyone indoors. But no one is in the fale when we arrive, and the quiet house surrounded by the tapping of rain is eerie.

"We made the others clear out," Robbie says,

standing in the doorway. "Wanted to give you a bit of downtime before they start bugging you."

"Right." I nod, glancing around the vacant room. "Thanks."

"No problem," Robbie says, standing with one foot already outside. He needs to check in with Mrs. Buxley, to let her know we've made it back and update her on the status of my arm. But he hovers on the threshold, watching me for signs I need further assistance.

"I'm good," I assure him, waving my right hand.

He nods, pausing a few seconds more before darting into the rain. I watch him through the foggy window and, when he's out of sight, I slump onto the nearest couch.

Less than a minute passes before Meander appears. He must have been waiting, watching for Robbie to leave before he snuck in. I'm glad he's decided to ignore the warning about giving me space.

"You're back," he says, the words a sigh of relief.

He pulls off the sweater soaked with rain from his wait outdoors and, when I stand, he steps towards me like he's coming for a hug. When he sees the sling, he stops, frozen a foot too far away.

"They haven't told us anything," he mumbles.

His eyes slide along my arm until they fix on the spot where my fingers hang free from the white-bandaged cast. I glance down at the sling and offer him a smile.

"A *minor* fracture," I say. He doesn't return my smile, so I step forward, closing the gap between us. "I'm fine."

He touches my good arm, his fingers gliding past my elbow and over the small definition of muscle that's been my reward for a summer of hard mornings with Althea.

"You're not fine," he says as he drops his arm back to his side. "You're hurt. *Again.*"

"What can I say, I'm a natural klutz," I joke, my attempt to be cheerful half-hearted.

A new kind of pain blossoms in my chest. I don't like the way he's so serious. Four days have slipped by since I talked to Meander. I didn't bring my cell phone with me to the cave, figuring it'd be pointless to drain the battery. I'm glad it wasn't in my pocket when we crashed into the water but, without it, we've been disconnected. Which means he's had more than half a week to brood by himself and crawl back into his hermit hole.

"You didn't get hurt because you're clumsy," he says. His eyes are still fixed on the sling and the cast within it.

I reach forward and take his chin, pulling his face up until his gaze shifts to meet mine. "You didn't hurt me, either," I say, knowing what thoughts are rattling around in his head.

He holds my stare but, try as I might, I can't make the dark dejection dissipate from the ring of jade in his eyes.

"You were hurt *because* of me," he says. "Which is pretty much the same thing." He tightens his jaw, and swallows like he's forcing down something he knows will make him sick. "Everything that happened in that damned cave is because of me. You were wrong, Cal. You told me I couldn't hide away, but I can... I *have* to."

I shake my head, my fingers sliding from his chin to his neck. "Mim knew what she was doing when she asked you to be a part of the exorcism," I remind him. "I know things went wrong, but she wouldn't have had any chance of success without you."

"A total failure would have been better," he scoffs.

"If you had said as much to Mim before we went to the cave, she would have disagreed. You know she would."

"And now?" His whole body stiffens with tension. "What would she say if we could ask her now?"

I don't have an answer, but I won't let his cheap shot be the end of the conversation.

"She asked you to go with her," I press. "She knew there were risks, but she wanted you there, anyway." I stroke his neck with my thumb. "Besides, if anyone shouldn't have been there, it was me. I'm the one who caused trouble."

Meander relaxes as he shakes his head. "You're not to blame," he says.

"Neither are you," I counter. I try for a smile again, even though I know it won't do any good. "Things like this happen to Senders. And we two seem to make a particularly *active* pair."

He holds my gaze for a long moment, his expression grave. Then he lowers his head. "You're right," he says, each word hesitant. "Which is why we shouldn't... We shouldn't stay so close."

My thumb halts, although my hand remains on his neck in stunned bewilderment. I expected him to blame himself for what happened in the cave, and I was prepared for a new onslaught of reasons he wouldn't return to camp—and would instead devise some ludicrous plan for keeping away from ghosts.

But never did it occur to me his ill-considered

obsession with self-sacrifice would extend to us.

"Meander, you can't—" I start, but he doesn't let me finish.

"I can't let you get hurt again," he says, raising his head.

"I'm *fine*," I repeat, panicked and angry that he won't believe me. "It's just a minor fracture. It's nothing."

"And last year it was just a minor concussion, yeah?" he asks, his voice rising. He steps back, leaving my hand to slip into empty air. "When does it stop being minor, Cal? When you wind up like Mim? When you wind up worse?"

He paces the short distance between the sofa and the door to our room.

"I don't..." The words catch in his throat, and he takes a deep breath before continuing. "I don't want anyone to get hurt on my account. But you... I *won't* let you get hurt because of me."

"Don't be stupid," I snap, my teeth gritted in frustrated fear. "I can take care of myself, and it's up to me to decide what's dangerous. Besides, if you're so worried about your abilities, you should be around people who understand the risks. You should stay close to someone who gets it."

"But you *don't* get it!" Meander explodes, his eyes shining. "Things are getting worse, Cal. And apparently next year, a fresh hell will be unleashed. I don't understand the risks of my talent's development, so how can you?"

"Well... I..." I stammer, unsure how to stop the imminent crash headed in my direction. "Shouldn't I get to take the risk if I want to, even if I don't know what it is I'm risking?"

To my surprise, Meander laughs, a gentle sound that would be lovely if it weren't for the tears in his eyes. He walks over to me and touches my arm again.

"You're the kind of fantastic idiot who'd risk everything if you thought it'd help," he murmurs.

His gaze is soft, his fingers are warm, and this moment brims with surreal confusion.

"I'm not—" I start, but the argument hangs unfinished. I *would* risk everything, if it was worth it. I wasn't lying when I told Mim as much.

Meander is worth it. Whatever we were creeping towards, whatever tingling brightness is ending now before it fully began, is only part of the equation. Even without any of that, Meander is my best friend. The only person I've ever felt honest, unflinching closeness with. Of course I'd risk everything for him. He's the first person who ever lifted the aching loneliness of my life. And if the tables were turned, he'd risk whatever it took to keep me safe. He's trying to right now, in his stupid, misguided way.

I lean into him and he mirrors the movement until our foreheads are touching.

"I'm sorry," he whispers, the words worse than any of the piercing shocks of static a spirit has ever shot through my ears.

I start to shake my head, but footsteps outside halt me from demanding he take those awful words back.

"We should let him be," I hear Kornelía saying from beyond the front door.

"I want to know what's going on," Dylan replies. His voice is annoyed, likely because Kornelía is trying to stop him from coming in. She interrupted the last important conversation I had with Meander, and I'm sure she knows I'm in here with him now.

Not that it matters. When we hear the others talking, we step apart. As soon as Dylan manages to throw the door open, Meander retreats another several steps.

Dylan locates me, opening his mouth to speak before he notices I'm not alone. When he sees who my company is, his eyes narrow.

"What the hell are you doing here?" he hisses at Meander.

"He's talking to me," I say, confused by his apparent fury.

"I'm leaving," Meander says in a dry voice.

"No you're not," I blurt.

"Good," Dylan replies, ignoring me.

I stare at Dylan, baffled by his behavior and wondering what vital piece of information I'm obviously missing. But then I realize what must have transpired while I was in the hospital. Kornelía would have filled Dylan in on what happened in the cave. If this is how Dylan's reacting now, it must mean he's decided to lay the blame for Mim's condition on a specific person.

No wonder Meander's been brooding. If my assumption's correct, Dylan's been making things worse by telling him it's his fault Mim got hurt.

"Dylan, stop being an ass," Kornelía mumbles.

"No," I say at the same time, turning to Meander. "Don't leave."

But Meander doesn't listen. He heads for the door, until Dylan tries to block him in a ridiculous show of threat. Kornelía pushes Dylan out of the way with a sigh, and Meander slips out the door without another word.

"What the hell, Dylan?" I growl. I'm too tired and sore to deal with him being a jerk. I'm confused, too. And, I suspect, something akin to heartbroken.

"He caused all this," Dylan says, falling onto the far sofa. He crosses his arms over his chest, his hair shaggy and mussed, the hollows of his eyes more gray than usual.

"He did not," Kornelía says, her voice simultaneously scolding and gentle.

"She's right," I say, walking over to the window. I pull back the sheer curtain and stare outside, but Meander's already out of sight. "He didn't do anything. Mim's condition isn't anyone's fault."

"That's what we came here for," Kornelía cuts in before Dylan has time to respond. "We were told to give you space, but... We wanted to know how you were. And if you've been told anything about Mim."

I turn back and spend a moment glaring at Dylan. But as much as his anger fuels my own, I know it comes from a place of worry. Staying here talking about Mim is not what I want to do. But giving Meander time to cool off might be the better solution.

With a pained sigh, I leave the window and sit on the couch adjacent to the others. Pushing aside my fears and the weariness of travel, I tell Kornelía and Dylan what little I know about Mim.

# 37

MEANDER IS GOOD AT BEING INVISIBLE. ONCE, HE TOLD ME HE COULD skip classes without his school even registering the absence. After witnessing his latest disappearing act, I no longer doubt his claims.

Once Dylan and Kornelía leave, I'm unable to resist another dose of pain killers followed by a short nap. When I wake mid-afternoon, I start hunting for Meander. Like last year, he's nowhere to be found. But unlike the isolated château in France, our current location offers many hiding places in close proximity to camp.

I'm upset, though unsurprised, when he misses dinner and doesn't show up later in the evening. I'm too drowsy to pull an all-nighter, so I set my alarm for five in the morning to ensure I'm up long before him. When the buzzing of my phone sends me rolling onto my left side and groaning with pain, I clench my teeth and set my bleary sights on Meander's bunk—only to find the sheets flat and tucked, no mound of blankets exposing a mop of curly hair.

My concern grows when I don't see him the next day, or the next. Courses are finished, so I have no schedule to track him. He doesn't appear in the fale, the dining hall, or the library. I walk the beach a dozen times, going up to the treehouse and over to the dock leading to Swallow's Cave. I trek through the nearest neighborhood and stop in every shop and restaurant with no result.

I'd talk to an instructor about his absence, except he only seems absent to me. On Friday, Sefa says he saw Meander in our room, getting something from his suitcase. On Saturday, Sabeena says he was in the library during a brief downpour. On Sunday, I walk into our room to find Reed grumbling about how we didn't even invite him to attend Mim's ill-fated exorcism, his tone petty but laced with genuine concern about the girl who's been tutoring him. When Naasir's sharp gaze shushes him, Reed reddens, then shrugs and tells me Meander was making tea in the dining hall earlier that morning.

By Monday, I've figured out that he must be more or less tailing me, watching me search for him so he can ensure I never get ahead. Which is why I've decided to do some spy work myself. I stay in the fale all morning, moving to the beach around noon. Sitting with my face towards the water, I keep a compact mirror I borrowed from Sabeena angled on my shoe so it reflects our front door.

I can't let him go unseen for another day because I don't have another day to waste. Camp is officially finished at the end of this week, but campers are trickling out over the next five days. Dylan and I are sharing a flight back to L.A., and we'll be leaving on Wednesday. But Meander departs for England today, and I don't think he's planning any grand farewells. So, I'm waiting, and watching. He's not slipping away that easily.

"Hey," Dylan says after a while, sitting next to me.

"Hi," I grumble, not taking my eyes off the mirror.

"What are you doing?"

I'm sure he's noticed the compact but, as curious as I bet he is, I don't provide an answer. The two of us have chosen to ignore all talk of Meander, at least until we're back at home. I'm mad at him for what he thinks and—more to the point—what he's been saying aloud. But it'll be a long flight home if we're not on speaking terms.

Besides, I know Dylan is as morose as I am right now. Mim is in Guatemala, still unconscious, the state of her life uncertain. And I'm not going to pretend I'm some valiant hero who would never stoop to his kind of judgment. If Meander was the one in a coma because Mim gave some spirit a dangerous burst of power, I'd be convinced she was to blame, too.

I *am* furious with Dylan, and I can't wait for us to be in separate countries. But my fury is quiet, and I'll suppress it for a few more days. If not for his sake, then for Mim's.

After a few seconds of silence have passed, Dylan draws his knees to his chest with a sigh. "You know, I did try this year," he says, speaking as if we're in the middle of a conversation, not one he's beginning without prelude. "When Mim said she didn't want me at the exorcism, I thought I'd try my hand at doing something on my own."

I almost look away from the mirror, but I stop myself before I break contact. "What did you do?" I ask instead.

"That dog. The one from the initiation. It's been following me around all summer," he admits.

"Really? I didn't know that," I say. I'm apologetic, until I remember why I'm mad at him.

In my peripheral vision, Dylan shrugs. "He's been around me off and on since that night," he clarifies. "Not all the time, but enough to be freaking annoying. You were off with Korni releasing spirits, Mim was off planning her stupid exorcism, and Reed kept complaining about being surrounded by water and *still* not seeing anything. So, I thought I'd give it a shot and try to help."

"What happened?"

Someone exits the fale and, in the brightness of the day, it takes a minute to distinguish Sefa's dark hair. If my observations have been accurate, our quarters are now empty.

"I followed the dog for days," Dylan says in a moody voice. "Whenever I had a moment. At least, I tried to follow it. Every time it noticed me, it took to following *me* around instead. But then I got an idea. I thought maybe the dog just wanted someone to play with it. While you guys were in the cave, I was on the beach, throwing sticks and telling a dead dog to go fetch."

"I take it by your tone it didn't work," I mumble.

A volleyball lands nearby, and Dylan gets up to kick it back to the players. Camp Wanagi held a volleyball tournament last week while I was in the hospital. A camp game missing at least three members. More than three. Between Isabis's early departure, our disaster at the cave, and whatever tasks the Wraith kids were up to this year, the number of absent campers was likely closer to ten.

"No, it didn't," Dylan says with a huff as he sits back down. "The dog is still here. Nothing's changed. Which pretty much proves what I've been saying all along. My talent is worthless. This whole summer sucked."

"It was only one dog," I say, while a figure appears in the distant reflection of the mirror.

I feel ridiculous leaning forward to get a closer look in the compact resting against my shoe, but it's worth it when I know for certain the person is Meander.

"I've got to go," I tell Dylan, snapping the mirror closed as soon as the fale's door shuts.

I scramble up and hurry back to the fale without waiting for a reply. I don't care if Dylan had more to say about the dog or this summer. He's not the one I'm worried about.

Reaching the fale takes no time at all but, when I arrive, I enter as silently as possible. I want to make sure I don't give Meander advanced notice so he can sneak out the back or something. The idea is absurd. But, if the last few days have taught me anything, I can't predict what insane measures he'll use to stay hidden.

He doesn't hear me, a fact I'm entirely too proud of considering the circumstances. When I reach our room, he's packing so he can take the water taxi to the nearest island with a large enough airport to get him out of the kingdom. The taxi is set to leave in less than an hour. My heart is dreary when I think of how close his departure is.

"You really going to leave without even saying goodbye?" I ask at last.

He doesn't startle, which makes me wonder if I've been as stealthy as I believed. He finishes packing his bag, placing the last couple of items in a neat pile before zipping his suitcase. Then he turns to me.

"That was the plan," he says, working hard to be emotionless.

My face flushes, anger swelling through my throat until it bursts between my teeth. "Why the hell have you been avoiding me?" I half-shout as I step into the room. Raising my voice was not part of my careful plan, but I can't control my frustration. The worst part is, I'm sure this is what he wants. He's hoping I'll be mad at him because he thinks if I am, I'll let him go.

My outburst doesn't make him flinch. "So we didn't have to do this again," he says, almost succeeding at sounding like he doesn't give a damn. The act would be flawless if it weren't for the crack on his last note, a falter that makes him avert his gaze.

"Don't pretend not to know who I am or what I'm like," I snap. "I'm not giving up on you."

Pink blooms on his cheeks, and he bites his lower lip. I can't tell if he's embarrassed by his attempt to act like we're still strangers, or pleased by my affirmation that I'm not going to surrender to his stupid plan. I hope it's the latter, even if he won't admit to it now.

"I have to go soon," he says, eyes downcast. "And I'm not changing my mind about what I said. So, don't pretend you don't know me, either. I'm nothing if not a stubborn bastard."

My mouth twitches towards a smile, but I force it down.

This argument will not be resolved in the next twenty minutes. Part of me wants to fight it out until the last second. And part of me wants to do something drastic like twist him around and kiss him before he has a chance to get away. But I don't want my last moment with him this summer to be full of yelling. And as much as I'd love it to be full of kissing instead, I don't want to force him into something he's clearly trying to escape, sound reasons or no.

I'm useless. I should be doing something more. But I only manage a pathetic, irresolute sigh.

"At least say goodbye," I say, the words more pleading than I intended.

He presses his hands against his suitcase as if he's struggling to fit everything inside, despite the fact it's already zippered shut. After a beat, he straightens and turns, crossing the space between us and pulling me into a hug.

When we hugged at the beginning of this summer, I marveled at how full and warm the embrace was. Wrapping my uninjured arm around his neck now, I am aware of the subtle way everything has morphed. This embrace is not happy, nor is it as warm. But it's fuller, more intimate and meaningful—and much more painful.

Meander holds me tight. I close my eyes and breathe the scent of sunscreen and sandalwood, listening to the drum of my heart as it mixes with the quiet exhale of his breath close to my ear.

He doesn't say goodbye, which I'm thankful for. Despite asking for it, the lack of words between us feels less like an ending and more like a promise things still have a chance to turn out right in the end.

He squeezes me hard for a final few seconds, and then he walks away, avoiding my eyes as he collects his suitcase and leaves.

# 38



The Kingdom of Tonga fades into a world of water below us as our plane sets a course towards Fiji.

I'm not sad to see it go.

"Beautiful, isn't it?" Daniel asks from beside me.

The plane to Fiji is full of campers, a good portion of us travelling this stretch together before we take bigger airlines back to our homelands. I was supposed to be sitting next to Dylan on this flight but, when I saw Daniel, I swapped seats with one of the Entity campers. I'll be sitting beside Dylan the entire flight from Fiji to LAX. A small break from his company is a relief when the two of us are still only half-speaking.

"It's a nice place," I offer with a vague nod.

Daniel sits by the window, watching the dotted islands with content. "I wonder where we'll end up next year," he says, elbow on the seat rest and chin in his hand.

"Don't you know?" I ask. I figured the leads were

privy to information the rest of us weren't.

Daniel laughs. "Nope," he says, glancing at me before facing the window again. "I won't know until next spring. Only about a month before you do. Truth be told, I don't think the Oracle plans Wanagi too far in advance. All depends on what spirits are of interest at the time."

"Yeah, but… Do you ever get a say, now that you're a lead?"

"Yes and no," Daniel shrugs. He looks at me again, his blue eyes a bright contrast to the dark hair sweeping across his forehead. "We can suggest places, of course. But it all depends on what's promising and how many spirits are nearby that might be of use to the campers."

I think about our unproductive scouting mission earlier this summer, an unsettling episode that was, ultimately, the catalyst for Kornelía's decision to tackle the treehouse.

"Did you ever do anything with that spirit we found?" I ask. "The one that bothered Kornelía?"

"No," Daniel says with a frown. "No one seems to be able to communicate with him. At least no one at camp. But the spirit Isabis interacted with during the initiation was released by two Entities, so that's good. In fact, all seven Entities were part of successful groups for their final task, which is even better."

"Shade wasn't so lucky," I mumble.

Our encounter with the children in the treehouse went okay, but Dylan failed his private attempt to communicate with the canine spirit, and Mim's in a coma after her disastrous attempt at an exorcism. Reed never found a ghost to interact with and, although Mim's intended group attempted their project without her, Sefa's interaction with the elderly spirit was unsuccessful as well. The only person I'm not sure about is Lu. She did her own project. I've seen so little of her this summer, I have no idea what she chose to do.

Last year was so promising. But maybe that's because last year we had help. This year we were on our own, and the results suck.

"The second summer is hard," Daniel says with a sigh. "So is the third. It does get easier, but it takes a while."

I don't want to think about things getting worse. Thinking about *how* they might get worse makes my head swim.

Daniel considers me, taking in the cast and the sling. Then he smiles. "Make sure you're on guard," he says, his voice a soft warning. He draws in a long breath and nods his chin towards my arm. "You seem to be accident-prone."

"I'll be fine," I mutter.

I slump down in my seat, holding back a wince of pain. I know what Daniel's getting at, and I don't want to hear about how I should be cautious when I'm around *certain* individuals. The suggestion I can't take care of myself is sickening, and I'm tired of having injuries to give everyone proof I need constant rescue.

Daniel turns back to the window while I sulk about my arm and the ridiculous, yet still kind of wonderful, reason it broke in the first place.

Last year, I made up an excuse about falling on a rock during a soccer game so my parents wouldn't wonder whether letting me return to Wanagi was a good idea. This year, I don't give a damn what they believe. They've known about my arm since I was checked into the hospital but, if my suspicions are correct, it'll be up to me to fill in the details of how the injury was sustained.

I won't lie this time. I'll tell them what happened and inform them about Mim, too. Hell, I might even let it slip that I found a couple of corpses this summer. And if they freak about it, I'll shrug my shoulders, put in my earbuds, and drown them out with the loud crashes of Stravinsky's "The Rite of Spring."

I take out my phone to listen to music now. Before I make it to my playlists, the photo app catches my eye, taunting me with a promise of bittersweet torture. I haven't looked at my photos since before the exorcism. My finger hovers over the button, my heart speeding a fraction of a beat. Looking at the photo of Meander and I will be brutal, but I can't force myself to avoid it. I will see it eventually, so I might as well look now.

I tap to open the app, prepared to face the picture I looked forward to obsessing over a week ago. But the photo that greets me is not the one I expected. I blink in confusion until the circumstances untangle themselves and fall into logical order. The picture of the two of us is still on the phone, one photo back. But someone's snapped another shot since then.

Meander.

It's a photo of him standing in the courtyard by the hammock. He must have taken it when he retrieved my phone, a quick shot before he joined me and Kornelía when we left for dinner and the cave.

My eyes sting, and I press a palm to them to keep the tears from welling up. The picture is simple, just him smiling at the camera. And that's what catches me off-guard. He's *smiling*. He took a photo of himself for my sake, and he's smiling because he knew I'd like it.

Dylan thinks Meander is a dangerous menace. And while Daniel's more reserved in his opinion, on some level, I suspect he believes it, too. Absolutely worst of all, so does Meander. But I don't. I can't, not with a treasure like this in my grip.

The boy in this picture is stubborn and scared. He's lived his life being ignored or ridiculed by most, and his biggest regrets are the pain and fright he's caused the few people who have treated him with kindness. His aunt in Paris moved apartments after our run-in with a spirit made her believe the place had been broken into. And his brother thinks he's sick, sending money each month for medications Meander can't convince him he doesn't need. Even his boss at the cemetery hasn't figured out why the otherwise obedient teenager refuses to work whenever a funeral is taking place nearby, lest a spirit be hanging around its loved ones, furious to see its body lowered into the ground.

And I—well, I keep winding up with cuts, bruises, and broken bones.

Wiping my eyes as discreetly as I can, I close the photo app before putting on my music. I don't flip to Stravinsky. I choose Chopin instead, pressing the earbuds in as "Piano Concerto No. 1 in E Minor, op. 11" begins. The sweet music flows through my ears while all around me Senders-in-training talk and laugh as the plane sails over the Pacific.

Things are going to get worse before they get better, and I've got my work cut out for me. Meander has his reasons for acting the way he does. But he's still foolish if he believes he can hide from spirits. And he's a full-blown imbecile for telling me to stay away.

I suck at being adventurous, and I don't make a good voice of reason, either. But if I have one thing going for me, it's persistence. I'm terrified to discover how my connection with spirits will change when I turn sixteen in February. But stronger is my fear of what will happen when Meander's full Sender abilities arrive next spring.

He wants to keep me safe, but he's failed to realize I want the same for him. And despite his insistence, I won't stop being—at the very least—his friend.

Not even if it breaks my body, or shatters something far more valuable than my bones.

THE STORY CONTINUES
IN BOOK THREE OF THE ORACLE OF SENDERS SERIES


WRAITH

# ACKNOWLEDGEMENTS

Many, many thanks to Martina McAtee for believing in the story, Molly Phipps for making it a beautiful sight to behold, and Megan for being an incredible editor. You are all amazing!

And a special thanks to everyone who read and loved *Shade*. We've been waiting for this together, and I can't wait to share the rest of the adventure with you as well.

# ABOUT THE AUTHOR

**MERE JOYCE** is a Canadian author of books for young adults. Her writing includes contemporary tales, high-action mysteries, and her personal favorite—ghost stories. When she's not writing, Mere can be found recommending books as a librarian, or spending time at home with her husband and two sons. She's also been known to be a selective, yet highly enthusiastic fangirl.

*Find her online at:*

**MEREJOYCE.COM**

www.ingramcontent.com/pod-product-compliance
Lightning Source LLC
Chambersburg PA
CBHW020917110726
47900CB00001B/175